"You know m... woman ever has, ... murmured. "B... you know yourself?"

A small lump of anxiety grew into fear as Sabrina watched him rise, slowly...so slowly...and move toward the bed where she lay, his gaze never leaving her eyes. She pressed back against the hard stone wall, feeling like a rabbit frozen in the blinding headlights of an oncoming vehicle. Spencer leaned down and eased his hand beneath the quilt.

The zipper at her breast slowly opened. His hand was warm, despite the chill in the room. And so gentle. Sabrina shivered.

"Think of last night, Sabrina," he whispered, leaning closer, closer. "Are you the kind of woman who could have given herself so completely—" his lips sealed hers with a long, probing kiss to which she couldn't help responding "—to a killer?"

Dear Reader,

Another month of eerily romantic reading has arrived, and you won't want to miss either of our spooky selections.

Reader favorite Barbara Faith is back with *Dark, Dark My Lover's Eyes*, a cautionary tale about marriage to a man with a mysterious past. In this case there's a first wife who died amid strange circumstances and who just might be jealous of the woman she thinks has taken her place.

Sandra Dark is a new author to the line, but you'll be eagerly awaiting more books from her after you read *Sleeping Tigers*, a story about a woman whose newest assignment lands her right in the den of a man who's as dangerous as any jungle beast.

You'll also want to keep an eye out for *Lovers Dark and Dangerous*, the third of our annual Shadows short story collections. This year's volume brings together stories by Lindsay McKenna, Rachel Lee and Lee Karr, and I promise you this—every one will haunt you.

So enjoy your time in the shadows—Silhouette Shadows.

Yours,

Leslie Wainger
Senior Editor and Editorial Coordinator

Please address questions and book requests to:
Silhouette Reader Service
U.S.: 3010 Walden Ave., P.O. Box 1325, Buffalo, NY 14269
Canadian: P.O. Box 609, Fort Erie, Ont. L2A 5X3

SANDRA DARK

Sleeping TIGERS

▼ SILHOUETTE® Shadows ™

Published by Silhouette Books
America's Publisher of Contemporary Romance

If you purchased this book without a cover you should be aware
that this book is stolen property. It was reported as "unsold and
destroyed" to the publisher, and neither the author nor the
publisher has received any payment for this "stripped book."

 SILHOUETTE BOOKS

ISBN 0-373-27044-5

SLEEPING TIGERS

Copyright © 1994 by Sandra Dark

All rights reserved. Except for use in any review, the reproduction
or utilization of this work in whole or in part in any form by any
electronic, mechanical or other means, now known or hereafter
invented, including xerography, photocopying and recording, or in
any information storage or retrieval system, is forbidden without
the written permission of the editorial office, Silhouette Books,
300 East 42nd Street, New York, NY 10017 U.S.A.

All characters in this book have no existence outside the imagination of
the author and have no relation whatsoever to anyone bearing the same
name or names. They are not even distantly inspired by any individual
known or unknown to the author, and all incidents are pure invention.

This edition published by arrangement with Harlequin Enterprises B. V.

® and TM are trademarks of Harlequin Enterprises B. V., used under
license. Trademarks indicated with ® are registered in the United States
Patent and Trademark Office, the Canadian Trade Marks Office and in
other countries.

Printed in U.S.A.

SANDRA DARK

lives in the rugged cross-timbers country of Oklahoma. Sandra and her husband share their house with a dog, three birds, an opossum (who lives under the back deck) and tons of books. A voracious and eclectic reader, Sandra has had a lifelong love affair with words which led her to take up the craft of writing at an early age. Nearly two hundred of her articles and short stories had appeared in national and international magazines before she turned to penning books full-time five years ago. One of the nicest things about writing books, Sandra thinks, is getting to meet so many other people who enjoy reading as much as she does.

To Lois Carnell Alexander—
with all my heart

PROLOGUE

A damp bone-chilling north wind whipped across the bleak cemetery, moaning dolorously through the dripping cedars. Spencer Bradley tugged the wool-lined collar of his trench coat higher around his chilled ears, and stared angrily at his uncle's rain-speckled casket suspended over the open grave.

Jeremiah Kellogg had lived a charmed life, Spencer thought—and he had lived every moment of it selfishly, with a total lack of remorse. That was clearly evident in the starkness of the brief graveside service. Far from being ushered into the hereafter with a level of pomp and ceremony that was to be expected for a man of Jeremiah's past stature, the old reprobate was about to be lowered into the ground like so much toxic waste.

The funeral director had dutifully recruited a preacher for the occasion. The cleric stood at the head of the dark mahogany casket, droning on about a man he'd never had the ill fortune to meet, as if his words mattered to a living soul gathered in that soggy upstate New York graveyard.

Spencer impatiently raked damp hair off his forehead and glanced around at the three black-clad carrion crows standing on the wet, wheat-colored grass. There wasn't a teary eye among them, he noted without surprise. Not even spare Conrad Lafever, Jeremiah's long-suffering but loyal secretary, could manage more than his usual tight-lipped frown, as if he smelled something rotten on the wind.

Next to Lafever stood Noble Wetherbee, thin wisps of silver hair dancing around his ruddy heavily jowled face. The attorney gazed down intently at his muddy wing tips,

perhaps mourning the demise of his most lucrative client.
Then again, perhaps not.

Beyond old Wetherbee, the Glade woman shivered in a
short coat that was far too thin for such a raw day. Besides
the preacher, she was the only one at the grave site whom
Spencer hadn't met until each of them arrived in separate
cars less than fifteen minutes ago.

He had to lean forward slightly now in order to get a
good look at her downcast, oddly striking face. Oddly
striking, because the ghost was a tad too thin for his taste,
her pale features too sharply cut. Nevertheless, there was
something about her that kept drawing his attention.

Luring it, he thought, although he was certain the attraction was not a conscious effort on her part. She hardly
struck him as the type to play the coy vixen, particularly at
a funeral.

She seemed to sense that she was being watched. Her
gaze lifted, searched for a moment, then met his with an
almost palpable impact. He just had time to glimpse that
remarkable depth of intelligence in the warm brown irises
that had so startled him when they were first introduced.
Then she ducked her head again, a thick curtain of sable
hair spilling forward to hide her face.

Sabrina Glade, Spencer thought with an unexpected
twinge of regret that he shoved quickly aside, *your days are
numbered.*

The hard corners of his lips twitched into an expression
of icy contempt. Old Jeremiah should never have brought
in an outsider to handle what never should have been begun at all. Now it was up to Spencer to send his uncle's
ghost packing. He looked forward to that final act of ret-
ribution with bitter pleasure.

Shoving his hands deeper into the wool-flannel warmth
of his coat pockets, Spencer cautioned himself to be patient. The long wait was almost over—and it was about
damned time. In one way or another, he'd been waiting for
this moment his entire life.

The hard, stinging rain began again, peppering down on the tight cluster of mourners huddled amid ranks of stained, mossy gravestones. Spencer Bradley hardly noticed. He had turned his back to the wind, hunched his shoulders, and retreated into a simmering caldron of pent-up rage.

CHAPTER ONE

The rain had let up by the time Sabrina Glade turned left off the country road and onto the steep, winding driveway that led up through the gloom to the Kellogg mansion. A dozen yards beyond the entrance gate, she took a right and continued along a narrow gravel track. Black branches of the estate's ancient winter-denuded oaks entwined overhead like the grotesquely twisted fingers of skeletons.

She felt heavy limbed, exhausted. The lead-lined blanket of depression that she had been carrying around for the past three days was finally getting to her. Sabrina tried hard to shrug it off as she nursed her decrepit car around the base of the hill toward the drafty stone cottage that she'd called home for the past three months. But it was no use. When disgusting old Jeremiah Kellogg unexpectedly went to his Maker last Friday, everything she had worked for all these months had gone straight down the toilet.

"Damn," she muttered, heartsick.

It was wrong to be thinking so ill of the dead, Sabrina told herself. Wrong and unfair. The poor man hadn't totally lacked redeeming qualities, even if the infirmities of old age had at times left them hidden beneath a patina of surliness. Besides, his death had been so chillingly horrid.

She wished she'd known Kellogg before he retired prematurely from public life twenty years ago—back when globe-hopping feats of shuttle diplomacy had lifted him to the stature of Nobel Peace Prize candidate. Back before the steep decline that had left him a broken and morose old man. He must have been something then.

Sabrina tried to recall her initial excitement over this project—money aside. To a struggling writer trying to recover from a devastating divorce that had shattered her belief in herself, being offered the chance to ghostwrite Jeremiah Kellogg's autobiography had appeared to be a major career leap. But the bad feelings had taken root the first moment she had set foot inside the mansion.

The place had been so different from what she had anticipated—so instantly and totally dispiriting—as if the esteemed Jeremiah Kellogg had been secretly leading a double life. She should have known right then and there that signing the contract with Sampson Books had set her on a course headed straight for disaster.

Now she was right back where she'd been last summer, a month after Darryl had stolen her spine and run off with a bleached-blond cocktail waitress, leaving Sabrina at the cold mercy of his creditors.

Nowhere.

And destitute.

The overhanging boughs parted abruptly and Sabrina came out into a weedy clearing a hundred or so yards southeast of the mansion. The stone cottage squatted near the back of the sloping ground, its sharply canted slate roof reaching almost down to shoulder height on the uphill side. A crooked, soot-blackened chimney jutted above one end of the roof, reminding Sabrina of the smelly cigars that Jeremiah Kellogg used to worry endlessly between his nicotine-yellowed teeth.

The cottage was a singularly ugly structure, the sight of which never failed to make her feel vaguely unwelcome. Finding Conrad Lafever's black BMW parked in front, a steady stream of gray vapor pouring from its exhaust pipe, lifted her spirits only marginally. Conrad sat behind the wheel, as ramrod straight as a homely, tawny-haired haberdashery mannequin.

He had asked her to ride down to the cemetery outside Schuylerville with him, but Sabrina had made a weak excuse for taking her own car. She'd never been at ease in Conrad's company, although he had always been kind to her. Too kind, she sometimes thought. Darryl had taught her to be leery of considerate men.

When Sabrina pulled in next to the BMW, Conrad got out, put on his charcoal gray felt hat, and strode over to open her car door for her. It was one of the many old-fashioned courtesies that she had come to expect from Kellogg's private secretary.

She slid out of her car, noticing that Conrad had left the BMW's engine running. She took that as an indication that he didn't intend to stay long, and was glad. She wasn't in the mood for company.

"Your left front tire has no tread, Sabrina." Conrad had the dulcet voice of an undertaker, the height of a professional basketball player and the temperament of an aged Saint Bernard. Twenty-five years in the service of Jeremiah Kellogg had prematurely aged the man. Sabrina continually had to remind herself that Conrad was only in his late forties.

"I've learned to live without tread, Conrad. You could read the Sunday paper through the spare."

His expression shifted into another version of deadpan. "Wet roads and bald tires are an especially dangerous combination."

So are creditors and an empty bank account, she thought, straining to maintain her false smile. Darryl's creditors had quickly devoured the entire initial advance that she had received from Sampson Books.

Up until three days ago, she had almost convinced herself that she could see the light at the end of that dismal tunnel. The book project was moving right along on schedule, carrying her steadily closer to receiving additional money from the publisher upon the book's completion. Then Jeremiah Kellogg had quite gruesomely gone to his reward on a dark and seldom-used back stairway of the mansion, sending an avalanche of cold reality thundering down to block the tunnel exit.

"Ah, well." She sighed. "You know what they say. Danger is the spice of life."

Conrad's gaze shifted to the tire, his thin lips pursing. For one horrible moment, Sabrina feared he was about to offer her money to buy a replacement. She prayed that he wouldn't do that to her last remaining shred of pride.

His cheek twitched. He slipped a long-fingered hand inside his suit coat. She winced, waiting for him to haul out his calfskin wallet—then relaxed as he produced a thin sheet of paper folded lengthwise.

"You received a fax from Sampson Books this morning," he said. "I didn't read it."

Sabrina believed him—Conrad was nothing if not discreet. She wasn't sure her own insatiable curiosity would have stood the test had their positions been reversed.

A heavy weight settled in her chest and began to swell as she accepted the sheet. She had been dreading this moment for three days. Her cold fingers trembled slightly as she unfolded the message from Ira Sampson informing her that her ghostwriting contract for Jeremiah Kellogg's autobiography had been cancelled because of the retired diplomat's untimely death.

Sabrina had no idea what she was going to do now. Her parents were no longer living. Thanks to Darryl, she no longer had a penny to her name. She had a frightening vision of herself dressed in rags, pushing a cart containing all her earthly belongings along a crowded Manhattan sidewalk.

She quickly scanned the first two or three lines of the letter, then backtracked to read them more carefully. A gust of icy wind caught the flimsy paper, almost ripping it from her hands. She gripped it more tightly, feeling the color drain from her face as the clearing began to spin crazily around her.

"Bad news, Sabrina?"

She looked up at him, suddenly drunk with shock, grinning like an idiot. "Good news. Incredibly wonderful news." Sabrina took a deep breath to still the reeling sensation, and laughed as she exhaled. "The publisher still wants *The End of the Line*—if I can make his pushed-up deadline."

Conrad hesitated for what seemed like a very long time. "Will that be possible without Mr. Kellogg?"

She pressed chilled fingertips to her lips, exhilarated— and frightened. The contract was still on. But she wasn't at all sure she would be able to fulfill it. Old doubts began to stir inside her like remnants of a not-quite-vanquished virus.

"I think so," she said finally. "But I'll need your help with the research, Conrad. The bits and pieces that I'd expected to get straight from Mr. Kellogg. Even then, it'll be a tight squeeze to get it all pulled together in six weeks."

His prominent Adam's apple lurched, then his tongue flicked out to wet his thin lips. Sabrina was suddenly, unaccountably certain that Conrad was about to lie to her.

"I will be most happy to assist you," he said, "if I'm still here following the reading of Mr. Kellogg's will next month."

Sabrina stared at him for a moment. It had never entered her mind that Conrad Lafever wasn't an integral component of the Kellogg estate, like the mansion itself and the venerable oaks. Now that it did, she hardly knew what to say.

"Conrad, surely you won't be let go after all these years."

"That's entirely up to Mr. Wetherbee, as executor of the estate—"

"Oh, of course. That's a relief. Wetherbee has seemed almost as keen on the book as Mr. Kellogg—"

"—and Spencer Bradley, as sole heir." Conrad pronounced the name with distaste.

As his meaning soaked in, Sabrina experienced a hideous sensation that the roller coaster had reached its apex and was plummeting downhill. And that she'd just fallen out.

"Oh, God, I'm dead," she murmured. "After the will is read, we'll both be here at Spencer Bradley's suffrage." She clasped a hand over her suddenly clammy forehead. "Did you notice the way Bradley looked at me when Wetherbee introduced us at the cemetery? I felt like something unspeakable stuck to the bottom of his shoe."

You also felt... Sabrina's hand drifted to her throat. She blinked again, this time in dismay. No—impossible, she thought. She couldn't possibly have felt *those* kinds of stirrings. Not under the baleful glare of Spencer Bradley.

"I'm sure that wasn't his intention," Conrad said unconvincingly.

"And all through the service, he looked mad at the world." She waited for more reassurance. When it was not forthcoming, she added, "Bradley hasn't shown his face around here since I've been at the estate. What can you tell me about him?"

"Not a great deal that's current, I'm afraid. He hasn't been back in twenty years. The last I heard, Bradley was a private security consultant with a rather exclusive international clientele."

The profession, at least, perfectly fitted the impression Sabrina already had of Spencer Bradley. She could definitely see him as the sort who would gravitate toward padlocks and sentry dogs. "Where does he live?"

"Hartford, London, Tokyo. And, I believe, Abu Dhabi."

"Sounds like his home is a suitcase."

Conrad merely shrugged.

"I'm dead," she said again. "Spencer Bradley isn't about to let me stay here and finish the book. Once he's on the premises, I'll be out on my ear."

"According to Mr. Kellogg's instructions, the will won't be read until the end of next month."

"Barely four and a half weeks." She shook her head. "Not enough time to finish the research." With the research completed, she might have persuaded Ira Sampson to grant an extension on the contract to give her time to do justice to the actual writing.

"I suppose not."

There didn't seem to be anything either of them could add to that dismal conclusion. The silence that settled between them quickly became awkward. Sabrina glanced toward the cottage door, but couldn't bring herself to invite Conrad inside out of the biting wind. His fossilized personality made casual conversation with him next to impossible.

His thin lips parted as if he was about to say something more. But then he touched a finger to the brim of his hat and moved toward his waiting car.

"By the way, Conrad..."

He stopped with the car door half-open and looked back at her.

"I was surprised that the Shaws didn't attend the graveside service," she said.

Orrin and Maria Shaw hadn't exactly endeared themselves to Sabrina during these past three months. But the taciturn old man and his equally reticent sister had been in Jeremiah Kellogg's employ even longer than Conrad, albeit as domestics. Their absence at the cemetery had seemed odd, to say the least.

"Maria hasn't been herself since Mr. Kellogg passed on," Conrad said. "Orrin thought it best if she didn't venture out in the weather and risk a chill. I suggested that he remain with her. At their age, you know..."

"Of course."

All the same, Sabrina thought it sounded like a weak excuse. Even in their sixties, Orrin Shaw was a sinewy bull of a man, and Maria had the constitution of a draft mule.

The housekeeper had in fact seemed singularly dry-eyed these past three days. If anything, Sabrina decided, Maria had appeared . . . worried. But that shouldn't have come as a surprise. Jeremiah Kellogg's sudden demise had robbed them all of job security.

Conrad folded himself into his car and nodded a farewell from behind the tinted glass. Sabrina watched him drive off down the gravel track toward the main driveway. When the BMW was out of sight, she glanced up the steep hill toward the mansion, nearly hidden from view by a dense stand of dark cedars. With a sigh, she turned toward the cottage.

The weathered door was unlocked—Sabrina had never bothered to inquire about a key. The hinges whined as she entered. As she pushed the door shut behind her, a shape darted from the shadows of the small front room, accompanied by a rasping sound like a screwdriver being pulled across sandpaper.

"Spying on us from the window were you, Quetzal?" She reached down and drew the big Siamese tom into her arms. He glowered at her with crossed eyes, his tail lashing testily. "It's freezing in here."

She crossed the front room, with it musty-smelling upholstered furniture and dark mahogany tables, and checked the antiquated propane heater in the corner. Tiny blue nubs of flames glowed behind the safety grate. She frowned, certain she had left it turned up higher. But when she examined the setting, the gas was almost fully off.

"What the devil?" Sabrina turned it up and dropped Quetzal onto the sofa. "Sit tight, my man. It'll warm up in a jiff."

In the kitchen, she placed a pan of water on the burner of the old range before hurrying off to change clothes. There was work to be done, and it wasn't in her nature to let things slide, regardless of her mood. If the ax was going to fall, it would have to catch her on the run.

Minutes later, Sabrina was back in the kitchen, having traded her black skirt and gray blouse for a comfortable maroon corduroy jumpsuit and soft ankle boots. When he heard the lid come off the tea tin, Quetzal came yowling in from the front room, his brown-black tail standing as straight as an exclamation point.

"I don't have time to join you." She poured steaming water through the tea strainer into a chipped saucer, blew on the pale liquid, and placed the saucer on the worn linoleum in front of the stove. "Enjoy."

Quetzal darted forward, purring like an out-of-tune engine. While she pulled on her coat, Sabrina watched him lap up the fragrant herbal tea. At the moment, the raggedy-eared old tom was the one bright spot in her life. She loved him dearly, and in his aloof feline way, she supposed he cared for her, too.

"I'll be up at the big house the rest of the day." It had been long months since she'd last had qualms about carrying on one-way conversations with a cat. "Be a gentleman."

His tail twitched once, marking a throaty break in the purring. Sabrina left the kitchen, grabbed her battered briefcase from the bench near the front door, and let herself outside.

The raw wind whipped her hair around her face as she struck off down the track that led around the base of the hill to the main driveway. Gravel crunched softly underfoot, the only sound other than the near-gale moaning through the trees. She pulled the collar of her coat higher, involuntarily shuddering at the eerie sensation that she was the only human being on the face of the planet.

Before coming here, she'd always had a particular fondness for the earthy smells of the countryside. But after three months in this gloomy place, Sabrina was aware only of the odor of decay. It filled her nostrils and embedded itself deeply in her spirit.

She picked up her pace, trying to ignore the cold. By the time she reached the juncture with the main driveway and turned right on the paved surface, her legs had begun tingling. She had gone perhaps another dozen yards when she heard a car turn off the highway behind her. She moved over to the edge of the driveway, but kept walking.

The vehicle caught up, then slowed, keeping pace with her. Sabrina moved farther to the left, almost off the pavement. The car nosed forward until she glimpsed a high black fender and a shiny, brass-colored wheel. Then she looked back, saw the driver, and halted in her tracks.

"Good afternoon, Sabrina." Spencer Bradley's tone was pleasant enough, in spite of his veiled expression.

He inched the Grand Cherokee forward another foot, then stopped, one elbow hanging out the open window, his right wrist draped over the steering wheel. His eyes were every bit as blue as Sabrina remembered from their earlier meeting at the cemetery—his gaze just as disturbingly invasive. His hair bore the look of an expensive cut. The way it fluttered around his face in the gusty wind somewhat softened the masklike hardness of his features. Even so, Spencer didn't strike her as being the sort of man who smiled easily. He had that in common with his recently deceased uncle and Conrad.

"Get in. I'll give you a lift up to the house," he said.

"No, thank you. I always walk, for the exercise."

"Do you now? Rain or shine?"

"Sleet or snow."

At that moment, Sabrina couldn't have explained why she was so astounded to see Spencer just then, or what she found so unsettling about the way he looked at her. But she knew without a shadow of doubt that a gang of armed thugs couldn't have persuaded her to get into his car with him.

She noticed metal cases, cardboard boxes and black leather suitcases jammed into every available square inch of space behind the front seat. When her gaze returned to

Spencer, she discovered that he was scowling at her brief-case.

"I understand you're staying in the cottage," he said. "The old man wouldn't offer you a room under his own roof?"

"Of course he did. I preferred the privacy of separate accommodations."

"Couldn't stand being in close proximity to the damned lowlife twenty-four hours a day, is that it?"

She stiffened, shocked. "No, that's not it."

He seemed to be waiting for her to elaborate—and Sabrina really did think she should come to the defense of the recently deceased. But at the moment, she couldn't come up with a single thing to add.

Finally he let her off the hook by asking, "How do you find the old cottage?"

"It isn't the most comfortable place I've ever lived in," she said truthfully.

Spencer nodded. "A refrigerator in the winter, and hot as hell all summer. Does the roof still leak like a sieve every time a wet Blue Norther blows in?"

Sabrina arched a brow. "How do you know about that?"

"I pulled drip-pan duty when I was a kid."

She almost dropped her briefcase. "You used to live in the cottage?"

"My mother and I. You didn't know?"

Spencer rubbed the back of one fist slowly across his chin and got an odd look in his eyes. A dozen questions flew into her mind, but Sabrina sensed this was not a good time to voice them.

Besides, she was too peeved. No one had so much as mentioned to her that Spencer and his mother, Zena, had once lived on the estate. The glaring omission couldn't possibly have been inadvertent—she would have caught it in her research. Sabrina clearly had to have been conspired against at every turn—certainly by Jeremiah Kellogg and

Conrad Lafever, possibly by Noble Wetherbee and others—for reasons she couldn't begin to understand.

Kellogg's abrupt retirement from public service had followed Zena's death by only weeks. He had spoken little of his only sibling, but Sabrina had assumed that Kellogg's sense of loss over Zena's passing had triggered his precipitous decline into reclusiveness. Learning that Zena and her son had lived in the meager little cottage—and not in the mansion—made her wonder if there had been more to the sibling relationship than met the eye. Though, God knew, she couldn't imagine what that might be.

Spencer seemed to catch himself wool-gathering, and returned his attention to her. "You're determined to hoof it all the way to the top of the hill?"

"Yes." She glanced at the packed cargo area once again. This time Spencer took notice.

"I'll be seeing you shortly then," he said. "I'm moving into the old mansion."

"Today?" The briefcase hit the pavement with a solid *whump.* Sabrina didn't even glance down at it. She couldn't seem to get her mouth shut. "But the will hasn't been read yet."

Spencer startled her with a harsh, mirthless laugh that actually made her take a step back off the edge of the pavement.

"Possession is nine-tenths of the law, my dear." He squinted through the windshield toward the mansion, still out of sight up the winding driveway. "Besides, I'm not about to let Conrad Lafever have sole tenancy on account of a technicality."

With a parting look that sent an alarming quiver through Sabrina, he put the Cherokee in gear and continued up the driveway. She stood motionless in the sodden leaves, gaping. Before he reached the first curve and disappeared, she snapped out of her trance, grabbed her briefcase, and hurried up the hill.

* * *

The hulking Kellogg mansion loomed cheerlessly out of
the trees, its mold-streaked limestone facade overgrown
with a creeping mass of Boston ivy. Three rows of narrow
glassed slits, looking more like gun ports than windows,
peeked through the greenish black foliage. Even on a sunny
day, Sabrina couldn't round the final curve in the driveway and catch sight of the big house without her heart
sinking a little.

Today, rain was threatening again, teasing with brief intermittent flurries of enormous drops as she huffed around
the last bend. She slowed to a sedate—though winded—
walk when she saw the Cherokee pulled under the protection of the deep portico.

Spencer was busy unloading his baggage onto the wide
steps leading up to the front door. Conrad Lafever stood
rigidly on the top step, watching. As she drew near, Sabrina sensed Conrad's fury, and was perplexed by it. She
paused for a moment in spite of the impending deluge, then
moved cautiously toward the portico as if approaching a
ticking bomb.

"You can't do this," Conrad said stiffly. Sabrina noticed with alarm that his normally pale face was flushed almost purple.

"Hide and watch, Connie." Spencer bared his teeth with
strain as he hauled a heavy aluminum case from the back
of the Cherokee.

"I'll ask you not to call me that," Conrad said icily.

"Ask away...Connie."

After lugging the case up the steps, Spencer deposited it
at Conrad's feet without so much as glancing at him, then
trudged back down to the car.

Sabrina stood just under the overhang, watching,
dumbfounded by the level of animosity that seemed to hum
between them like an electrical current. For two people who
apparently hadn't set eyes on each other for twenty-one

years, they were behaving as if they'd been carrying on a lifelong blood feud.

Spencer toted a suitcase up the steps and dropped it next to the aluminum case. Apparently he really did intend to move into the mansion, and he didn't seem to care at all about how bad an impression he made in the process.

"But the will hasn't been read yet," she said, unable to resist once more pointing out the obvious.

Spencer reached into the Cherokee and slung a leather suit bag over one broad shoulder before facing her. When he did, he was smiling.

Her first thought was that she'd been dead wrong—the man definitely knew how to smile. It started down around his collarbone and went all the way up to his piercing blue eyes. Her second thought came as even more of a surprise—Spencer wasn't half-bad-looking in a fierce sort of way.

"Spencer, I'm warning you. You have no right to live here until after the will is probated." Conrad nudged the aluminum case closer to the edge of the step with one foot.

His gaze stayed on Sabrina, but the muscles in Spencer's jaw knotted at the sound of the case scraping against the limestone step. "I wouldn't recommend that you push that case—or me—one inch farther, Connie."

He spoke softly, but the underlying menace in his voice reminded Sabrina of a snarling dog with a wagging tail. She moved away from Spencer, up the steps to stand beside Conrad. Spencer followed, still smiling. But his eyes were hooded, watchful.

A clap of thunder reverberated under the portico at the same instant that a curtain of gray rain came sheeting down. Spencer glanced back down the steps to make sure his baggage was safely under cover, then looked at Conrad.

Sabrina realized that he actually had to look up. Although Spencer appeared to be close to six feet tall, Conrad was easily a head taller. And yet she sensed that Spencer was the more formidable of the pair, both physically and otherwise. Something about him was as elemental—and dangerous—as the storm raging outside the sheltering portico. The thought sent an incongruous thrill through Sabrina that disturbed her mightily.

"As for who has a right to be living under this roof," Spencer said evenly, "my claim is far more valid than yours at this juncture, Connie. Need I mention that Kelloggs have occupied this house in an unbroken line since before the Civil War?"

"The king is dead, long live the king?" Conrad said tightly.

"If that's how you prefer to view it."

Instinctively retreating from her peculiar and seemingly bizarre attraction to Spencer, Sabrina found herself driven into Conrad's camp. "Your name isn't Kellogg, Mr. Bradley."

His gaze shifted to her, his smile hardening into a brittle line, making her wish she had kept her mouth shut.

"Surely, Sabrina, you know that's by *my* choice," he said so gently that her skin prickled. "Or was my dear departed uncle holding out on you?"

"I don't know what you're talking about," she said truthfully, but his question stung. She was good at what she did for a living. It hurt to be just now beginning to get the news that she'd been the victim of a snow job these past three months.

Spencer held her gaze for an interminable moment before nodding slowly. "I see. Then let's just settle for bloodlines being more important than names. God help us all."

While Sabrina tried to make sense of that last sentence, he pivoted on one foot and marched through the open front doorway. Seconds later, she heard his footsteps ascending the main staircase from the foyer, sounding doggedly resolute, as if he knew exactly where he was heading.

She closed her eyes and took a deep breath, which did nothing to quell the wave of nausea washing through her. *All that work down the tubes,* she thought miserably. *As soon as Spencer has the power, he'll boot me off the estate and never look back.*

CHAPTER TWO

"Damned mausoleum," Spencer muttered, surveying the second-floor hallway.

The drab walls were hung with age-darkened family portraits in heavy gilt frames, dimly illuminated by antiquated brass sconces that hadn't been polished in years, from the looks of them. The ornate Persian carpet runner in bloodred, black and gold had seen better days. But more than anything else, he was aware of the odor.

It was the stench of death.

In this case, it was the house that was dying. He frowned, inhaling the musty redolence of deteriorating wood, motheaten rugs and crumbling wallpaper. The mansion's inexorable slide toward the wrecker's ball hadn't yet progressed to the point of no return—of that, he was certain. But the creep of potentially mortal ruin was obvious at every turn.

For all his worldly achievements as a government diplomat, Spencer thought sardonically, the esteemed Jeremiah Kellogg had been a less-than-responsible steward of the family heritage.

To his right, a second set of stairs much narrower than those leading from the marble-tiled main foyer curved up toward the third floor. Spencer peered up, trying to remember if he had climbed two flights of steps the one and only time he'd previously ventured into the mansion. He had been no more than ten. Nearly thirty years had blurred his memory of that singular occasion—but not the emotions that had accompanied it.

His stomach spasmed now, as it had then.

Most of all, he felt . . . rage.

He gripped the carved walnut newel with a sweating hand, startled by the depth of searing anger that surged through him. Beneath it, quivering in its own private dungeon, lay humiliation.

"Damn you, Jeremiah," Spencer whispered through clenched teeth. "Damn you to the hell you so richly deserve."

Then it passed. The heat seemed to pour out of him in a rush, sending a single rivulet of sweat racing swiftly down the hollow of his spine. He jerked his head to one side as if shaking off a bad dream, and drew the back of one hand across his mouth.

A dim image of his mother drifted into Spencer's mind. He tried to concentrate on it, wishing she could have been here to savor their revenge. But if she were here, revenge wouldn't be necessary.

Without another conscious thought—responding to some deeper awareness rooted in his childhood—Spencer turned his back on the second staircase and moved confidently to his left along the threadbare carpet runner. Dark, deeply paneled walnut doors bracketed the hallway, all of them closed. He had no inclination at this time to find out what lay behind them. His attention was focused straight ahead on a set of double doors at the end of the passage.

He barely broke stride when he reached them. His hand slapped down on the brass lever of the door on the right, and he shouldered the door open with such force that it slammed back against the wall.

Spencer didn't know why he suddenly remembered it with such clarity, but Jeremiah's sitting room was just as it had been all those years ago. Shades were drawn over the narrow, deep-set windows, but he could still make out the two wing Queen Anne chairs, the claw-footed couch, the marble-topped table in front of the blackened maw of the stone hearth. Over in the corner, a small rolltop desk stood on ball casters, its myriad cubbyholes jammed with papers.

He crossed to the windows and reached behind dusty lace panels to raise the shades. Very little light penetrated the wavy hand-blown glass panes. He moved on through a door, which stood open to the left of the desk.

The high-ceilinged bedroom was smaller than the sitting room by about half, but spacious, nevertheless. It had to be in order to accommodate a huge sleigh bed and an armoire the size of a '57 Chevy standing on its bumper. The bedclothes had been removed, laying bare a jarringly modern, pillow-topped mattress quilted in pale blue satin. A narrow door in the opposite wall led into a bathroom—he glimpsed an old-fashioned claw-footed tub through the opening.

Spencer went straight to the row of windows to raise the shades. Holding the leather suit bag over a shoulder by two fingers, he struggled with one hand to shove open one of the narrow casement windows. It finally swung out with a harsh, grating sound, admitting a gust of damp, chilly air.

He turned to find a thickset old man watching him from the doorway to the sitting room, both hands thrust deeply into the pockets of gray coveralls. They stared mutely across the room at each other for a long moment, until Spencer was convinced the old man could stand there all afternoon without uttering a word.

"Do you work here?" he asked finally, shifting the suit bag to his other hand.

"For nigh on forty years," the old man grumbled, barely moving his lips. He reached up to claw at his thinning iron gray sideburns, then returned the gnarled hand to his pocket.

Spencer started involuntarily at the vaguely familiar gesture, recognition hitting home like a hard fist in his gut. The last time he had seen Orrin Shaw, the handyman had been a veritable ox, with a deep barrel chest and only a salting of gray in his short black hair. But with his robust middle years well behind him now, Shaw seemed to have buckled. His shoulders were hunched, and his sallow skin hung on the bony framework of his face like the papery hide of a deflated toad.

"You've changed...Mr. Shaw," he said, more graciously than he would have thought possible.

"You haven't much...*boy,*" the old man flung back, effectively quashing Spencer's budding suspicion that Shaw might have mellowed with the years.

Spencer leaned back against the windowsill, giving himself time to adjust. He had prepared himself to deal with Conrad Lafever, but he simply hadn't expected Shaw to be still around after more than two decades. "Is Maria, er—" *among the living?* "—well?" he asked.

One side of Shaw's mouth twisted sourly. "Sister is tolerable."

More tolerable than you, old man, Spencer thought, although his expression registered nothing. When Shaw fell silent again, he began to lose patience.

"Did you want something?" Spencer plucked absently at peeling paint on the windowsill. "Other than to satisfy your curiosity, of course."

The old man's jaw worked as if he was chewing on something tough. "Reckoned I'd see if you'd be needing me for anything."

"Ah." He smiled thinly, carefully inspecting a tiny shard of paint. "You thought I might enjoy having my backside kicked up between my ears for straying too close to the big house? Just for old times' sake?"

Shaw glared at him from beneath a shelf of bristly eyebrows. Spencer kept smiling, belying the fact that another part of him was suddenly going on point. He studied the old man more closely, detecting something he had missed earlier—something that had lain hidden beneath the predictable surliness. At first he thought he surely must be mistaken. Then he knew he wasn't.

Behind the crusty veneer, Orrin Shaw was scared spit-less. It showed in that great window to the world that no one could completely shutter, if you just knew where to look—the eyes.

While Spencer was still mulling over that remarkable bit of observation, Shaw started backing out of the doorway.

He quickly stepped away from the window. "Since you're here..."

Shaw halted, half-turned away.

"I'll be taking over this suite of rooms," Spencer said. "And I want that thing out of here before nightfall." He indicated the big sleigh bed.

The handyman looked abashedly at the bed, then at Spencer, as if he'd just been ordered to burn the piece of furniture to the floorboards where it stood. "How come?"

"Because I heard Jeremiah was brought back up here after his accident and died in his bed."

"He did."

"Well, I'm just superstitious enough not to want to sleep in someone else's deathbed."

That, too, seemed to catch Shaw by surprise. "Every head of this house since the place was built has slept in that bed."

"Not this one. Break it down and get it out of here. Replace it with something from one of the guest rooms. I'm not particular."

A slight tick tugged at Shaw's left eye. Spencer watched it, waiting, wondering if the mangy dog really could bring himself to ignore the past and take orders from him. The old animosity was still there as strong as ever. Shaw didn't want him around now any more than he had before. But, as before, the choice wasn't Shaw's to make.

After what appeared to be a good deal of internal struggle, the old man finally seemed to reconcile himself to the situation as it now presented itself. He hunched his shoulders higher beneath his long-lobed ears and cast a sidelong glance at the bed. "Have to go fetch my tools," he said sullenly.

"Is there someone who can give you a hand hauling out that mastodon, too?" Spencer nodded toward the monstrous armoire. He didn't fancy waking up to it every morning.

"Can't take it out."

"Can't?" He leaned forward, his free fist on his hip. "Or won't?"

The tick worsened. Shaw refused to even make eye contact with him now. "It's the closet."

It took a few seconds for Spencer to catch on. When he did, he glanced around the bedroom, searching for another door besides the one opening into the bathroom. There was none. The house predated built-in closets. But it hadn't occurred to him that no one had bothered to remedy that situation in more recent times.

"Right." He grudgingly made a closer inspection of the armoire. The door pulls were inlaid mother-of-pearl. Inside, the cabinetry smelled of mothballs. "Jeremiah used this?"

"He did."

Spencer was tempted to ask if his uncle had gone to his grave reeking of mothballs. At least someone—most likely Shaw's sister, Maria—had removed Jeremiah's clothes. He closed the door and hung his suit bag from a filigreed hook on the outside.

"This whole blasted place needs a good airing." He threw open another window and leaned his head out. The room was already turning cold, but he no longer felt as if he were breathing through a musty shroud. "Tell me, does Lafever still live on the premises?"

"In the servants' quarters."

"You don't say." Spencer straightened. "And where would that be?"

"Downstairs, off the pantry."

"Then where do you and Maria call home these days?"

The old man hesitated, then jabbed a thumb toward the ceiling.

"On the third floor?"

Shaw drew down the corners of his lips sourly, as if he had just been accused of something underhanded. Without another word, he turned and shuffled off into the sitting room. Seconds later, Spencer heard the door to the hallway close with a pronounced thump.

"Old coot," he muttered, wondering if the Shaws were still the only live-in help on the estate, and how much day help would be at his disposal. "Damn little, from the looks of it."

He leaned out the window again, squinting at the sting of rain on his face as he peered at the unkempt grounds below. The lawn hadn't been mowed at the end of summer, and autumn leaves had been left to rot among the tall weeds. But the foundation beds directly beneath the window had been turned so the soil could mellow over the winter, and an old pear tree down near the foot of the lawn showed the pale scars of a recent pruning. Apparently the estate wasn't being allowed to go completely to seed.

Hissing a sigh through his teeth, Spencer ducked back into the room. His gaze fell upon the sleigh bed, and he had to stretch his imagination to grasp the certainty that his uncle had actually bedded two wives there—and outlived both of them. Had Jeremiah grieved? Or had he simply ordered a new mattress and turned his back on that chapter of his past, just as he had turned it on his own sister while driving her to the ultimate desperation?

Painful images fathered a dull ache at the base of his skull. Spencer angrily shoved them away and returned to the sitting room, where he stood staring blindly into space for some minutes, deep in thought.

He hadn't heard a peep about old Jeremiah's autobiography until Noble Wetherbee had told him about it just before the funeral that morning. Sabrina Glade had come as yet another nasty surprise. How much did she know, or even suspect?

The fact that Spencer and his mother had lived in the cottage when he was a kid had clearly come as news to Sabrina. That led him to the perhaps optimistic conclusion that his uncle probably had been less than candid with his ghostwriter regarding certain aspects of Kellogg family history. But that didn't make sense. Surely the old man hadn't expected to keep a lid firmly on the family secrets while giving someone else a hand in preparing his memoirs.

Spencer cursed softly under his breath. After two decades of living like a hermit, he couldn't imagine what had possessed Jeremiah to risk stirring up the past. But then, maybe the old man hadn't viewed it as a risk. Maybe Jeremiah had viewed it as a chance to make a final, cruel slap at Zena before he, too, left this world.

Spencer pushed his lower lip pensively over its mate. Sabrina Glade was a threat, all right. He had seen that in her eyes the moment he mentioned having lived in the cottage. She would scratch at that tiny trickle of information until she drew blood—unless he got rid of her first.

With Jeremiah dead, it shouldn't be difficult to get the entire book killed. For all Spencer knew, the publisher might have already dropped it. But if that was the case, why was Sabrina still hanging around?

There was no better time for finding that out than the present, he decided.

A low cascade of thunder reverberated through the house, sounding like a row of distant skyscrapers tipping over. Spencer tugged a wool sweater over his dress shirt and raked the hair off his forehead as he started down the main staircase. He halted his descent when he saw Maria Shaw cross the foyer below.

The housekeeper still wore her hair in a long thin braid coiled around the crown of her head. Like her brother's, it had turned iron gray. But unlike Orrin, Maria hadn't knuckled under to the years. She still held her back as straight as a regimental drill instructor's, her heels clacking like pistol shots on the tiles as she hurried along with a double armload of linens.

Only when she started up the staircase did the ravages of time become more apparent. The once-milky skin of her face had shriveled, pulling downward to bitterly pursed lips that seemed to be drawing away in distaste from the sharp blade of her nose. In middle age, Maria Shaw had been a plain woman. During the ensuing years, Spencer observed, her difficult temperament had exacted a heavy toll.

When she noticed him standing in the shadowy upper reaches of the staircase, she halted as if she had walked into an invisible wall. Her expression didn't change as she took him in. He wasn't at all sure that it could. Her features appeared to be permanently frozen like corrugated ice.

"Maria," he said, slowly working his shirt collar out from the sweater's crew neck.

She nodded, a carefully measured lowering of her inadequate chin. No greeting. Nothing. She knew how to make someone feel unwelcome without putting herself out in the least.

"You'll be wanting bedding," she said.

"Good idea."

He could trust her with that. But it suddenly occurred to him that he couldn't trust her not to spit in his soup. There were limitations to the virtue of old enemies.

For now, he would have to be satisfied that, as with her brother, Maria apparently had reconciled herself to Spencer's right to assume Jeremiah Kellogg's recently vacated position. He would deal with the question of their continued—or, more likely, their discontinued—employment on the estate when he had the legal right to do so.

"How much day help do you have?" he asked, trying to get a handle on the place.

"None."

He grunted. No wonder the estate was so run-down. The very idea of trying to manage a place this size without a small army of domestics and gardeners was nothing short of ludicrous.

"Is Sabrina Glade still here?" he asked, resuming his descent.

"In the library—as usual."

Did he detect a note of disapproval in the housekeeper's response? Or had that been just her normal acid tone? He couldn't be sure. He did notice that she moved close against the wall as they passed each other, as if loath to come into contact with him.

Spencer moved quickly down the remaining stairs, smiling grimly at the thought that he was safe in at least one quarter. Maria didn't have the sense of humor to try short sheeting his bed.

The foyer was warm. The air felt surprisingly close for an old house of that size in the dead of winter. No drafts to speak of. The heating bills must be horrendous. He almost wished he hadn't worn the sweater.

There was also the silence. He stood perfectly still on the marble tiles, listening.

As incredible as it seemed, he would rather be in his present state of perplexity than to have admitted to Maria Shaw that he hadn't the foggiest idea where to find the library. It didn't much matter that she undoubtedly already knew that, he thought, and cast a quick look up the curving staircase in time to catch a slight movement of shadow on the second-floor landing.

A wide hallway opened off the back of the foyer. Spencer headed down it, past a matched pair of waist-high Chinese vases that looked ancient and extremely valuable. They would be his soon, but he barely glanced at them. His main objective at the moment was to remove himself from Maria Shaw's line of sight.

A lace-curtained French door on the right proved to give access to a long windowless room that might once have been a private parlor. Now it looked more like an elephant boneyard of old brocade sofas and dark gateleg tables draped with fringed cloths that appeared to have come straight from Queen Victoria's boudoir.

Spencer had seen very little of the interior of the mansion on his single previous visit inside. But he knew he wasn't remembering it with misty-eyed nostalgia when he realized it hadn't been like this then. Something had happened to the place—to Jeremiah.

A sickness of the soul, he thought. Spencer quickly closed his mind to the possibility that the same sickness might have infected him long-distance.

Farther along the hallway, a set of pocket doors stood half ajar. He slowed, hearing a quiet murmur of voices on the other side. As he drew nearer, he heard Conrad Lafever's muffled intonations, then Sabrina's soft response, but couldn't quite make out what they were saying.

Lafever's voice stopped abruptly, to be followed by the sound of a closing door. Spencer stepped silently into the partly open doorway and looked inside.

Floor-to-ceiling bookcases filled with leather-bound volumes covered three walls of the library. The north-facing fourth wall was mostly mullioned glass with a view of the broad sweep of rain-drenched lawn and—some fifty yards in the distance—a fieldstone stable that had been converted into a six-car garage before Spencer's time. Three green leather club chairs were spaced around a long oak library table laden with at least a foot of neatly stacked papers, folders and books.

Wan light from the glass wall penetrated only a few feet into the room. Two Venetian-glass ceiling lights cast a muddy glow over the library table. A brass desk lamp with a green glass shade shone at the far end, where Sabrina Glade sat frowning intently at a portable computer. Lafever was nowhere to be seen, apparently having departed through a paneled door across the room.

Spencer started to clear his throat—started to, but didn't. For a moment, he was oddly mesmerized by the way the lamplight lay warmly across Sabrina's slightly downcast face and turned her sable hair to glossy silk. She had on a soft, oversize corduroy jumpsuit that made her look even smaller than she was, and almost fragile. Her thin-soled boots swung gently, barely brushing the Aubusson rug beneath her chair.

His gaze lingered on the delicate slope of her cheek, the nearly imperceptible twitch of her softly parted lips, the way the tip of her index finger lightly, absently traced the curve of her chin. She shifted in her chair and sighed—a vague sound of distress that stirred Spencer and so startled him that he lurched back from the doorway, drawing a fist across his dry lips.

He stared at the floor, swallowing with effort, his expression drifting somewhere between stunned and bemused. It wasn't like him to have so little self-control around women. He suddenly felt parched. And beneath the thirst, a deep, gnawing hunger.

CHAPTER THREE

Sabrina was having trouble focusing on her work following the brief but mystifying exchange with Conrad. She had sensed from the hesitant manner in which he had followed her to the library that something unpleasant was preying on his mind.

Considering the tense little scene that had just played itself out at the front portico, she supposed it was only natural for her to have assumed that Conrad's problem was directly related to Spencer Bradley. But when she had tried to broach that subject indirectly by mentioning Jeremiah Kellogg's sister, Zena, Conrad had suddenly remembered that he needed to be elsewhere. She hadn't had a chance to ask why she had been left in the dark regarding the past occupants of the cottage.

"Weird," she whispered.

It wasn't like Conrad to be so jumpy. Spencer's audacious storming of the estate seemed to have thrown him for a loop. She couldn't decide which bothered her most—Conrad's unprecedented discombobulation; the discovery that he had apparently conspired with Jeremiah Kellogg to deceive her; or her own Spencer-induced conviction that she was no longer wanted on the property.

She unfastened the top button of her jumpsuit and fanned the collar. The library was uncomfortably warm and stuffy, as usual. Kellogg had possessed an old man's aversion to the cold, although he hadn't thought twice about exposing others to it. Sabrina tried to picture Spencer Bradley sleeping in the drafty stone cottage with a hot water bottle at his feet, as she had done this winter. But she just couldn't get her imagination to grab hold of the idea.

Bradley's revelation that he and his mother had once lived in the ramshackle cottage had come as a shock. Sabrina could almost understand why Kellogg and his intensely loyal private secretary apparently had gone out of their way to keep it from her. Almost, but not quite.

Bradley's mother had been Jeremiah Kellogg's only sibling. With Zena's death many years ago, Spencer had become Jeremiah's last living relative on this earth. That Zena and her son should have been compelled to live in what must have been a kind of internal exile on the estate, while Kellogg basked in the international limelight and played lord of the manor, simply didn't fit the tapestry Sabrina had been weaving of the former diplomat's life.

She stared blindly at the glowing screen of her laptop computer while tracing the line of her chin with a fingertip. While working on his memoirs, she had developed a biographer's empathy for Kellogg. Even so, she'd had trouble capturing his "voice"—getting into the subliminal groove that would have allowed her to relate his life's story in words that read as if they'd come straight from his own mind.

What's more, crucial doubts had begun taking shape. Sabrina now admitted to herself that she had begun to suspect weeks ago that she just might be dealing with a deception—that Jeremiah Kellogg might not be the man she'd thought she had come to know so well. On several occasions, she'd even had the odd impression that he had begun to intentionally encourage such conjecture.

He wore a mask, she thought with a sigh. *The old fraud was as two-faced as a crafty politician up for reelection.* Which begged the question: Had the real Jeremiah been more than she had thought he was, or less?

From that intriguing point, Sabrina's train of thought slid smoothly on to Spencer Bradley. Her frown deepened. The private Jeremiah Kellogg beneath the former world-class diplomat hadn't been the most likable person Sabrina had ever met. But that alone wouldn't explain why his own nephew apparently despised him.

Suddenly sensing that she was being watched, Sabrina glanced toward the partially open door to the hallway. No one was there. Nevertheless, she felt an eerie *awareness* of someone—a prickly sentience that inexplicably filled her veins with icy needles.

"Maria...?"

The housekeeper didn't answer.

Suddenly Sabrina knew who it was. She knew—and hoped with all her heart that he would go away.

From the hallway came the sound of a decidedly masculine throat being cleared restrainedly. Seconds later, Spencer Bradley appeared in the doorway.

He had traded his suit and tie for a well-worn fisherman's-knit pullover. His hair had tumbled across his wide forehead—he reached up now and raked it ineffectively. Quite apart from the appealingly casual decline of his heretofore immaculate appearance, however, there was a peculiar disarrayed look about him that defied description.

"Didn't mean to interrupt you." He pawed his hair again, eyeing her severely. "I, uh, was on my way out to get the rest of my stuff."

He spoke in an almost library whisper. There was something extraordinarily intimate-sounding about his hushed voice in the stillness of the room.

Sabrina nodded slowly, her fingers gripping the edge of the library table. "You've missed the front door by a good ninety feet . . . Mr. Bradley."

His hand froze in his hair, then gravitated back down to grip his neck. *He's going to smile,* she thought uneasily, *all the way up to those devastating sapphire blues.* When he did, a rich current of heat flowed through her like warm honey.

"Please, call me Spencer." He glanced back at the hallway that led to the foyer and the front door. "You don't cut a man much slack, Sabrina."

"I'm only following your lead," she said, feeling as if she had blundered onto a tightrope.

Spencer dropped his hand, along with the smile. "Ah. You're referring to my little encounter with Lafever earlier."

"It didn't seem 'little' to him."

He stared into the middle distance for a moment, then shrugged. "We have a history together, Connie and I do. It's ancient, but well-defined."

"Aren't you being a touch enigmatic?"

"Not at all. You see, Connie's the son Uncle Jeremiah always dreamed of." Spencer clasped his hands behind him and rocked back on his heels. "I'm the nephew he never wanted."

I wonder why, she thought dryly. "But Mr. Kellogg left you everything. Or so go the rumors."

He gave a caustic laugh. "Now *there* lies the real enigma."

Sabrina flinched at his tone. There was a barely concealed volatile quality about him, like very old and unstable dynamite. Every now and then, Sabrina caught a glimpse of pent-up fury lurking just beneath the surface. She was leery of Spencer Bradley—and he seemed to know it just as a predator senses prey.

"You really don't feel the least bit morally obligated to speak kindly of the dead, do you?" she asked quietly.

The question obviously didn't sit well with him. "Surely, Sabrina, in the course of your research you've noticed that morality isn't a dominant trait in this family."

"Would you care to give me an example?"

"Certainly. Jeremiah's father, my grandfather—"

"Layton Kellogg."

"Right. Old Layton was just as amoral as the rest of us, in his fashion. The way Layton went through wives made Henry VIII look like Husband of the Year."

"You seem proud of that," she said.

All traces of his smile vanished. He looked grimly resigned. "Let's just say I harbor no grand illusions regarding my bloodlines."

After advancing another step into the room, he pivoted on one heel as he took in the rugs, the books, the rain-bleared view out the windows as though he was seeing them all for the first time. Maybe a twenty-one-year absence did that to you, Sabrina thought.

He turned slowly to look at her. She mentally braced herself for the instant his gaze would meet hers, realizing she was perilously close to being afraid of Spencer Bradley. Only when the full force of his deep-set blue eyes seemed to drive into her did she realize her anticipation had not been dread—but excitement.

Remember Darryl, she warned herself. *He excited you once upon a time, too. Then he wiped his feet all over you.*

With narrowed eyes, Spencer studied her for a moment, as if he were examining a painting that both interested and bewildered him. His lips parted, and he seemed on the verge of smiling again. She braced herself for that, too. But then he cleared his throat, and his gaze drifted on to the organized clutter covering the library table.

"You haven't stopped working on Jeremiah's book." A sharp edge had crept into his voice.

"The publisher intends to honor the contract." Sabrina didn't mention that it all hinged on whether she could meet Ira Sampson's pushed-up deadline without the help of Jeremiah Kellogg.

"But what if I don't want the publisher to be so...decent?" he asked. "What if I'd prefer to see the contract canceled?"

That was exactly what Sabrina had been afraid he would say. Her grip on the table tightened. For a moment, she felt as if she couldn't get a deep breath. Then her survivor's instincts kicked in, and she forced herself to go on the attack.

She managed to look Spencer squarely in the eye as she said, "That's between you, your lawyer and Sampson Books. Frankly I suspect that Ira Sampson would like nothing better than to go to court over it."

He didn't look as impressed as Sabrina had hoped. "That could be a mistake," he said. "I have a very good lawyer. Several, in fact."

"So does Mr. Sampson." She pried her fingers off the table and clenched them in her lap where Spencer couldn't see them. "He also has a flashy Park Avenue public relations firm at his beck and call. Before you knew it, they'd have the entire English-speaking world wondering why you were so all-fired anxious to kill Jeremiah Kellogg's autobiography." *And I'd be at the head of that line.*

His lips parted on a retort, but Sabrina hurried on.

"Come to think of it, Sampson Books publishes in nine different languages. Considering Mr. Kellogg's lengthy career as a high-profile diplomat, any effort to block publication of his book would likely make the news from Rome to Rangoon."

His eyes narrowed. He waited several seconds, then asked, "Are you quite finished?"

Sabrina nodded, clenching and unclenching her hands in her lap. This would be much easier to handle, she thought, if she wasn't sitting there impaled by that penetrating gaze.

"Rome to Rangoon." If it wasn't for the arctic glint in his eyes, he would have seemed to be savoring the alliterative phrase. "Are you threatening me, Sabrina?"

"Threatening?" She tried to look horrified by the suggestion, but that was precisely what she'd had in mind. "Mr. Bradley...Spencer, I'm only trying to point out some of the pitfalls you might encounter. Tabloid journalism is getting way out of hand these days, you know."

His jaw muscles knotted. He rocked on his heels again. Finally he gave a small, almost courtly bow, and said, "Consider me forewarned."

The abrupt—if mildly sarcastic—capitulation caught Sabrina by surprise. Her hands relaxed. She glanced down and saw that her fingernails had clawed small red crescents into her palms.

"So it's all right if I continue coming here to work?" she asked.

Spencer hesitated, then shrugged. "There isn't a whole lot I can do about it until after the will is probated."

"And then?"

"'Then' is on down the road, Sabrina. Let's not get ahead of ourselves."

That's it, Spencer, she thought, dryly swallowing a hard knot of frustration. *Leave me hanging on by the skin of my teeth.*

"If you don't mind my saying so," she said, "you seem a good deal more disturbed by your uncle's book than by his untimely demise."

Spencer appeared remarkably unruffled by her observation. "What did you expect?"

"I don't know. Grief."

"Jeremiah didn't deserve it."

"You really believe that, don't you?" Sabrina shook her head. "Mr. Kellogg wasn't the totally fiendish ogre that you seem to be trying to paint him as being."

"Which only proves that it isn't possible to develop every mean-spirited trait known to man in one lifetime." He spread his hands mockingly. "So you'll have to forgive me if I'm not inclined to wear a black arm band." He shifted his gaze to the dreary view through the window. "Grief is like friendship, Sabrina. You get what you give. And that old man never cared enough for anyone to grieve for one blessed second."

The chill in his voice shook her. "You know that for a fact, do you?"

Spencer returned his gaze to her, his expression stony. Long seconds later, he nodded. "For a fact."

It was a harsh, damning judgment of his uncle. It was also the gospel truth, at least as Spencer viewed it. Sabrina could see that conviction in his eyes and in the granite set of his jaw.

The problem was, it couldn't be true. It all came back to Jeremiah Kellogg's premature decline having begun soon after Zena's death. In the face of that, Sabrina couldn't much credit Spencer's contention that Kellogg cared for no one but himself. The old man must have loved his sister deeply to have been so devastated by the loss.

"Are you against memoirs on general principles?" she asked. "Or are you afraid this one might turn out to be a fluff piece that won't do justice to your concept of Jeremiah Kellogg as an odious villain?"

He just looked at her as if her question wasn't worthy of a response.

"My grandmother always told me that we hate most about others the things we like least in ourselves," she said. "I can't help wondering if you see too much of Mr. Kellogg in yourself, Spencer."

He blinked rapidly—Sabrina's only visual clue that her remark had registered on him at all. For several seconds, he stood so still that he might not have been breathing.

"Wonder whatever you want to," he said slowly, with a kind of savage quietness.

The brutal edge to his voice gave her a powerful urge to flee. At the same time, an indefinable something swam into his deep blue eyes, making her want to reach out and hold him the way any decent human being would move to comfort a suffering animal—warily, for fear of being bitten.

Spencer stood more than ten feet from her. And yet she suddenly had an almost tactile sense of his body heat that sent her blood racing. She couldn't begin to understand this strange pushed-pulled feeling, nor why she was so drawn to the man when he was making it so hard for her to even like him.

"Your uncle hurt you to the quick," she said. It was a statement, not a question.

"No," he flung back too quickly, "not me."

Sabrina didn't believe him for a second. Her instincts told her that she had stumbled onto a deep and festering wound that represented Spencer Bradley's soft underside. She sensed that, like his uncle, he was a fraud—only of a different kind. Recalling the stirring quality of Spencer's transient smile, she found herself wondering what manner of vulnerabilities lay hidden behind the elaborate facade that he presented to the world.

She toyed with a pen while mentally triaging a rapidly accumulating string of follow-up questions. Before she could lay the first one on him, Spencer drifted over to the far end of the library table. He raised the cover of a file folder and studied the laser-printed copies of photographs inside.

"Candidates for the cover photo," she said.

"They don't really show the man's true character, do they?" He let the folder cover slide off the tips of his fingers. "It's a shame you don't have one of Jeremiah all decked out in chains like Jacob Marley's ghost."

"That's sick."

"Why? Don't you believe in ghosts?" He threw up both hands. "Sorry, I forgot. You are one."

Sabrina put down the pen, gazing at him across the length of the table. "Honestly, Spencer. Cheekiness doesn't become you."

Ignoring that, he continued fingering the research materials on the table. Sabrina stiffened. She had always prided herself in being systematic and thorough in her work. That trait had taken on near-manic proportions since the divorce, as if maintaining rigid control of her work would somehow mend her ravaged emotions. She watched warily now, lest Spencer shift something out of place and disrupt her carefully designed system. At the same time, she was mentally opening a large new file with "Spencer Bradley" on the label.

"I don't recognize your name," he said. "Have I ever read anything you've written?"

Sabrina hated that question. She had never managed to come up with an answer that didn't make her sound either like an egomaniac or an underachiever.

She settled for "I don't ghost and tell."

"Admirable. How did you manage to land this job?"

"Luck." *And a certain amount of hard-earned skill with the written word,* she added to herself.

Spencer snorted. "Then as the saying goes, if you didn't have bad luck, you wouldn't have any luck at all."

"I don't see it that way."

In the face of Sabrina's financial woes of last summer, landing the Kellogg contract had been like being thrown a life raft. Though the vessel had sprung a huge leak these past few days, she still clung to the slim hope that it might carry her to safe harbor.

Spencer stopped prowling and braced both hands on a stack of books, leaning forward and hunching his shoulders. His disturbingly tactile gaze fixed on her once more. Feeling as if she were being physically pressed back in her chair by his stare, Sabrina struggled to keep her own gaze leveled on him without blinking.

"I can't keep you from finishing this book, Sabrina," he said evenly. "Now I'm not so sure that it would be a good idea, even if it was possible."

"It would be a terrible idea."

"You're prejudiced." Spencer smiled fleetingly. "But that's your problem. Anyway, if it's convenient for you to continue working here in the library, you have my blessing."

"Thank you."

"But I would prefer that you come to me if you need anything, instead of going to Lafever. In fact, I'm going to insist on that."

Sabrina did blink then. "You what?"

"It's a peculiarity of mine. I don't like the sound of whispers behind closed doors. Especially not in my own house."

Sabrina bristled, realizing that he must have been lurking outside the library door when she had had the brief exchange with Conrad earlier.

"But that's absurd, Spencer. Conrad worked closely with Mr. Kellogg for more than twenty-five years. He can provide information that you couldn't possibly know anything about."

She didn't mention that, having stumbled onto the deception-by-omission regarding the cottage, she no longer possessed total confidence in Conrad Lafever's veracity. At the moment, Sabrina was mainly concerned with preserving her research options.

"Don't make the mistake of selling me short, Sabrina. I'm not a total babe in these woods."

"Now that you bring it up, it hasn't exactly escaped my notice that you have certain wolfish traits."

He straightened slowly. "Just looking out for my own interests."

"And that involves putting your agenda ahead of Conrad's."

"There's something wrong with that?"

"No," she conceded. "Not as long as we agree that you're both trying to protect something. Conrad is and will always remain intensely loyal to Mr. Kellogg. And as you've already said, you're looking out for...yourself."

"And what about you, Sabrina?" His voice had once again fallen to that oddly intimate near whisper as he studied her with hooded eyes. "Whose music are you dancing to?"

He was playing with her. Her temper flared, but she managed to rein it in behind a smile that felt like plastic. The man was a frightful challenge, no doubt about it.

"I'm just trying to finish the job I started out to do, Spencer. So let's say I'm out to protect my integrity as a writer."

His head cocked slightly. "Really?"

She caught the glint in his eye, and her temper got the bit in its teeth and burst through the gate. "I resent that look."

"What look?"

"The one that says you think ghostwriters don't have integrity." She slammed a fist down on the table. "That we're some kind of creative prostitutes."

He gave a short, almost appreciative laugh. "Temper, temper."

"Don't you dare patronize me."

"Wouldn't dream of it."

"And while we're discussing agendas, Spencer Bradley, need I remind you that you have no right to be telling me whether I can or cannot work here." She pounded the table again. "Let alone decide whom I can speak with. Until Mr. Kellogg's will is read, those decisions are in the hands of his attorney."

Spencer said nothing to that. He just stared at her with that maddeningly sphinxlike expression that he could pull up like a shield. Meanwhile, her anger cooled sufficiently for Sabrina to recognize that she hadn't simply shot herself in the foot—she'd quite probably blown the stupid thing clean off.

There was absolutely no way that she could manage to complete her work in the four and a half weeks remaining before the will was probated. As if that wasn't bad enough, she now had effectively ensured her own speedy eviction from the estate as soon as Spencer Bradley officially came into his inheritance.

Before she could even attempt to beat a hasty retreat from this pit of smothering quicksand, Spencer nodded almost imperceptibly, executed a crisp military about-face, and strode from the library.

Sabrina sat perfectly still as a deathly silence filled the room.

Spencer hated his uncle clear to the bone, she thought, *even though he's about to inherit everything.* For the first time in the three days since Jeremiah Kellogg had been found sprawled in a pool of his own blood at the foot of the back staircase, she wondered if the old man's death really had been the result of a stroke. The beginning of doubt sent a shudder of dismay through her.

The antique grandfather clock in the foyer chimed four o'clock, somberly tolling each hour with the ponderous solemnity of a death knell. Sabrina tapped away at the computer keyboard in another grim-faced burst of energy. After having indulged herself by playing the hopeless victim of circumstances for a short while, she had decided hours ago that there was too much at stake here to give up without a fight.

Besides, the shot in the foot might not have been mortal after all. On the contrary, she had already begun to think of it as the starting gun, marking the beginning of the race of a lifetime. If she could persuade Ira Sampson to grant her an extension on the book's deadline, it was just possible that Jeremiah Kellogg's autobiography might turn out to be much more than anyone had bargained for.

"Especially old Jeremiah," she murmured.

Sampson would be a hard nut to crack. The flinty publisher wouldn't give an inch unless Sabrina could show him something special. No—something spectacular. Since her tense conversation with Spencer Bradley, she could smell that something. She could almost taste it. Somehow she had to get her hands on it in time to save her own hide.

Until just hours ago, Sabrina had believed she was on the homestretch with the project. But that was before Spencer Bradley had waltzed out of the library and left her chin-deep in rubble. From that humble perspective, she had begun to view her predicament quite differently—and had arrived at the astonishing conclusion that, before his untimely death, Jeremiah Kellogg had only begun to tell his story.

"Zena." She said the name aloud.

In the course of this one day, the vague specter of Kellogg's long-deceased sister had worked its way into Sabrina's psyche like some kind of haunt. She sensed that ridding herself of it would not be an easy task—nor did she want it to be. With Conrad's help—possibly with Noble Wetherbee's, as well—Jeremiah Kellogg had managed to keep his sister in Sabrina's blind spot for three months. It was time Zena came out and let the world get a look at her.

"Warts and all," Sabrina said under her breath. She had a sneaking suspicion there were a lot of those, considering the amount of trouble Kellogg must have gone to in order to keep them hidden.

If Zena held the key to Sabrina's fate, it stood to reason that the woman's son was the lock—and a tantalizingly complex one at that. Spencer had raised far more questions than he had answered today—not to mention at least one ugly suspicion. In the process, he had stirred the pot so vigorously that the contents would never be the same again. The crazy thing was, Sabrina wasn't sure she would ever be, either.

Closing the file on which she'd been working, she pushed the computer away and rubbed her eyes. She still had a shot at this. But when she let herself think about the seemingly insurmountable obstacles that lay in her path—as she did right now—a wave of nausea quivered hotly through her stomach.

Of course you're queasy, knothead, she thought. *You haven't had a bite since breakfast.* Well, that was hardly an incurable affliction. She switched off the computer and stood.

Along with the library, Sabrina had been granted free range of the kitchen when she came to work at the estate. For the most part, she had chosen to take her meals at the cottage, preferring Quetzal's company to anything the mansion had to offer. But one glance at the cold gray rain drumming down outside the window was enough to persuade her to put off venturing outside until she was ready to head home for the day.

The house seemed even more quiet than usual as she made her way along the deeply shadowed passage toward the kitchen. Maria hadn't bothered to turn on the hallway lights despite the early twilight brought on by the storm. For once, Sabrina wasn't bothered by the gloom. The awakening presence of Zena was becoming too pervasive, filling her with edgy excitement.

The hallway angled past the high-ceilinged dining room where a banquet-size mahogany table stood beneath a formerly white dustcover that had turned gray with age. Glancing at it as she went by, she couldn't help wondering for the umpteenth time how much more of the three-story mansion had been relegated to more-or-less permanent mothballs during Jeremiah Kellogg's waning years.

She paused at a short hallway leading off to the right. Conrad's rooms were down there. Sabrina was half-tempted to see if he was there now, and if so, to confront him about the deception concerning Zena. In the end, she decided it might be better if she first gave more thought to her strategy of attack.

Straight ahead, swinging double doors with tarnished brass push plates opened into a big kitchen that must have been on the cutting edge of modernity forty years ago. But the stainless steel surfaces had gone dull. A ceramic-tiled work island in the center of the room was chipped and badly marred. A stale, greasy odor hung in the air.

Sabrina wrinkled her nose as she crossed to the adjoining pantry. The kitchen wasn't exactly Maria Shaw's favorite place, and it showed. The contents of the walk-in pantry in turn clearly reflected Jeremiah Kellogg's Spartan taste in foods. She plucked a can of tomato soup from one of several identical cases lined against the wall as well as a canister of oolong tea off the back shelf.

As she stepped out of the pantry, the door to the hallway swung open. Conrad Lafever halted abruptly just inside the kitchen, clutching an empty glass in one long-fingered hand. At first, she couldn't figure out why he looked so startled at seeing her. Then she noticed his bloodshot eyes and the way he listed just a shade to one side.

Sabrina tried to dismiss her first impression—it was so unlike Conrad. But when he came over and leaned heavily on the center island, she couldn't deny the obvious. The man was drunk.

"I'm making myself a cup of tea and some soup," she said quietly. "Care to join me?"

"Pass. But thank you very much."

His undertaker's drone had become clipped and precise. He was overcompensating, trying to hide the mushy syllables. She caught an unmistakable whiff of bourbon all the way across the work island as he slid the empty glass back and forth between his fingertips.

"How about a cup of black coffee then?" she asked, getting a soup pot from the cabinet.

"Pass."

His eyes flicked to one side. Sabrina followed his gaze to a corner cabinet as she put the soup on the gas range to heat, and lit a burner under the teakettle. She would have been willing to bet there was at least one bottle of alcohol behind that cabinet door. Which would explain how Conrad had reached his current state without making runs on the teakwood liquor cabinet in the library—something he must have been reluctant to do practically under her nose.

"I'll not offer to refill your glass for you, Conrad. It appears you've been doing a pretty thorough job of that on your own."

He straightened with a jerk. The glass spun out of his hands and would have rolled off the countertop if Sabrina hadn't made a lunge for it. She turned to place it in the sink. When she faced him again, Conrad was making a valiant effort to straighten the knot in his tie, managing to pull it even more askew.

"I've had a few," he admitted.

"I gathered."

She nudged a tall wooden stool against the backs of his legs. He finally took the hint and sagged onto the edge of it.

"I had no idea you, er, indulged," she said.

"Extenuating circumstances."

Sabrina started to move away, then changed her mind. "Sorry if I sounded insensitive, Conrad. I know how close you felt to Mr. Kellogg. But you can't drink the grief away."

She almost preached the point that alcohol was a depressant—that it would only drive the despair deeper, making it more difficult to let go of the pain. A second later, she was glad she had hesitated.

"Nothing to do with Mr. Kellogg," Conrad said. "It's that no-good bastard."

Sabrina raised a brow at his language. He didn't have to explain to whom he was referring. She pressed her lips together and eased back around the island to check on her soup.

"Spencer indicated there was no love lost between the two of you," she said, although she had already deduced that from their encounter under the portico. "I guess I took it for granted that the...attitude was more his than yours." She opened the tea canister and filled a tea ball. "Do you want to talk about it?"

"Nothing to talk about." Conrad scowled at his pale hands fidgeting on the counter. "He's a spoiler, that's all. Hates every last thing Mr. Kellogg stood for."

Without thinking, Sabrina reached into her pocket and brought out the miniature tape recorder she always carried. After activating the Play/Record buttons, she placed it on the counter in front of Conrad. They both stared at it for a moment—Conrad sullenly, though his expression seemed to have little to do with the recorder.

By now he ought to have been accustomed to her habit of taping any and every conversation they'd had concerning Jeremiah Kellogg. Still, she was relieved when he didn't object to her recording this one.

"Why do you suppose Spencer has such a low opinion of his uncle?" Sabrina asked, deciding on a gradual approach to the subject of Zena Bradley.

"Because he's totally worthless, that's why."

"Spencer? He's worth a bundle, isn't he?" She was momentarily distracted by a thought that should have occurred to her before—that Spencer Bradley did not covet the Kellogg estate for the obvious financial gain that it represented. According to Conrad, Spencer was well-heeled in his own right.

Conrad snorted. "I mean *character... blood.* He's just plain jealous."

"But he's Mr. Kellogg's nephew."

"He's a bastard."

"You're beginning to repeat yourself, Conrad. Besides, that's a little rude."

"It's the truth."

He lisped wetly, reminding Sabrina of comedian Lily Tomlin's waspishly petulant Edith Ann character. Since it was coming from Conrad, she wasn't even tempted to find it humorous. Still a long way from fully understanding the bad blood between Conrad and Spencer, she was just glad she wasn't living under the same roof with them.

"What did Mr. Kellogg think of his nephew?" She already had a good idea but wanted to hear it from Conrad's mouth, anyway.

"He never said."

"Never?" The soup had begun to boil. Sabrina reached over and turned off the burner without taking her gaze from Conrad. "Come on, he must have mentioned Spencer now and then over the years."

Conrad shut his eyes for a full minute, then opened them and shook his head. "Mentioned him maybe once or twice, but that's all."

"What about Zena?"

His cheeks twitched. "Called her a slut once."

Thinking she must have misunderstood, Sabrina said, "Pardon?"

"Mr. Kellogg called her a slut."

The teakettle began to hiss. She fumbled for the burner knob and turned it off. "You're serious? Mr. Kellogg called his own sister a slut?"

He gave a single deep nod. "Heard him say it right to her face."

"What could he have meant by that?" she wondered aloud.

"A slut is a woman of flawed moral fiber," Conrad enunciated carefully as if explaining to an idiot.

"Oh, for heaven's sake, Conrad. I know what slut means. I just can't imagine why he would use the term on his one-and-only sister."

Conrad looked mildly offended by her tone—and became suddenly watchful. "Mr. Kellogg was not a man given to the use of superlatives," he said, visibly sobering. "Therefore, the shoe must have fitted her."

"But that doesn't make sense. Didn't you tell me Mr. Kellogg's health began failing right after her death? And that's when he started becoming so reclusive?"

"Indeed."

A vital thread had come loose in the image of Jeremiah Kellogg that she had so carefully woven together. Sabrina had a strong feeling that if she pulled at that thread just a little, the whole scheme of things would come unraveled.

She wasn't sure she was prepared for that right now. But ready or not, she didn't have the luxury of waiting.

"Conrad, did Mr. Kellogg love his sister?"

He shifted on the stool, rearranged his tall frame in his suit coat, and looked straight into Sabrina's eyes. She strained under the prolonged eye contact before suddenly realizing that Conrad had lost none of his anger. It was now directed at her.

"Mr. Kellogg was as fine a man as I've ever known," he said flatly, without a trace of slurring.

His statement sounded almost defensive. It also effectively halted the unraveling of the thread, terminating that line of conversation. Sabrina sensed that this would be a particularly bad time to ask why he had deceived her about Zena and Spencer having lived in the cottage. But time and the tape were running out. So as Conrad slid off the stool, she hurriedly tried another tack.

"Conrad, why do you suppose Mr. Kellogg was toting his own dirty dishes down to the kitchen the evening he had his stroke and fell down the back stairs?" The question of Zena aside, she had known Kellogg well enough to be convinced that he wasn't in the habit of picking up after himself.

He shrugged. "Ask Mr. Wetherbee. He was here."

Sabrina veered in yet another direction, trying not to let her growing irritation show. "Are you going to have Spencer removed from the premises?" she asked.

His bloodshot eyes clouded. She sensed his anger slipping away from her and focusing elsewhere. He pressed his lips together in a thin white line and shook his head.

"You could, you know," she said. "I think Mr. Wetherbee would have to agree that Spencer has no right to be here until after the will is probated."

Conrad's face reddened. He seemed on the verge of saying something—most likely a curse, from the looks of him. But then he suddenly exhaled and his shoulders sagged as if the rage had all poured out of him like air escaping a ruptured balloon.

"Fighting him would serve no purpose, Sabrina. I've seen Mr. Kellogg's will. As distasteful as it is to me, Spencer's being here is inevitable."

Conrad had gone from pent-up fury to gray-faced defeat with one profound sigh. Neither frame of mind suited him. Sabrina put his erratic behavior down to stress, grief and the incipient terror of the soon-to-be unemployed. After burying a man he had practically worshiped, it must be rough on him, she thought, to face the end of a job into which he had poured his life for a quarter of a century.

"I wish there was something I could say that would make all this easier for you, Conrad."

She meant it in spite of the as-yet-unexplained deception. Conrad had never been anything but polite to her. Even the fleeting blast of anger directed at her a moment ago had been born of pain, so it wouldn't be fair for her to blame him for that. Besides, even in light of his deception regarding Zena, she knew she couldn't complete *The End of the Line* without him.

"It's been a difficult day." He sounded weary to the soul. "I believe I'll go to my rooms for a while and have a rest."

"Do that."

But when he got up and started out the kitchen door toward his quarters behind the pantry, Sabrina called him back. She went to him and took his hand. His hand was soft for a man's, and in its own way, as lacking in vitality as his face in its natural, subdued state.

"You've been a good friend to me since I've been working here," she said. "I want you to know how much I appreciate all your kindnesses. And I really do care that you're hurting right now."

Conrad nodded awkwardly, and Sabrina realized she was embarrassing him. She released his hand.

"Off with you now," she said. "Have a nice nap. Would you like me to ask Maria to bring you an ice pack later, in case you wake up with a hangover?"

The very idea that he might suffer ill effects from his communion with spirits seemed to catch him by surprise, reinforcing Sabrina's hunch that Conrad's postfuneral tippling had been an aberration. In some ways, the man was a babe in the woods—so very different from Spencer Bradley, the wolf.

Conrad was the sort who could live in another man's shadow his entire life and never feel deprived of the sun. The words "male spinster" came to mind. She rejected them at once, ashamed.

After he was gone, Sabrina returned to the stove. Her soup had gone tepid. She turned the burner back on, then reached for the miniature tape recorder. After rewinding the tape, she listened over and over to the recording of her conversation with Conrad.

Each time, his anger and pain sounded more clearly defined. The mild profanity made her wince—not so much the words as the way he said them. The words, the emotions—both were as out of character for Conrad as had been the drinking. It occurred to Sabrina that the words, at least, might not have been truly his. They merely might have been Jeremiah Kellogg speaking from the grave.

"Okay, genius," she murmured, pouring the steaming soup into a big pottery mug, "if you're so smart, explain why the old man left the whole ball of wax to a nephew he couldn't stand?"

The answer didn't leap out and grab her by the throat while Sabrina arranged the mug, a cup of hot tea and a stack of saltine crackers on a small wooden tray. It didn't rap her between the eyes in a single staggering burst of revelation as she carried the tray back to the library. But when she had settled down at the work table with her mostly liquid dinner and the sheaf of laser-copied photographs, one of which would be chosen for the cover of *The End of the*

Line, three thoughts arranged themselves in such a way as to bring her to a dead stop with the soup mug raised halfway to her lips.

The private Jeremiah Kellogg had not at all matched his own public image.

Contrary to Sabrina's earlier assumption, he apparently had not much mourned the loss of his sister, Zena.

Assuming that those two conjectures were accurate, it stood to reason that Spencer Bradley, too, might not be what he seemed.

CHAPTER FOUR

The chilly air stung Spencer's face as he moved along an overgrown trail, lashing irritably at the underbrush with a crooked hickory stick. The stormy weather had finally passed, leaving gray fog in its wake.

Unaccustomed to being pent up indoors for days on end, he had sought relief through long, solitary walks in the winter-blighted countryside surrounding the estate. The exercise had done little to work off the edginess that gripped him when he was in the mansion, much less improve his state of mind.

The more days he spent trekking the highlands overlooking the nearby Hudson River, the more Spencer found himself chewing on the knotty problem of his Uncle Jeremiah's ghostwriter. But as vicious circles would have it, pondering Sabrina Glade only served to feed the smoldering fires of his restlessness. The irony of it all, he feared, was that those hungry fires were swiftly scorching away his common sense.

He muttered irritably to himself. For over twenty years, Spencer's life had been ruled by two obsessions—a relentless drive to build his own financial power base, and an almost morbid desire to get his hands on the Kellogg estate. With the first goal achieved and the second nearly within his grasp, he had expected to feel a sense of supreme triumph. Instead he'd discovered that he had been seized by yet another governing passion. Because it involved his long-neglected personal life, it was one that he was pathetically ill equipped to handle.

Every atom of his intellect desperately wanted his uncle's ghostwriter to be gone from the estate, and the blasted book quashed. At the same time, Spencer's body had quite independently come to the decision that it wanted Sabrina—period.

He thwacked the hickory stick rhythmically against the side of his leg as he unconsciously chose a fork in the path that would lead him back to the mansion—and to a woman he barely knew. This dangerous reshuffling of priorities couldn't be happening to him, he thought. He wouldn't let it. He had always prided himself in having better self-control than this.

Shouldering his way through the skeletal ruins of a privet hedge, Spencer came out onto the scruffy, wet lawn. The fog-shrouded mansion loomed in front of him, shadowed in murky twilight. He hadn't meant to be out so late. He was damp and cold and out of sorts when he spotted the light glowing in the library.

He slowed then stopped a dozen yards from the library window. With hands jammed into his coat pockets, he hunched his shoulders against the chill and squinted through the swirling mist. The woman was a workaholic, all right—Spencer knew the breed as well as he knew himself.

He could see Sabrina through the clouded glass, bent over her portable computer with all the intensity of a neurosurgeon probing an ailing brain. The analogy brought a bitter smile to Spencer's cold-blanched lips. Probing a brain was precisely what Sabrina was doing, even if the brain in question had been committed to its well-earned grave days ago. And that was precisely what worried him most about this whole book business—she kept right on grinding away at the research as if her life depended on it.

While he watched, Sabrina straightened, rubbed her eyes, and pushed herself up from her chair. She was wearing a short brown skirt, matching tights and a bulky, pumpkin-colored chenille pullover. She glanced toward the hallway door as if to make sure she was truly alone, then lifted the pullover above her waist and fanned her bared midriff.

The glimpse of smooth, pale flesh sent a current of heat flowing through Spencer's body in marked contrast to the bleak winter chill. He parted his lips, a faint sigh whistling through his teeth.

She dropped the pullover, resettled the skirt on her slender hips, and moved toward the door. Only after she had disappeared into the hallway did it strike Spencer that he had been playing Peeping Tom.

"God in heaven," he murmured. This was getting entirely out of hand. Head down, frowning, he started around the mansion toward the front entrance. Snapping the end off his hickory stick, he paused for some time in the deepening shadows beneath the portico to scrape mud and rotting leaves from the treaded soles of his hiking boots. He pulled off the boots before opening the front door, and placed them on the tile floor just inside the foyer.

Spencer stood there in his wool socks for several minutes, conscious of having traded gloomy winter fog for the equally depressing environs of the decaying mansion. At least the place was dry and warm. Too warm, in fact. He resolved to make an adjustment to the mansion's furnace—then turned right around and gave that task a low priority as he recalled Sabrina hiking up her pullover to fan herself.

The pale flesh. The graceful curve of her narrow rib cage. Spencer could almost feel ...

A sharp rattle of glass on metal spun him around. Sabrina stood frozen on the other side of the foyer, her back to the hallway leading to the kitchen. She was carrying a tray covered with a cloth napkin.

"Sorry if I disturbed your woolgathering." Her startled expression faded quickly. "I didn't know you were back."

Spencer arched a brow. "Disappointed?"

She pressed her lips together, apparently trying to decide how to answer that. Their conversations had been minimal since the day of Jeremiah's funeral, which was just as well. For some reason, they couldn't seem to resist throwing darts at each other.

Finally she said, "Let's not start."

He nodded slowly. "Good idea."

Her frown made Spencer wonder if she was having second thoughts. But she surprised him.

"You look half frozen." Sabrina eyed his reddened hands, which he had been rubbing together, then raised the tray a few inches. "I have hot tea and soup that I'm willing to share. Come on back to the library and take your pick . . . if you want."

Spencer was caught off guard—and warmed—by her concern. He smiled. "I want."

She turned away before he could move to take the tray. He followed her to the library, his gaze fixed on the bulky pullover, his imagination caressing the sleek flesh beneath. When she halted to settle the tray on the end of the library table, he almost walked right into her.

"Tea or tomato soup?" she asked, removing the cloth napkin.

He glanced at the two steaming containers and the stack of saltines, distracted by the delicate scent of her perfume. "I'll take the tea. You look like you could use all the calories you can get."

Sabrina glanced at him, then down at herself, as if he had spilled something on her. "Thanks," she said dryly. "That's just what I needed to hear in the middle of a hard day's work."

"Hey—I meant it as a compliment. You have the figure of a girl half your age."

She took a step back, fists on her hips. "We're getting a bit personal with our barbs now, aren't we?" she said coolly.

Spencer raised both hands in a placating gesture. "I swear, Sabrina, I'm not trying to insult you. Hell, you offered me your tea. I'm trying to be nice."

"Really?" She squinted one eye. "I'd have thought you would've developed a smoother line than that ... at your age."

He winced, then smiled crookedly. "I have more money than I know what to do with. That's all the line some women need."

"Do tell? And when did you make this fascinating discovery?"

"When I got rich."

"Ah." Sabrina glanced around at the richly appointed library, her head cocked to one side. "I guess I've been assuming you were born rich."

An alarm went off in Spencer's head. Sabrina was fishing. She had managed to shift the conversation very close to forbidden territory. He backpedaled quickly.

"I'm a self-made man, for what it's worth." His hand trembled slightly as he reached for the cup of tea. He was pretty sure the reaction had nothing to do with his still being chilled. "You'd better eat up before your soup gets cold."

Spencer could feel her eyes on his back as he walked over to peer out the windows. His own indistinct reflection stared back at him from the glass as if mocking him.

"Remarkable," she said after a while. "A self-made rich man who doesn't know the first thing about making a decent pass at a woman."

"I wasn't trying to make a pass at you, Sabrina."

"Oh. And you weren't tossing barbs. So, what were you doing, might I ask?"

Spencer turned to face her. She had settled into one of the heavy oak chairs alongside the library table and was studiously crumbling saltines into her soup. He wondered if she had any idea how exasperating she could be.

"I was taking a stab at civilized conversation," he said. "Apparently I was wasting my time."

Sabrina took a sip of soup, then crumbled in a few more crackers before looking at him. He tried to hold her gaze—

to plunge right into the rich brown depths of her eyes—but she wouldn't let him this time.

"You're so outrageously self-assured," she said. "I guess I thought . . ." She shook her head, then changed tack with a swiftness that left Spencer off-balance. "Is the tea all right?" she asked. "I like it kind of strong."

"It's fine."

"How do you know? You haven't tasted it."

"I can tell by the smell." Spencer raised his cup and inhaled deeply. "Oolong, with a mix of dried citrus fruits and a touch of cinnamon."

Sabrina looked impressed.

"I own half interest in a tea import shop in Hartford," he explained. "The place was losing money when I bought in. At the time, I needed to show a loss for tax purposes. But we did a little advertising in the right places, and business went right through the roof last year."

"It takes money to make money."

"Usually. Anyway, now my partner wants to open another shop in London. But I'm more inclined to try Tokyo—it's a harder nut to crack."

"Then what? Somewhere near your home in Abu Dhabi?"

Spencer tensed, his mind suddenly racing. To cover that, he took a long, slow swig of tea without taking his eyes off Sabrina.

"How did you know I used to live in Abu Dhabi?" he asked quietly.

"Used to?" She shrugged. "I thought you still did sometimes."

He shook his head. "It's been five, six years. I had a contract with the emirates." He waited several seconds, then asked again, "How did you know? Did Jeremiah tell you?"

One corner of her mouth curled sardonically. "No. You and your mother weren't exactly a common topic during my talks with Mr. Kellogg." Her expression grew pensive.

"In fact, he barely mentioned either of you until the last few days before his . . . accident."

Spencer drained the cup and returned it to the tray. "My understanding was that Jeremiah died of a stroke."

"That played a part in it. But the bottom line was, he died of a cake plate."

"I can't wait to hear the rest of that."

She ran a fingertip along the rim of her soup mug, then placed it on the tray with a sigh. "Your uncle had a stroke while carrying a stack of dirty dishes from his rooms down the back staircase to the kitchen. He fell partway down the stairs. Broke an arm and some ribs, the doctor said. But all that was probably survivable. What killed him was a cake plate that broke during the fall. It sliced through the jugular vein in the left side of his neck. He bled to death."

Spencer leaned back against the table and crossed his arms over his chest, doing a fair job of hiding the fact that he was suddenly shaking inside. He scowled down at the rug, waiting for his gut to settle. A bloody accident on the back stairs was a long way from dying of a stroke. But it seemed like a mere hop and a skip from that nightmarish day in the cottage just weeks before Spencer's eighteenth birthday.

"I thought Mr. Wetherbee had already given you all the gory details," she said. "He was here when it happened."

"He probably didn't have the nerve." Spencer caught the curious lift of her eyebrow and covered his slip by quickly adding, "Noble has always been big on looking out for his clients' feelings. Even when it isn't necessary."

"I'd be a little put out with my attorney if he colored the facts that way."

"So would I. But Noble is Jeremiah's lawyer, not mine." He glanced down and picked up a dove gray business card from the corner of the table. "Speaking of the devil."

"Mr. Wetherbee sometimes stops by the estate if he's in the neighborhood. If he misses me, he's kind enough to leave his card."

"How thoughtful." Spencer flipped the card back onto the table and mentally shelved the entire matter of Jeremiah's lawyer for the time being. Right now, he had to find out just how seriously Sabrina had been nosing around in his past. "So how about it? How did you know I used to live in Abu Dhabi if Jeremiah didn't tell you?"

She drew her fingers slowly back through her hair and lifted it off her neck as if she was thinking. The library was stuffy. Spencer reminded himself to do something about the furnace—then reminded himself of the way Sabrina had raised her chenille pullover to fan her body, and waffled. Maybe she liked the heat.

"Abu Dhabi." She closed one eye, concentrating. "I believe Conrad mentioned it the other day."

He snapped a curse through his teeth. "I should have known Lafever wouldn't miss a chance to stick it to me behind my back."

Sabrina eyed Spencer for a moment. Then, moving deliberately to make a statement of it, she got up and moseyed down the table to the chair in front of her computer.

"You needn't get paranoid over it," she said frostily. "As a matter of fact, before that day, Conrad had never so much as mentioned you . . . or your mother."

That came as a relief. Even back at the time of his mother's death, Spencer had suspected that Lafever had known more than he had let on. Then he gave closer attention to what Sabrina had just said, and the uneasiness returned. "Before that day?" He stepped away from the table. "Then, I take it, Lafever's had more to say about me since. I'd be curious to know just what."

"I'm not that indiscreet, Spencer."

"I see." He smiled tightly. "Connie called me some pretty raw names, did he?"

She confirmed that with her silence. As Spencer moved down the table toward her, Sabrina's fingers danced over the computer keyboard. Before he thought to look at what was on the display, a kaleidoscopic screen-saver graphic swirled into view.

"My, my," he said. "You don't trust me at all, do you?"

Again, her answer was in the silence.

Spencer almost reached out and touched her sable hair, aglow in the lamplight. An ache rose inside him. He walked around to the other side of the table to give himself room to breathe, thinking this was ridiculous. The woman didn't even like him, yet just being in the same room with her was incredibly distracting.

"You're one to talk about trust," Sabrina said to his back. "I've yet to find anyone around here who *you* feel is trustworthy."

"If you're suggesting that I put one ounce of faith in Conrad Lafever, forget it. I'm not inclined to buddy up to someone who calls me the scum of the earth behind my back."

"Bastard."

He whirled and looked at her. She was squaring the keyboard precisely with the edge of the table.

"Conrad didn't call you scum," she said evenly. "He called you a bastard."

Spencer swallowed dryly, turning away again to hide the new surge of apprehension that he thought must be apparent in his expression. How could it not be? A bead of sweat slipped from his hairline and ran down the side of his face.

"What do you think about that, Sabrina?" he asked, surprised by the unruffled tone of his voice.

After what seemed like a long time, she said, "The jury's still out. If you try hard, we could talk about upgrading you to a garden-variety jerk."

Spencer was still trying to decide whether she was joking when he heard a wry chuckle. He closed his eyes for a moment, and the smile returned. He pivoted on one heel. Sabrina was watching him intently as if she was taking another reading of some kind. He made a real effort to keep the smile intact but felt it buckle under the strain.

"I'll work on it," he said.

She inclined her head to one side. Her expression didn't actually change, but her gaze lost its razorlike intensity. He sensed that something about her had relaxed—opened up—just a little.

"That's a start," she said, squelching a smile of her own.

He nodded, and tried to let go of some of the tension that was drawing at the back of his neck. But it had been so long since he had relaxed that he'd forgotten how. The only release Spencer had ever known had been in work.

Leaving his company in the capable hands of well-trained subordinates while he came up here to settle accounts had been a mistake. He could see that now. He would not weather this as well as his company would. But if he hadn't come, he wouldn't have found out about Jeremiah's book, and that could have been disastrous. It still could be, depending on just how much of a bloodhound Sabrina turned out to be.

The light from the lamp washed warmly down her cheek, highlighting the delicate line of her neck. He realized how much he wanted to reach out and stroke the back of a finger along that alabaster line, to feel its warm, satiny texture. The *need* to touch her for the first time stirred Spencer deeply, while filling him with an eerie sense of impending jeopardy.

A dim, haunting image crept out of the darkest recesses of his mind. Frowning, he stared at Sabrina's pale neck, the sense of danger growing like a dirty chunk of ice in the pit of his stomach. Her skin was so milky pure. Spencer could almost see the thin line of her jugular vein—

He blinked away a startling, crimson-tinted vision of horror that made his gut lurch.

"Are you all right, Spencer?" Her tone was equal parts concern and wariness.

"Fine." And he was, he told himself. It was just that for a moment there...

Spencer licked his lips, trying to shake the feeling that he had just stuck his hand into a black hole and touched something cold and slimy. His fingers twitched, absently stirring through a sheaf of papers stacked neatly on the corner of the library table. A dozen or so pages spilled onto the rug at his feet. Sabrina gasped, but said nothing.

"Damn." He bent to scoop them up, trying to shuffle them back into some kind of order. "I hope these aren't something vital."

"Every slip of paper on this table is vital," she replied edgily.

Spencer looked at her sharply, feeling a touch frayed himself at the moment. Their gazes locked in a mute challenge. He knew he could make her blink if he tried.

"You could haul all this down to the cottage and work there," he said instead, taking his own sweet time returning the papers to the table. "Then you wouldn't have to worry about clumsy...bastards messing up your playpen."

The suggestion came out sounding harsher than he had intended. Spencer started to apologize, but the damage was already done. Sabrina bolted to her feet, flushed with anger.

"Now don't overreact," he said too loudly.

"I wouldn't dream of it," she retorted, all trace of their tentative approach toward amity of a moment earlier obliterated. "You've already made it crystal clear to everyone in this house that you don't approve of me or of Mr. Kellogg's book. But in case you weren't paying attention when I mentioned it before, Spencer Bradley, let me repeat—I have as much right to be here as you do until your uncle's will is read."

A spark exploded in the knotted muscles at the base of Spencer's skull. The feeling of being wired that had gripped him since his return to the gloomy estate intensified. He tried to keep his mouth shut, to halt the cascading effect that was carrying them both toward the brink of a deep precipice. But the chemistry in the room was too volatile.

"You don't know what this is all about, dammit," he heard himself say.

That was all it took. She lost it.

"Don't swear at me, dammit yourself!" Sabrina picked up a pencil and flung it across the room. "I came here to do a job, and by God, I'm going to do it or die trying. End of discussion!" She snatched up a piece of paper, wadded it into a tight ball, and ricocheted it off Spencer's chest, defiant tears in her eyes.

His hands curled into white-knuckled fists. He felt it coming—that monstrous sense of rage that had dwelt at the very center of his being all these years. It had been rising closer and closer to the surface from the moment Spencer had set foot on the old estate. It pressed hotly against the taut skin of his civility now, like a huge boil ready to be lanced.

He wanted to scream at Sabrina that she had no rights in that house—that she should get down on her knees and thank the powers-that-be that she didn't. But the words remained locked behind welded jaws. He took two quick steps toward her, bent on casting her out of the library, out of the mansion and out of this absurd sham of an existence that he called his life, before her stubbornness laid her low.

Her eyes widened. The sudden look of fear stopped him cold. Sabrina searched his face as if trying to find a touchstone of familiarity in Spencer's contorted features. He knew he was frightening her, knew he had that power at his command. And still he wanted to take hold of her. Wanted to.

Wanted her.

A bone-deep shudder quaked through him. He wasn't sure what had caused it. Rage. Frustration. A kind of fear that he had never known before. And something else— something like a small voice crying out in the wilderness.

I'm going mad. It started—this insane feeling that I'm crumbling apart—the day I found out Jeremiah was dead. And it got worse when I found out about the damned book.

With enormous effort, Spencer managed to unclench his fists. He raked his fingers through his hair. His throat made a clicking sound as he tried to swallow the fiery acid that had perked up from his stomach.

"Sabrina." For some reason, just saying her name had a calming effect on him. He cleared his throat and said it again. "Sabrina, if you must stay on this estate, move your work down to the cottage. Please. Do it...for your own good. Don't come up here to this house anymore."

Spencer backed off a step, then another. When he reached the end of the table, he turned and stalked toward the door.

"Is that a threat?" Her voice sounded far away.

"No, Sabrina. It's a warning."

He didn't look back.

Three days later, Sabrina's dispute with Spencer Bradley had settled into an uneasy standoff. Convinced that the impasse was destined to be of short duration, she was determined to make as much headway as possible on *The End of the Line* before they inevitably locked horns again.

Her stomach grumbled. She hadn't paused to eat since grabbing a Spartan breakfast with Quetzal. Her head felt fuzzy in the overwarm library, and her eyes and shoulders ached. Sabrina squelched a yawn with the back of her hand and glanced over at the windows. The light outside was failing. She had better get moving if she was going to make it back to the cottage before darkness fell.

That was the one small concession she had made in the face of Spencer's warning. She no longer hung around the mansion after dark. There was no point in pretending that Spencer was incapable of intimidating her, she thought, as she unplugged the laptop computer and slipped it into its carrying case.

In point of fact, his performance in the library three days ago had scared the hell out of her. Looking into the man's eyes had been like staring down the molten gullet of an active volcano. The heat of his inexplicable rage had incinerated her own anger, along with the biggest part of her courage—at least temporarily.

If Spencer had walked out of the library at that moment, Sabrina probably would have heeded his warning to stay away from the mansion. She might even have fled the estate altogether. But he had lingered for a few critical seconds. Because of that, she had seen perhaps the one thing that could have restored her courage at that moment. It had been there in his eyes, holding the heat of his anger barely in check.

Spencer was just as afraid as she was.

Oddly enough, Sabrina wasn't sure Spencer was even aware of his fear. In the final analysis, perhaps it didn't matter. Recognized or not, in a man who was as difficult to fathom as Spencer Bradley, it represented an unexpected vulnerability that made him suddenly seem bigger than life to her. Darryl had never let her so much as glimpse his soft side. In Spencer's case, she reluctantly admitted, it somehow compounded his powerful allure.

She had no idea what drove Spencer's fear. Whether he was afraid for her, or of her, or of himself. But she had already decided that not knowing might be an integral part of his undeniable animal magnetism. Sabrina brushed her hair out of her eyes, worried about herself. How could she be so blasted attracted to a man who scared her out of her wits? Had Darryl's endless mind games totally destroyed her emotional perspective where men were concerned?

That bothered her to no end. Because she had begun to suspect that Spencer Bradley was at the center of a dark undercurrent in the Kellogg family history.

With a weary groan, Sabrina pushed herself up from her chair. Singing shut the zipper on the computer case, she began gathering up the research materials to work on at the cottage that evening. She hurriedly fanned through a stack of random notes clamped together with a bull clip. Lips pursed, she paused to flip through the notes again, more slowly this time. Frowning, she glanced around and under the table.

She distinctly remembered having jotted a list of questions to herself yesterday regarding Jeremiah Kellogg's fatal accident, the circumstances of which had begun to nag her more and more each day. She just as clearly recalled having slipped the list between the jaws of the bull clip. And now it was missing.

"Well, well. I see you've been at it again," she muttered, drumming her fingers on the library table.

Whether by happenstance or design, Spencer had kept out of her sight since their fractious encounter of three days ago. That wasn't difficult to do in a place the size of the Kellogg mansion. But out of sight clearly was not out of mind.

In recent days, it had become apparent to Sabrina that someone had begun prowling through her research materials during her absences at night. Someone less compulsive about the careful arrangement of books and folders might not have noticed. But she spotted the signs immediately when she returned each morning. A book askew on its stack here. Pages spilling from a folder there.

The clandestine intrusions were particularly evident in the scribbled reminders that Sabrina kept organized with big metal bull clips. She was fastidious about how she fitted the odd-size scraps of paper into the clips. The prowler was not.

She had no way of knowing how long the nocturnal visitations had been going on before she began noticing them. But this was the first time she had ever been aware that anything was missing.

"Keep it up, Spencer Bradley, and I'll set a large rat trap."

She couldn't prove Bradley was the intruder. But the process of elimination had scratched Conrad off her short list of candidates, since he was already nearly as familiar with her research as Sabrina was. Besides, Bradley had an expressed interest in deep-sixing Jeremiah Kellogg's book project.

Dusk was fading fast now, settling like a blackout curtain over the library windows. Figuring out how to deal with Spencer's annoying stealth attacks on what she considered to be her territory could wait until she got back to the cottage.

Shouldering the computer-case strap, Sabrina picked up her briefcase and headed for the door. She was already out in the hallway when she remembered the key. Retreating three steps into the library, she eyed the tarnished brass key hanging on a hook next to the door. She had forgotten all about it.

Sabrina glanced over at the library table. There were far too many research materials to lug down to the cottage each evening. Nor was there handy closet space in the library in which to lock everything away. She looked back at the key.

The mansion wasn't hers. But it wasn't Spencer's, either—not until Noble Wetherbee and a probate judge made it official. In the meantime, it could be argued, Jeremiah Kellogg was still the master of the house. And he had given Sabrina certain rights and privileges that included this key, if she cared to use it—which she hadn't until now.

Smiling grimly, she plucked the key from its hook and hurried across to the other door on the far side of the library. She inserted the key into the keyhole, and twisted. The lock tumblers resisted briefly, then snapped into place with a satisfying click.

Retracing her steps, Sabrina pulled the door to the front hallway closed behind her and locked it, as well. Withdrawing the heavy brass key, she glanced around quickly to make sure no one was watching. Then, standing on tiptoe, she slipped the key onto the deep, dusty cornice above the door. She wasn't about to risk losing the thing.

CHAPTER FIVE

Soapy, jasmine-scented water gurgled noisily down the drain of the claw-footed bathtub. Sabrina toweled herself vigorously until her skin was flushed, then pulled on a pair of baggy wool socks before slipping into her bathrobe. As she left the steamy bathroom, the cool air of the bedroom hit her like an unfriendly wall.

Quetzal lay waiting at the foot of the bed, next to her bulging briefcase and laptop computer. He yowled at her as she reached for the one-piece velour lounging suit that she had pressed into service as pajamas that winter in the drafty cottage.

"Hang in there, my man. I'll fix us some tea as soon as I get into my warm fuzzies."

Sabrina had started back toward the bathroom when something crashed against the front door in the living room. She gave a startled cry, and Quetzal shot off the bed with a hiss.

Before she could collect herself, the crashing came again, in triplicate. Sabrina tossed the jumpsuit onto the bed and scurried into the living room, pulling the belt of her robe tighter as she crept up to the small round window high in the front door. There was no outside light. She couldn't make out a thing in the pitch darkness beyond the fogged glass.

She had never had a nighttime caller at the cottage. That, and the horrendous pounding, filled her with inexplicable dread, reinforcing her innate sense of caution.

"Who is it?" she called.

"The jerk."

Sabrina hopped back a step and stared at the door for a moment. The door was unlocked. For the first time, she regretted never having asked Conrad for the key.

"What do you want?" she asked.

Silence. Then, "Give me a break, Sabrina. I'm freezing my can off out here."

She hesitated before reaching out and turning the paint-caked knob. The door whined open, admitting a gust of frigid air along with Spencer Bradley. He barged past her as if he owned the place.

By the time she got the door closed behind him, he was standing next to a gateleg table in the middle of the room with his back to her. Water droplets shone in his hair and on the shoulders of his coat. His ears were bright red from the cold.

"I didn't know it was raining again," she said.

"It isn't... quite."

Quetzal leaped onto the high back of a threadbare arm-chair over by the bedroom door, where he sat, tail twitch-ing, eyeing the new arrival. Sabrina edged toward the big tom, winding the belt of her robe tighter and tighter around her hands.

"It's late, Spencer," she commented.

"I didn't mean to get you out of bed."

"Considering the way you hammered on my door, I sin-cerely doubt that." She didn't mention that she hadn't yet made it to bed—or that she had planned to spend at least the next three hours plowing through research materials. "What do you want?"

Spencer looked at her, his gaze drifting down over the tightly belted robe to her wool socks. Her skin prickled hotly. Sabrina told herself that he couldn't know that she wasn't wearing a stitch beneath the robe, but she didn't quite believe it.

Beneath the flush of cold, he looked pale, almost hag-gard. He stood there with one hand tucked inside his heavy coat, absently massaging his stomach, oddly reminding

Sabrina of a tall, heavily maned Napoleon. He didn't utter a word for a full minute, seemingly unaware of how his silence unnerved her. Finally he stretched his free arm toward her and opened his fist. A brass door key lay across his wide palm.

"Come now, Sabrina. What did you think you were gaining by locking the library doors?"

She just managed to keep her expression impassive. "Apparently nothing. I didn't know you'd stoop to spying on me."

"When you so imaginatively hid the key?" His tight smile didn't come close to reaching his eyes. "You leap to conclusions too fast. The first place any idiot would look for a door key is up on the cornice." His smile broadened. "On the other hand, I'll bet you keep the key to this cottage under one of the stones right out there on the front stoop."

Sabrina kept her mouth shut, hoping he wouldn't find out that she had no key to the cottage.

Spencer flipped the brass key into the air and caught it with a downward swipe of his hand. "Didn't it occur to you that Lafever had master keys for the entire house?"

"Maybe." She raised her chin defiantly. "Then again, maybe I figured that if Conrad was curious about my work, he'd have enough integrity to come right out and ask about it, instead of sneaking around at night to sift through my research materials. Not that there was anything there he didn't already know about."

His expression turned to granite. Spencer stood perfectly still, bombarding Sabrina with silence until she was ready to jump out of her skin.

Then his gaze shifted past her to the open bedroom doorway. Sabrina tensed as something in his expression seemed to turn inward, and his eyes visibly darkened. Again noting his odd pallor, she was struck by the absurdly irrelevant thought that she had forgotten to get her flu shot last fall.

Suddenly he turned and slapped the brass library key down hard on the gateleg table. She watched him move restlessly around the cramped living room, his hands buried deeply in his coat pockets. Two paces to the couch. A half turn to the left. Three paces to the corner.

Spencer reminded her of an enormous Siberian tiger she had once seen pacing the cruel confines of a cage no larger than this room. That was the last time she'd had the heart to visit a zoo.

"You walked down from the big house?" She hadn't heard a car drive up before he'd banged on the door.

He nodded, still moving, his gaze taking in the low ceiling, with its exposed beams, the water-stained wallpaper, the nap showing through the area rug in front of the sway-backed couch.

Sabrina still found it hard to believe that this man had ever lived in this cottage. "Why haven't you been back to the estate in twenty years?"

"Why didn't you ask Jeremiah when you had the chance?"

"I didn't know enough about you then."

"You still don't."

He ran a finger around the lip of a cheap vase on an end table next to the couch, then dusted his hands together.

"Your mother was probably a better housekeeper than I am," she said, still fishing for an opening. He would make the kind of teeth-pulling interview that writers despised.

Spencer didn't comment. He just continued his wandering, inspecting faded pictures on the walls, touching a lop-sided lamp shade. Each piece of shabby furniture and dime store bric-a-brac in that room must have its own history for him, Sabrina thought. He had that far-off look she'd seen before—the one that made her curiosity itch way down deep.

She watched with growing interest, wondering what manner of memories the man kept walled away inside himself, raging to be set free, like that Siberian tiger. *They must be something dark. Happy memories would show on his face.*

Quetzal spat and shot down off the back of the chair, darting around behind the couch. Sabrina belatedly realized that she had been twisting his tail in with the belt of her robe. She dropped the ends of the belt and moved away from the chair, refocusing her attention on her visitor.

"How long did you and your mother live here in the cottage?" Now that she had stopped torturing the belt, she had trouble deciding what to do with her hands.

"Seventeen years."

Spencer sounded so distracted that she wasn't sure he was even aware he had spoken. He had stopped in the far corner to nudge an old platform rocker into motion.

"No kidding?" Sabrina could almost stretch her imagination around his having lived there as a small child, but that was the limit. "How old were you when you left?"

"Seventeen."

He was beginning his second or third circuit of the room. She had been trailing along behind until he murmured that last word. Sabrina stopped, uttering a short laugh of disbelief.

The dwelling had been barely fit for habitation when Sabrina moved in three months ago. As far as she could tell, it hadn't reached its current state of decrepitude in recent years. For one thing, according to the meager hints that Spencer had dropped about the place, roof leaks had been a common occurrence since at least as far back as his tenancy.

"Spencer, you surely don't expect me to believe you were practically *born* in this dump."

He turned and took a step toward her. The distant look had left his eyes. He caught and held her gaze. "You ask a lot of questions, Sabrina."

She nodded. Her heart rate seemed to slow.

"But you don't answer many," he added.

"Such as?"

"Why you've sunk your teeth into this venture so deeply. Why the only phone calls you've made from the estate since you came here have been to your publisher. Why you've received no mail here." He paused. "Why you're afraid of me."

Sabrina licked her dry lips, wondering why she was so surprised to learn that Spencer had been checking up on her. "Since you know the questions, I'm amazed that you haven't dug up the answers."

"I'm not a detective."

He was doing a pretty good job of throwing Sabrina off balance, which she suspected was precisely what he intended. She gave herself time to come to terms with that, then doggedly attempted to wrench control back from him.

"I can't imagine why you and your mother lived here all those years and not in the mansion."

Spencer took another step toward her. Barely an arm's length separated them now, and still she could not look away from those penetrating blue eyes. A danger signal went off somewhere in her mind, as loud and insistent as a fire-station klaxon.

He moved again, one more step at last breaking the barrier of her psychological territory. The inner alarm became deafening. Sabrina tried to back up, but her heel hit against an immovable object. She couldn't tear her eyes free to check out what had gotten in the way of her retreat.

"Let it go, Sabrina." His tone was at once demanding and entreating. "Please, for the good of all, just let it go."

Her head twitched from side to side like an automaton with a bad set of bearings. Her tongue had grafted itself to the roof of her mouth, forestalling intelligible speech. The klaxon had begun to lose some of its overpowering volume now as she caught a faint whiff of Spencer—a blend of damp wool and leather, and an expensive brand of aftershave—and another set of sensations threatened to take over altogether.

His lips parted. Sabrina sensed rather than saw the rise and fall of his thick chest as he breathed. The riveted intensity of his gaze reached deeper and deeper. Beckoning.

"I think you'd better leave," she managed in an alien voice.

He nodded, and his lips soundlessly seemed to form the words, "So do I."

When he didn't move, Sabrina once again tried to step back, forgetting about the unseen barrier, her mind hopelessly entangled by wildly contradicting emotions and sensations. Quetzal coughed a throaty protest at her feet, and she went tottering backward, arms flailing. She felt the belt loosen at her waist, and the soft fabric of her robe shifted.

They both gasped.

Spencer's hands jerked out of his pockets and he made a catlike lunge at Sabrina. His arms encircled her, lifting her off her feet and halting her backward tumble as her arms instinctively clamped around his neck. Sabrina felt the harsh rasp of his wool coat against her bared flesh, sensed the quivering heat of his breath on the side of her face.

For a moment, he held her suspended in a powerful embrace. She was acutely aware of the clean smell of his hair and the hard knot of jaw muscle bulging just below his earlobe. Then, with a sigh, he gradually loosened his grip, and she slid down the length of his body, coat buttons and pocket seams combining with the firm grip of his hands to send myriad shock waves of confused pleasure through her.

When her feet were firmly planted on the floor between his, Spencer took her shoulders and gently eased her away from him so he could see her. Sabrina was stunned by his expression. No man had ever looked at her with such dumbstruck hunger.

The force of it rushed through her like a river of fire, driving away all traces of embarrassment and drowning out the screaming klaxon. She waited for his touch, wanting it more than she had ever yearned for Darryl's selfish groping, sensing that Spencer's touch would be a huge leap into a totally unknown experience.

He inclined his head toward her, and Sabrina's lips tingled in anticipation. His Adam's apple bobbed. He slid his hands gently, gently down the rolled lapels of Sabrina's robe... and drew them closed.

She blinked as if snapping out of a trance. When he reached for the belt of her robe, an awakening bud of humiliation blossomed. Sabrina spun away from him, clawing the robe tightly closed. Putting the chair outside her bedroom door between them, she whirled and glared at him.

"Get out," she rasped.

Spencer spread his hands in a mute gesture that only added to her confusion. Neither of them spoke again. But when he finally moved toward the front door, tears burned like acid down her cheeks, etching the sense of humiliation ever deeper.

He stopped at the door and looked back one last time at her robe... or what lay beneath it. He lifted his gaze to her face, and Sabrina could make absolutely nothing of his expression.

When he had gone, Sabrina closed her eyes and gripped the back of the chair, shivering with disgust and anger. Disgust at her shameless behavior. Anger at Spencer for what he had not done.

A helpless moan escaped her. In his powerfully gentle embrace, the sense of overwhelming desire had felt so incredibly, purely... *right*. Now, in the cold grip of solitude, Sabrina was shocked by how much she had wanted the dreadful man's touch.

Quetzal stroked his sleek body against her legs, purring righteously, then trotted off into the bedroom. After a while, she followed.

Misty rain whispered against the window. Spencer tossed fitfully, stared into the impenetrable darkness of the bedroom ceiling and tossed again. The sheets caressed his naked body the way he wanted Sabrina to, turning his every movement into exquisitely maddening torture.

Dolorously, the clock downstairs bonged once. It was twelve-thirty. Or one. Or one-thirty. Wide awake, he offered a pathetic curse to the black night. He should never have gone down to the cottage. Never. But the truth was, Spencer hadn't been able to stop himself.

He couldn't blame the colossally stupid move on nostalgia. As strolls down memory lane went, the cottage represented a personal back road to unspeakable nightmares. His willingness, no, his *eagerness* to go there hadn't even had much to do with the issue of the locked library. That had only provided the excuse.

Take all that away, and Spencer was left with the simple fact that he was falling head over heels in lust with Sabrina Glade. Unfortunately there was nothing simple about it. Not with the specter of Jeremiah Kellogg's damnable book looming in the background.

Spencer threw back the covers and sat up. He hadn't had a decent night's sleep since moving into the mansion, and tonight was going to be no exception. There was no point in dragging out the ordeal. Besides, he was about to give himself another headache. He got out of bed and pulled on his clothes.

The house was dark and still. Spencer refrained from switching on lights as he made his way downstairs, though he was unconcerned that he might awaken anyone. The Shaws were beyond sight or sound up on the third floor, and Lafever's rooms were all the way at the back of the ground floor behind the kitchen pantry.

Spencer had come to prefer the darkness. It sharpened his awareness of the decrepit smell of the place and focused his hearing on the faint settling sounds the old mansion made in the night. Little by little, this growing familiarity was helping him to shed the feeling that he was an outsider in his own house.

He paused at the foot of the stairs and leaned against the newel post, unsure of where he was headed. His head actually did hurt, sort of, and he was a tad queasy. He realized that at times he hadn't felt so great lately. Spencer moved on across the pitch-dark maw of the foyer, impatient with himself. This was no time to be coming down with the flu.

Near the end of the hallway leading to the kitchen, Spencer began to detect food smells mingled with the pervasive odor that he had come to think of as basic house rot. Maria Shaw had been spending more time in the kitchen the past day or so. As it turned out, she was a surprisingly talented cook, particularly with the spicy hot foods that he preferred.

The end of the hallway formed a right angle. The kitchen lay straight ahead. In the deep shadows off to the right was the door to Conrad Lafever's quarters. Spencer had never been beyond that door. Giving way to impulse now, he turned in that direction, the sound of his footsteps silenced by an ancient carpet runner.

He stopped at the door. Funny, he thought, how clearly he remembered first meeting Lafever nearly twenty-five years ago. In his mind's eye, Lafever had been exactly as he was now—a perfect match for Jeremiah Kellogg. Stiff, puritanical, secretive.

Favored.

Wrapping a hand around the porcelain knob, Spencer turned it slowly and carefully. The door was locked. Having had no intention of actually entering, he carefully reversed the turn, his curiosity satisfied. He was about to release the knob when a telephone jangled, then abruptly stopped in midring as if Lafever had snatched up his private phone to answer an expected call.

A thin ribbon of light appeared under the door. Spencer released the doorknob and froze as the indistinct murmur of a voice filtered through the door. Several minutes passed before he heard a quick rattle that must have been the tele-

phone receiver being returned to its cradle. Then the light
went out.

He moved silently back down the hallway to the kitchen
and flipped the switch beside the door. The overhead light
came blindingly on. Spencer crossed to the sink, not even
trying to be quiet now, and stood frowning at his ghostly
reflection in the window.

The call could have been a wrong number. If Lafever
happened to be a light sleeper, he might have snatched up
the phone in the middle of its first ring. Spencer had done
so on more than one occasion, but he seriously doubted
that Lafever's reflexes were that quick. Besides, if the call
had been a wrong number, Lafever wouldn't have talked so
long, and surely not in such muted tones.

Spencer checked his watch. Ten after one. Not a totally
ungodly hour, by his standards. But for the likes of Conrad Lafever, it smacked of high intrigue, regardless of
whether the call involved business or pleasure.

"You're a sneaky one, Connie," he murmured, his
hackles rising.

Next to his reflection in the window, Spencer noticed a
narrow paneled door. He turned and looked at it on the far
wall. The door stood slightly ajar. The pantry was to his
left. He wondered if, in the labyrinthine arrangement of the
mansion's corridors, this other door might somehow give
access to Lafever's rooms.

He went over, pulled the door open wide, and stared into
a void. A light switch was just inside the door. He flicked
it and peered down a set of sturdy wooden steps into a deep
basement. A ripe, somewhat repellent odor of damp,
soured earth wafted up to him.

Spencer drew back with a grunt, as satisfied as he cared
to make himself that the basement was a dead end. It
seemed only appropriate to him that a crumbling old mansion such as this should have such dank, moldering bowels. He switched off the basement light, closed the door,
and returned to the sink.

Getting a glass from the cabinet, he filled it at the tap. After the first swallow, his stomach rebelled. Spencer plunked the glass down on the counter and gripped the edge of the sink for a moment, head bowed, waiting for the wave of nausea to pass.

Maybe it wouldn't be a bad idea to drive over to Schuylerville and see if the hamlet still had a doctor, he thought. Find out what he was coming down with and get some antibiotics before the bug got a firm grip on him. He made up his mind to do that if he didn't feel better by morning.

Spencer took a deep breath, and his gut settled unreliably down out of his throat, leaving him clammy. The headache was still there, somewhere around the periphery. The muscles in his arms and legs twitched, annoying evidence of an uncommon fatigue that weighed more ponderously on him with each passing day—further proof that he was fighting a bug. Even so, he knew that if he went back upstairs to bed, he wouldn't sleep.

He stretched both arms, bridging his back until it popped, trying for any relief he could find. It didn't help. He tried to recall the old adage—starve a cold and feed a fever. Or was it the other way around? He didn't have a fever. Was his bug a cold?

Maria had left a foil-covered pan of her homemade gingerbread on the kitchen worktable. Heavy on the cinnamon, the way he'd mentioned that he liked it. He wondered if the housekeeper had remembered—or even known—that he had a lifelong addiction to the stuff.

After a bumpy start, Maria seemed to be making a genuine effort to meet Spencer halfway. That was more than he could say for either her brother or Lafever—not to mention Sabrina Glade.

He lifted a corner of the foil. Through no fault of its own, the spicy cake didn't look or smell nearly as appetizing to him now as it had when it had been fresh from the oven at noon. If his gut couldn't even handle plain water, there was little hope of keeping this down. Even so, Maria's culinary effort left him tempted to think more kindly of her.

Tempted.

He rubbed his eyes. Temptation was going to be his downfall, if what had almost transpired at the cottage that evening was any indication. Tucking the foil back into place around the pan, Spencer shuffled off across the kitchen toward the hallway.

Warm gingerbread and Sabrina Glade, he thought. Both cravings were within easy reach. But sadistic fate had arranged it so that he didn't dare touch either one.

CHAPTER SIX

The library had been unusually chilly these past couple of days. Apparently the furnace was no longer being operated at full throttle. Sabrina didn't mind. The change was a relief from the stuffy atmosphere in which she had worked for over three months.

She slowly walked the length of the library table, tapping a pencil against her chin as she surveyed the orderly stacks of books and folders. Here was another thing that had changed for the better. She had stopped locking the library door—for whatever good it had done—and her research materials had remained undisturbed for two days running. Either Spencer had found what he had been looking for, or she had made her point the night he had come uninvited to the cottage.

Her thoughts drifted back to that night, and she felt what was by now an all-too-familiar stirring. Sabrina shoved the disturbing recollection of Spencer Bradley's lascivious coat buttons from her mind before her barely latent sense of humiliation could come riding in on its coattails.

A clipped bundle of notes lay beside her laptop computer. She picked it up and plucked a random note from the stack.

"Tomato soup," it read. "Did J.K. always have such monastic tastes?"

She had made the note to herself the evening after Jeremiah Kellogg's funeral, when Conrad Lafever had gotten smashed and revealed for the first and only time that Kellogg had held his sister in less than reverent esteem. Sabrina was still convinced that Zena's death some twenty

years ago had precipitated the onset of Jeremiah's sudden
decline. The timing of both events had coincided too neatly
not to be related. But thanks to Conrad's momentarily
loose lip, she was no longer so sure that the old man's
downturn had been caused by sibling bereavement.

"If Spencer is any indication," she muttered under her
breath, "the men in this family wouldn't recognize grief if
it grabbed them by the throat and threw them on the
ground."

She tapped the pencil on the note, lips pursed. Jeremiah
Kellogg had called his only sister a slut. Conrad's inebri-
ated detonation of that little bombshell had blasted Sabrina's preconceived notions about the old man completely
out of the water. Ever since then, she had been trying to
piece together a new concept of what had made Kellogg
tick.

Kellogg's passion for tomato soup might have been simply an eccentricity brought on by old age. Unless, of course,
his tastes had radically changed in that direction around the
time of Zena's death. If that was the case, the stockpile of
canned tomato soup stacked in the kitchen pantry might
indicate something more than just an old man's monoma-
niacal taste buds.

"That shouldn't be difficult to clear up." She tucked the
pencil behind her ear and went off in search of Maria Shaw.

Some time later, Sabrina stood on the second-floor
landing, eyeing the shadowed staircase that led up to the
Shaws' living quarters on the third floor. She'd never had
either a reason or an inclination to climb those stairs. For
some reason, she had a spooky reluctance to do so now—
the old mansion sometimes did that to her. But she had already searched most of the lower floors. Unless Maria had
gone out on an errand or was in Spencer's rooms—both
highly unlikely—she had to be up there.

Shoving past her ineffable sense of trepidation, Sabrina
grabbed the handrail and moved resolutely up the carpeted
flight of stairs. Shadows closed in around her, fostering a

not altogether absurd anticipation of cobwebs. At the third-floor landing, she found her progress blocked by a wide mahogany door.

"Hmm." Sabrina knocked smartly on the barrier.

And waited, fidgeting.

When no one answered, she tightened her fist and knocked more loudly. Waiting again, she smiled uneasily as she recalled the way Spencer Bradley had hammered on the cottage door the other night. In the process of bringing her the brass key, he had somehow managed to unlock something more than just the library door. She felt the stirring once more, and snapped her attention back to the mahogany door in front of her.

Still no response.

"Hmm," she said again.

And opened the door.

That was as far as Sabrina went—and it was far enough. Without crossing the threshold, she could take in Orrin and Maria Shaw's entire spacious living room.

A thick Persian rug of an intricate red, black and gold design covered most of the polished hardwood floor. Near its center, two Queen Anne chairs and a matching settee were grouped around a low glass-topped table with a thick, black marble pedestal. Directly over the table hung a brass and crystal chandelier with three tiers of prismatic lusters.

Oil paintings in massive gilt frames graced the immaculate ivory-colored walls. Even to Sabrina's untrained eye, the artwork appeared to be genuine collector's items, undoubtedly appropriated from other parts of the mansion. Through a gracefully arched doorway, she could see enough of the dining room and an inlaid cherry sideboard to make her jaw drop.

She leaned against the doorjamb, feeling as if she had just fallen through some kind of time warp. Once upon a time, this was how the entire mansion must have looked, she thought, dazzled. Then she reminded herself who lived up here amid all this splendor and jolted back to reality.

Sabrina took another long look at the Shaws' less-than-humble abode, compared it with Conrad Lafever's minuscule rooms crammed behind the kitchen pantry, and decided that Jeremiah Kellogg must have held his housekeeper and handyman in far higher esteem than made any sense at all.

"Go ahead and say it," she whispered. "This is more than tomato soup. This is insanity."

She eased the door shut and quietly descended the stairs, trying to figure out how she was going to broach this to Conrad without hurting his feelings. With that preying on her mind, she didn't notice Spencer at the foot of the stairs until she almost ran into him.

He had been watching her from the landing, a deep frown line between his narrowed eyes. She slowed, forcing herself to meet his gaze steadily in spite of her wildly quickening pulse.

"What were you doing up there?" He unzipped his fur-collared bomber jacket, glancing up the staircase suspiciously.

"Looking for Maria." She could feel the chill of the outdoors in the air around him and was angered by an answering surge of heat within herself.

"She's down at the garage, cleaning out Jeremiah's old Mercedes. I'm going to sell it after the will is probated."

"Then I'll catch her later."

Spencer flashed another look up toward the third floor as she brushed past him. She felt a stab of guilt, wondering if he had seen her open the door to the Shaws' upstairs quarters. Sabrina was almost to the main staircase when his hand clamped her upper arm, stopping her short.

"Shall I tell Maria you're looking for her?" he asked.

"No." She met his gaze and saw the pupils in his sapphire eyes dilate dramatically as his grip relaxed, his fingers shifting a bare inch down the sensitive flesh on the inside of her arm. In a strained voice, she repeated, "No."

He nodded, and dropped his hand. Sabrina moved quickly down the curving staircase, feeling his gaze on her all the way, melting her like butter. But when she reached the bottom and glanced back, he was gone.

Back in the library, Sabrina sank into a chair and stared blankly at the screen saver swirling on the monitor of her laptop computer. After what seemed like a very long time, her head cleared enough for her to realize that the encounter with Spencer had been purely happenstance. He had just come in from outdoors. He hadn't been lurking in the shadows, spying on her.

"Get your head screwed on straight," she muttered through her teeth.

Blinking away sensually disturbing flashes of sapphire blue eyes, she wrenched her thoughts willfully back to the astounding opulence that she had discovered on the third floor. It was crazy. Conrad Lafever had been Kellogg's trusted right arm for twenty-five years. And yet he put up with tiny rooms behind the pantry, while the Shaws lived in the lap of luxury. How could he have remained so loyal to the old man all that time in the face of such inequitable treatment?

Jeremiah Kellogg had blatantly taken Conrad for granted. Sabrina could think of no other explanation. Maybe that was what a man like Conrad needed, she thought—the opportunity to prove his loyalty with subservience. Lafever was like a nineteenth-century English butler, lost in time.

If Spencer Bradley had been in Conrad's shoes, he wouldn't have put up with it.

"Ah, we're back to that," she murmured, wondering if Spencer had been up on the third floor since his return to the estate. Probably not, she decided. If he had, she surely would have heard the fireworks.

She suddenly straightened. Squaring the laptop in front of her, she dumped the screen saver and pulled up the file she was slowly accumulating on Zena. After scrolling

through its meager contents, she stored Zena and pulled up
Spencer's even-skimpier file.

There wasn't much volume in either, but both files contained not an ounce of fat. They were all meat and bone.

"And smoke. Maybe a few mirrors, too."

This past day or so, Sabrina had begun to recognize the
need to include this material on Spencer and Zena Bradley
in the book. After all, Zena had been Jeremiah Kellogg's
only sister—and Spencer was his sole heir. *The End of the
Line* wouldn't be complete without fleshing out these two
significant peripheral players.

She sighed now, disheartened by the knowledge that it
probably was already a lost cause. There wasn't likely to be
enough time to complete the research she already had
mapped out, let alone do justice to an entire new chapter.
Besides, she knew without asking that Spencer wouldn't
approve.

But—should that matter?

Sabrina absently stroked her fingertips across her lips.
Until running into him on the landing a short while ago, she
hadn't set eyes on Spencer since he'd left the cottage two
nights ago. But regardless of what pundits claimed, out of
sight had been a long way from out of mind. Two minutes
in Spencer's arms had thoroughly scalded her emotions and
cursed her skin with a heightened awareness of everything
she touched.

Then he had grabbed her arm there on the landing,
sending through her yet another fire storm of a sort that she
had never before experienced. She didn't know how to deal
with it. How to fight it. Where to plant her emotional feet
to confront it. Dammit, she wasn't even sure what *it* was.

She shook her head and rubbed a fist down over one
breast as if to erase the scintillating memory of wool and
buttons scraping across her flesh. There was a distinct possibility that she was allowing her ridiculously inappropri-
ate physical attraction to Spencer Bradley to skew her
perspective.

The fact remained that he was dead set against her completing *The End of the Line*. There had to be a good reason for that. Finding out what Spencer was afraid of might be her best hope of persuading Ira Sampson to grant her a deadline extension. It might also dispel some of Spencer's mystique and help her to escape the magnetic aura that seemed to be drawing her inexorably to him.

Before noon, Sabrina made a discovery that set her back on her heels, and as far as she could tell, it had nothing whatever to do with Spencer Bradley. One hour and a couple of hurried phone calls later, she was on the road.

The highway was wet, and her battered car's tires were dangerously bald. But Sabrina crowded the speed limit, anyway, because she couldn't afford to be late. Not with just a few short weeks remaining before the reading of Jeremiah Kellogg's will would at last give Spencer the power to evict her from the estate.

With one eye on the treacherous road and the other on her watch, she sped south through Schuylerville and Stillwater and Mechanicville, paralleling the Hudson River. When she reached the bridge across the Mohawk, south of Waterford, she was well ahead of schedule. As she entered the outskirts of Albany and followed the scribbled instructions to Noble Wetherbee's house, she was doing even better than that. But she didn't breathe a sigh of relief until she pulled up in front of an imposing redbrick colonial and saw Wetherbee's drab green Jaguar parked in the circular driveway.

Grabbing her briefcase, Sabrina slid out of her car and trotted up the short walkway bracketed with topiary to the low front porch. The elegant symmetry of pristine white shutters on the multipaned windows of the house brought home to her just how far into depressing decay the Kellogg estate had sunk.

Noble Wetherbee himself opened the door before she reached the bell button. Clad in pin-striped suit pants and vest and a ragged brown cardigan with worn leather patches on the elbows, he greeted Sabrina with a smile that seemed just a little too tight around the edges.

"I really do appreciate your waiting for me," she said as he escorted her down a wainscoted hallway to his study. "I hope I'm not going to cause you to miss your meeting."

"Not to worry." Wetherbee smiled, pointing her to a chair in front of his big walnut desk.

The study was comfortable and masculine, but with a discernible woman's touch in the draperies and in the leather-trimmed throw pillows on the long couch against the wall opposite the door. An oil portrait of a strikingly attractive middle-aged woman hung over a bookcase at the end of the room. Wetherbee cast a lingering glance at the image of his late wife as he settled into a captain's chair near Sabrina.

"You were so mysterious when you called," he said, "I'm afraid my curiosity got the better of me, so I canceled my appointment."

"With the *lieutenant governor?*"

He chuckled. "Scouter and I are old golfing buddies. He knows I'm four-fifths retired and makes allowances for my idiosyncracies."

Wetherbee had called the lieutenant governor Scouter, Sabrina noted. The old lawyer was obviously remaining in touch with the mainstream in spite of his semiretirement. Unlike Jeremiah Kellogg, he hadn't crawled into himself and made tomato soup the focal point of his life. Wetherbee leaned back now and folded his hands over his vest.

"You've come on urgent business, I take it?"

"You know about my accelerated deadline with Sampson Books," Sabrina said. "Since Mr. Kellogg's death, everything having to do with the book has become urgent."

He nodded slowly, waiting patiently for her to continue. For all his genteel cordiality, Wetherbee gave away very little when it came to discussing his late client, even though

Kellogg had given him permission to be free and open with Sabrina. That was the lawyer in him, Sabrina thought, hoping she wasn't about to run up against a stone wall.

"Shortly before his fatal accident," she said, reaching into her briefcase, "Mr. Kellogg gave me a case of old files dating back prior to his father's—Layton's—demise in 1956. At the time, they appeared to contain fairly inconsequential documents. But I came across an item this morning that—well, see for yourself."

Sabrina opened a large manila envelope and drew out a sheaf of yellowed paper. Wetherbee produced a pair of reading glasses from his vest pocket, accepted the papers and, poker-faced, settled back to read.

When he was finished, he returned the glasses to his pocket and sat pulling at his chin. Unless her imagination was playing tricks on her, he seemed reluctant to look at her.

"I was told that Mr. Kellogg's marriage was childless," Sabrina said finally.

Wetherbee did look at her then. "You were told? Or you assumed?"

She wondered why he was making the distinction. "I was *told* by Conrad Lafever. I hadn't come upon any records before that would refute that."

"I see." He handed her the papers and watched as she slid them carefully back into the envelope. "Well, Mr. Lafever was correct."

"Really?" She tapped the envelope. "Then how do you explain this application for preenrollment of one Jeremiah Layton Kellogg II in a very exclusive private boarding school in Connecticut?"

Wetherbee plucked a bit of lint from his pants, then straightened the razor-sharp creases. He was stalling, gathering his thoughts. Her hand slid into her briefcase and curled around her pocket tape recorder. When she brought it out into plain view, Wetherbee stopped fussing over his pants.

"I'd rather you didn't use that," he said.

He had never objected to her recording their conversations before. But on this occasion, there was nothing in his tone to indicate that the matter was negotiable. Sabrina let him know with a look that she hadn't expected the restriction. Deciding there was nothing to be gained by making an issue of it at this point, she shrugged agreeably. His expression seemed to relax as she returned the recorder to her briefcase and took out a notebook.

"As you've undoubtedly noticed, Miss Glade, that application bears a 1954 date, with the child's actual matriculation set for the 1963 term." Wetherbee waited for her nod. "As you mentioned, the boarding school in question was—and still is—exclusive. Because it takes years for a prospective student to work his way up the lengthy waiting list, parents commonly preenroll their offspring at birth."

Sabrina waited impatiently, anxious for Wetherbee to cut to the chase. None of this was new to her. She had already spoken on the phone with the administrator of the boarding school.

"Are you saying now that Mr. Kellogg *did* father a child?"

Wetherbee nodded. "In the fall of 1963, Jeremiah Kellogg's stillborn son would have been six years old, had he lived."

"Stillborn—"

"Indeed. After the unfortunate birth, Jeremiah never spoke of the child again. Not even to me." He gestured toward the manila envelope in Sabrina's lap. "I seem to recall his showing me that application a month or so before Evelyn's doctors realized there might be something wrong with her pregnancy. Jeremiah had such dreams..."

Wetherbee shook his head slowly. "He was devastated. I do believe Jeremiah would have gone to *any* lengths to ensure a male heir."

"Did he and his wife try again?" she asked, scribbling notes.

"No. The birth was difficult. It took a lot out of Evelyn, physically and emotionally. She never truly recovered her health afterward."

Sabrina hugged the envelope against her, letting all those revelations soak in. Jeremiah Kellogg II had never drawn a single breath of life, yet he seemed to have played a major role in his father's life. Or had he? The elder Jeremiah Kellogg had gone on to achieve his greatest diplomatic triumphs and international acclaim during the nearly two decades following his son's ill-starred birth. Not until his sister Zena's death did he begin his sharp decline into oblivion. That somehow didn't jibe with the picture that Noble Wetherbee had just drawn.

"I take it that Mr. Kellogg never considered adopting a child," she said.

"Not for one moment. That wouldn't have served his purpose."

"Purpose?"

The attorney strove to maintain an impassive expression, but Sabrina was beginning to detect subtle indications of just how much of a strain that effort was for him. His jowls had grown ruddier, his eyes taking on a flintiness that made her pulse quicken.

"May I assume that you've never examined a copy of a Kellogg's will?" he asked.

"Which Kellogg?"

"It doesn't matter. Any Kellogg for, say, the past six generations."

She shook her head.

"Then you aren't aware of the one key condition that they all contain, without exception."

Sabrina leaned forward. "Being?"

"That the Kellogg fortune must always revert to the oldest male blood Kellogg in the line."

Sabrina thought, *How archaic,* and would have smiled if it hadn't seemed so tragically perverted. Then the ramifications of what Wetherbee was saying hit home, bringing the entire picture into cruel focus.

Jeremiah Kellogg had been able to carry on with his life after his only son was stillborn because his devastation had been not of the heart, but of the mind. His own son evidently had represented an item of vital genealogical importance to him. Period.

She smoothed her hands gently over the envelope, wondering if she was being too harsh on Kellogg—and knowing in her bones that she wasn't. With a feeling of unutterable sadness, she slid the envelope back into her briefcase.

"That's why Mr. Kellogg left his entire estate to a nephew he apparently despised?" She shook her head in disbelief. "Come on. Surely he could have left out the blood-lineage clause in his own will."

"Impossible." The word held a certain bite. "You see, Jeremiah was an incurable traditionalist at heart. Which always struck me as rather ironic, since previous generations of Kelloggs were notable for their tendency to march to their own drumbeat. With the exception of their wills, of course."

Sabrina's shoulders began to ache. She realized that she had braced herself rigidly in the chair as if to prevent a whiplash. Her carefully constructed image of the private Jeremiah Kellogg behind the public image had just slammed head-on into a cold reality that she hadn't even suspected until this morning. She had a sick feeling that it was going to take longer than her deadline permitted for her to reassemble the wreckage.

She took a deep breath and tried to relax. This wasn't just hearsay. She had the beginnings of hard documentation right there in her briefcase.

"Mr. Wetherbee, it appears that I've been wearing a blindfold these past three months."

He raised his hand, palm up, apologetically.

"Not your fault," she said. "You were here all along with the answers. It was my job to come up with the questions."

"I'm sure you weren't counting on Jeremiah's... oversights."

"Deceptions, Mr. Wetherbee. The stillborn child, the bloodline condition in the Kellogg wills, the way that information was held back by Mr. Kellogg—all a deliberate deception."

He shrugged again as if concurring.

"The same way," she continued, "that he and Conrad Lafever deceived me by concealing the fact that Mr. Kellogg's sister and nephew lived in the cottage right there on the estate for seventeen years."

Sabrina left unspoken her conviction that Wetherbee had taken an active part in both deceptions. She waited for him to respond. When he didn't, she searched his expression for any reaction whatever. But in his own way, the attorney could be just as stone-faced as Spencer Bradley when the spirit moved him.

She glanced down at the manila envelope in her briefcase. "What I can't figure out is why Mr. Kellogg handed over that last case of old files before he died."

"My guess is that Jeremiah had forgotten all about that application," Wetherbee said as if the subject of deception had never been broached. "He probably felt the same about the files as you did—that they were inconsequential."

"I don't know." Sabrina frowned. "If Mr. Kellogg thought the files were worthless, why would he have bothered to trot them out at all? Besides, he was a flawless practitioner of the art of omission right up until he handed over that box. It seems inconceivable that he gave them to me without having closely examined them."

Wetherbee nodded vaguely. "It almost seems as if Jeremiah wanted you to find that application."

"Yes, but I'm not sure that makes sense."

"Very little of the human condition does, I find," he said, with a cynicism that surprised Sabrina.

"Maybe he left the application in the files just to drive me out of my mind." She fingered the corner of the manila folder protruding from her briefcase. "Then again, he couldn't have known he would be dead just a few days later. Maybe he did expect me to find the application...and bring it to him, just like I've brought it to you."

"Perhaps."

She stared at him as if across a vast gulf, growing increasingly frustrated by the feeling that they were engaged in a game of twenty questions. Only by asking the right questions—whatever they might be—would she get a straight answer. Or not.

"Something has bothered me since the night of Mr. Kellogg's death," she said, marching doggedly on. "You were visiting in the mansion when the accident occurred. You might know. What in blue blazes was he doing carting a tray of dirty dishes down the back stairs?"

Wetherbee rubbed his eyes, then sat frowning for a moment as though he was trying to recall an event from long ago, instead of something that had taken place less than two weeks ago.

"I wish I knew," he said finally. "I had gone out to look for something in my car. The first I was aware that anything had happened was when Maria Shaw ran screaming out the front door."

Sabrina nodded. She had heard Maria all the way down at the cottage that night. The memory raised the hairs on the back of her neck.

Wetherbee had gone gray-faced. "I called the emergency medical team at once. Then I went and helped Orrin Shaw carry Jeremiah to his room."

Two old men dragging a third off to his deathbed, she thought. Neither of them must have realized that it would have been better to have left the injured man in place until the paramedics arrived. Not that it had mattered in the end.

In spite of Wetherbee's efforts to apply pressure to the severed artery, Jeremiah had bled to death before the ambulance had pulled up out front. Before Sabrina could even race up from the cottage.

She reluctantly decided that the curious puzzle of Jeremiah Kellogg and the dirty dishes was one that probably would never be satisfactorily explained. But she couldn't quite bring herself to completely let go of what was—to Sabrina—the single most peculiar aberration in Kellogg's behavior. For now, she filed that away for later consideration.

The attorney shifted, planting both feet squarely on the floor as if preparing to stand. Sensing that the end of their interview was drawing near, Sabrina hurried on. Like the winner of an all-you-can-grab-in-sixty-seconds shopping spree, she intended to rake in every bit of information she could before Wetherbee politely showed her to the door.

For some reason, the tradition of passing the family fortune down to the eldest blood-related Kellogg male again loomed large in her mind. Following her well-honed interviewing instincts, Sabrina took another quick look at the subject.

"Tell me, Mr. Wetherbee, did Spencer Bradley know before Mr. Kellogg died that the condition in the will concerning blood-related males more or less guaranteed that he would inherit his uncle's estate?" The question seemed to form itself on her lips with no conscious thought. As she heard herself speaking the words, she felt an unaccountable chill.

Wetherbee pulled a long face, thinking it over. "I can't be sure. I suppose that's possible."

"Really?"

Sabrina bit her thumbnail, squinting intently while considering the possibility that Spencer Bradley had known all along that he was sole heir to the Kellogg estate. Because of her disturbing attraction to him, she was particularly anxious to remain on solid ground where Spencer was concerned. So she added into the account two more firmly established certainties. First, Spencer's loathing of his uncle had not been one-sided. And second, Spencer had been hell-bent on assuming the role of lord of the manor before his uncle was cold in his grave.

As she totaled up the scorecard, the fine hairs rose on Sabrina's arms. Still, a part of her managed to turn its back on the implication. This afternoon, she had found out too much too soon about the shabby side of Jeremiah Kellogg's private life. She couldn't—wouldn't—let herself take it for granted that Spencer had a perfect motive for wanting his despised uncle dead. Not yet.

"Mr. Wetherbee, you mentioned that the Kelloggs were individualists—they marched to their own drumbeats, I believe was the way you put it."

"Yes. I remember old Layton—"

"What about Mr. Kellogg's sister, Zena?" she interrupted.

The attorney shifted in his chair again, turning slightly away from her. Wetherbee seemed to grasp the significance of his body language at once and quickly returned to his former position, his hands resting loosely on his thighs. He would be a cagey adversary in a courtroom, Sabrina thought.

"What about Zena?" he repeated. "Yes, yes. She most definitely inherited the Kellogg wild streak."

"And her brother didn't."

His chuckle sounded oddly brittle. "As a matter of fact, Jeremiah dedicated a good part of his life to extinguishing the trait."

"By making Zena and her son live in that dump of a cottage on the estate?" Sabrina asked.

Wetherbee took an intense interest in the crease in one pant leg.

"I have it from a reliable source that Mr. Kellogg had called his sister a slut," she said, scrupulously avoiding any mention of Conrad Lafever. "Was Zena really as wild as all that?"

"She was fast." Wetherbee seem to regret that statement as soon as it was uttered. "Please, don't misunderstand me, Miss Glade. Zena was a hard person to dislike. In her youth, she was a born risk taker, always searching for new thrills and challenges. There were times when I felt that Jeremiah actually feared that in her."

Feared. Sabrina scribbled a note.

He tucked both thumbs into his vest pockets and entwined his fingers. "I see a lot of Zena in Spencer. Not just the blue eyes, either. Unfortunately she was born too early in this century."

"Why do you say that?"

"As a rule, women weren't taken seriously in the business arena until recently—even women with Zena's spirit and intelligence." He sighed with regret. "Today, she might have climbed to the summit as an entrepreneurial wunderkind."

"Instead she lived at the bottom of the hill with her brother's foot on her neck."

Wetherbee raised his fingers from his thighs. His subtle gestures had a certain eloquence. But Sabrina wasn't fooled. They were also his way to avoid making a clear-cut statement.

"I have the impression that Zena's son inherited her entrepreneurial spirit," she said.

"Yes. Spencer seems to have done all right for himself," Wetherbee agreed after a pause. "He enlisted in the Marine Corps when he left home, and ended up serving with U.S. embassy security detachments in Moscow and Tokyo."

"He joined up right after high school?"

"Immediately after. The military put him through college. I believe he served about eight—no, it must have been ten—years before he was discharged. After that, he pretty much went right on with what he'd been doing in the Corps, only in the private sector."

"And now he's here."

Wetherbee drew a thumbnail slowly down the crease in one pant leg with an air of detachment. She watched him for a moment, thinking the distinguished attorney sometimes relied too heavily on his posturing. Her instincts told her that he was deeply bothered by Spencer Bradley's presence at the mansion.

"Has Spencer ever married?" The question came out of the blue. Sabrina was grateful to Wetherbee for not making more of it than she had intended.

"Not that I know of." He watched her flip quickly back through her notebook before making another notation. "To tell you the truth, he was so full of anger when he was a boy that I simply can't picture him in a domestic situation."

Nothing had changed. "Did he get that from his mother?"

"Not at all."

"Then what about the other side?" she asked. "What was his father like?"

Wetherbee shrugged. "Zena eloped when she was still in her teens. Not even her closest acquaintances ever met the man."

"The marriage must not have lasted until the water got hot." Sabrina fell silent for a moment. "Did the guy attend Zena's funeral?"

Wetherbee pondered that briefly. "No one knew where to find him—and there wasn't much time. The funeral took place less than thirty-six hours after Zena passed on."

Sabrina had always hated euphemisms for death. "She must have been pretty young when she died."

"Middle thirties," Wetherbee said. "Perhaps a year or two younger than Spencer is right now."

She had imagined Zena as withered and aged, as Jeremiah Kellogg had been at the time of his death. The product of one of Layton Kellogg's later marriages, however, she had been ten or more years younger than her half brother. Thinking of Zena as young and vibrant seemed to bring her to life for Sabrina for the first time.

"By the way," she said, "what did Zena die of?"

Wetherbee smoothed the front of his vest. "I don't really recall. I was down in Miami attending a bar association function at the time. Quite out of touch with everything."

Sabrina stared at him, bewildered. Wetherbee stared back, his expression bland. *He's lying through his teeth,* she decided, wondering why he had suddenly found that to be necessary.

She kept tossing questions at Wetherbee, trying to shake loose something else—she had no idea what. But she couldn't seem to get her thought processes to skip past the one fabrication that she had detected. When she realized they were drifting into a discussion of the weather, Sabrina thanked the attorney for his time and reached for her briefcase.

As he walked her to the door, Wetherbee rambled on about nothing of substance, once again playing the avuncular old gentleman-lawyer. Sabrina kept up her end of the chatter, being pleasant and deferential, hoping her responses didn't sound as mechanical as they were. The biggest part of her mind was already busily collating the information she had already gained during their meeting.

Taking it all at face value, it seemed that she was coming away with a great deal more than she had expected. But when he finally closed the door behind her, Sabrina couldn't shake the nagging suspicion that Noble Wetherbee had withheld a good deal more than he had revealed.

A light drizzle began falling as Sabrina pulled onto the highway and headed back north, driving on autopilot. She wasn't pleased. The farther she drove, the more she became downright fighting mad.

Jeremiah Kellogg had been manipulating her as an unwitting pawn in some kind of grand deception from the moment she signed on to ghostwrite *The End of the Line.*

If she had only suspected that before, she was certain of it now.

Sabrina hissed through her teeth and turned up the windshield wipers. She hated being used—*hated it.* The wiper blades slapped rapidly back and forth. Sabrina peered through the bleared glass, fuming. If she had a choice, she told herself, she would call Ira Sampson and tell him she couldn't possibly make the book's delivery date.

The problem was that she didn't have a choice. Even if she'd had a place to go to—*someone to go to*—she couldn't afford to get there. *The End of the Line* represented the absolute end of her rope—and it was growing more frayed with each passing day.

The driver of a passing eighteen-wheeler bapped his air horn. Startled, Sabrina swerved, then checked her speedometer. She was going barely forty, her already-battered spirits rebelling at the thought of returning to the dank cottage in the shadow of the Kellogg mansion. *In the shadow of Spencer Bradley.*

Her grip on the steering wheel tightened. From all indications, Jeremiah Kellogg had despised his own heir apparent, as did Conrad Lafever. Even close-to-the-vest Noble Wetherbee had seemed less than excited about Spencer being on the estate. Sabrina, too, wanted him gone, knowing that he had the power to eventually kill whatever nebulous chance she still had of completing the book.

The drizzle turned to cold rain. She chewed her lip savagely, recalling the simmering heat of Spencer's gaze flowing down over her bared skin on the night he had visited the cottage. Her foot bore down harder on the accelerator. As the car sped north toward the Kellogg estate, she felt like a moth sailing toward an open flame—inexorably drawn to Spencer Bradley.

CHAPTER SEVEN

The miserable rain let up a few miles outside Schuylerville, but the sky remained overcast and threatening. Minutes after taking the turnoff onto the road leading to the Kellogg estate, Sabrina glimpsed flashing lights in the rearview mirror and edged over onto the narrow shoulder.

A fire truck roared past, siren warbling, and rapidly disappeared up the road. As she pulled back onto the pavement, a sudden premonition slithered into the pit of her stomach. Sabrina gave chase. She was still several hundred yards behind when, sure enough, the fire truck slowed to make the right turn through the gate into the Kellogg estate.

A pall of sooty smoke drifted through the barren treetops onto the road, the sharp stench wafting in through her car's heater vents as Sabrina approached the entrance gate. Her vague sense of foreboding took on a fearful urgency.

She hit the brakes too hard, sending the car into a sickening skid toward one of the mold-streaked fieldstone gateposts. Sabrina instinctively turned into the skid, and the rear bumper missed the post by inches. Then a tire blew. The car careered in a full circle before the left rear fender slammed into a tree with a rending crunch of metal and plastic, bringing the wild ride to an abrupt end.

"You stupid...!"

Sabrina hammered her fists into the steering wheel, unsure whether she was referring to the car, the tree or herself. The engine had died. She turned the key in the ignition, to no effect, then vented her frustration on the steering wheel once more.

The stench of fire was getting stronger. Sabrina bolted out of the car and took off up the long leaf-littered driveway toward the mansion. From the looks of the smoke billowing through the trees, this was no minor kitchen fire. She half expected to see flames licking toward the low clouds from the top of the hill.

When she reached the fork in the driveway, Sabrina drew up short, momentarily confused. She realized that the smoke wasn't pouring down from the hilltop, but was drifting from the right, along the narrow gravel track that led around the base of the hill to the cottage. She stared at the black shroud for precious seconds, her heart pounding, simple fear transforming itself into icy terror.

"No!" Sabrina broke into a trot, then into a full-blown sprint, kicking up gravel. "No! No!"

The word became a frantic chant, fading to a whisper as the smoke grew thicker. She choked, but kept running even after she had lost both shoes. The sharp gravel tore at her stockings and cut into her feet. She didn't notice. Her entire consciousness had riveted on the horror toward which she was racing.

She burst into the clearing, saw the small cluster of volunteer firemen milling aimlessly around the fire truck, felt the roar of the conflagration through the torn soles of her feet. The cottage was gone. In its place was an unrecognizable inferno of charred stone and timber from which poured a hellish storm of flames, smoke and airborne embers.

Sabrina staggered to a halt at the edge of the clearing, winded, her lungs burning. A beam split with a loud crack, sending a shower of brilliant orange sparks skyward.

She opened her mouth, took a deep, searing breath, and screamed, *"Quetzal!"*

The firemen glanced her way, then returned to complacently watching the flames. Sabrina gaped at them, bereft, suddenly too weak with fury to move.

The smoke shifted on a gust of damp wind that fanned the flames like a bellows. She didn't notice the figure approaching through the haze until he was almost upon her. Even then, it took her traumatized mind a remarkably long time to register Spencer Bradley, perhaps because he looked so different.

Clear blue eyes peered from a soot-grimed face. His shirt and pants were filthy and torn. He carried what looked like a wet tweed sport coat all rolled up in a ball. As he drew nearer, she saw blood seeping through a series of slashes across the front of his shirt, and a nasty burn on the back of one hand. He looked angry enough to chew nails.

"Where the hell have you been?" he demanded.

Sabrina was speechless. He loomed over her like a tattered refugee from Hades, smelling of singed hair and sweat. She stared at him in disbelief with tear-stung eyes. Her beloved cat had just been incinerated along with all her earthly belongings, and the man was mad at *her*. At last, she mustered the only response she could at that moment.

She took a swing at him.

Spencer saw it coming and leaned back out of her reach. She hit the balled-up coat. The coat made a spitting sound and began bucking in his arms.

"Well, dammit, if that's the way you feel, take him," Spencer barked. "You two deserve each other."

He shoved the squirming bundle at her like a medicine ball, knocking her back a step. Sabrina gasped at the familiar shape inside the coat. A wet head popped out of the folds, still spitting.

"Quetzal!" Her voice broke.

The feline's whiskers had been singed, and he smelled even worse than Spencer. But he was beautiful. She planted a kiss between the tom's laid-back ears, almost blubbering now. She began to whirl around in exhilaration and almost fell down, suddenly dizzy with relief. By the time she got her bearings again, Quetzal was purring savagely, and Spencer was walking away.

Sabrina hobbled after him, aware now of her missing shoes, aware of a lot of things that she had been too blind to see just a moment ago.

"Wait up." She grabbed Spencer's arm and felt the hard sinew of muscle beneath his shirtsleeve. He stopped and looked balefully at her hand, but she refused to let go. "Spencer, I didn't... you went and... how can I..."

"Forget it." He tried to pull away.

She seized a handful of his shirt. "Hold on, will you? This cat is all I have in the world, and I just want to—"

The shirt tore down the front along the bloodied slashes, laying one side of his chest bare. Four ragged claw marks cut diagonally across his pectoral. A thin film of blood mixed with sweat covered his flat belly, disappearing under his belt.

"Oh, God, Spencer."

She feathered her fingers around the edges of the lacerations. He tensed and snatched her hand away. "Don't," he said sharply. Then his tone softened and was barely audible above the boom and crackle of the fire. "Please... don't."

Her fingers automatically curled around his. "You went in there and saved Quetzal, didn't you?" she said, looking past him at the burning cottage.

His hand fell away from hers, but he didn't deny it. Sabrina was speechless. The man had risked his life for a cat that couldn't have meant a thing to him. Her gratitude was boundless. If she'd had a free arm, it would have been around his neck.

"The cat isn't the only thing you have," he said.

She shook her head, uncomprehending, as his gaze slid down into her like warm quicksilver. In her mind, she leaned toward him as if drawn by a magnet. For a long moment, she couldn't move, couldn't even so much as draw a breath. Then Spencer blinked.

"I managed to drag a few other things out before it got too hot," he said. "Your computer. A duffel bag. A notebook, I think." He nodded over toward the south edge of the clearing, hidden behind a cloak of heavy smoke. "It's piled up over there."

Sabrina nodded dumbly and shifted the soggy tweed coat in her arms. Her thought processes seemed to have become as murky as the smoke. She couldn't make up her mind about Spencer's mood. One moment, he appeared to be ticked off at her. The next, his bright, probing eyes were mutely expressing quite a different emotion. It was as if he were two totally unrelated men sharing a single body. She was repelled by one and powerfully drawn to the other.

The problem was, she couldn't tell which was the genuine Spencer Bradley—the menacing troglodyte or the man she quite irrationally wanted to embrace. Sabrina couldn't bring herself to face the possibility that he might be both.

A remaining roof beam buckled with a hollow thud, plunging the last of the roof slates into the inferno. The flames began rapidly dying down. The firemen who had been watching the cottage burn edged closer now and began poking shovels at the edge of the smoldering rubble.

Sabrina was heartsick. As recently as half an hour ago, she wouldn't have believed that her situation could have gotten any worse. But within a matter of minutes, her worldly assets had been reduced to a cat, a wrecked car, the clothes on her back and whatever meager items Spencer had managed to rescue from the fire.

She turned her emotions on the firemen. "I can't believe they just stood around like a bunch of zombies and watched it burn to the ground."

"Don't blame those guys. The cottage went up too damned quickly." Spencer raked his hair off his forehead. "I had Maria call them as soon as I spotted the smoke from my window. By the time I got down here, the flames were already through the roof. Five minutes later, there wasn't enough left to waste water on."

"So fast?"

"Like a torch."

Sabrina resettled Quetzal in her arms again. The big tom was getting heavy, but nothing could have made her put him down.

The smoldering ruins were no longer pumping out great billows of black smoke. A gray haze had settled over the clearing, along with an unnatural hush. The firemen were talking quietly among themselves, their voices sounding muffled and far away.

Too damned quickly. Spencer's words seemed to echo in the eerie stillness.

"What could have started the fire?" she wondered aloud.

"Maybe you left a heater on."

"Of course, I left a heater on. You said yourself the place is a refrigerator in the winter."

Spencer raised his blistered hand. "Don't get all bent out of shape. I'm only suggesting a possible source of the fire. Maybe the stupid cat knocked something over into the flames."

"You can forget that. I've always been leery of space heaters. I don't—didn't leave anything near them. Besides, Quetzal usually sleeps all day when I'm gone." She hefted the bundle higher in her arms. "And he isn't stupid."

He raised an eyebrow, crow's-feet fanning out from the corner of that eye. It gave him a sinister look, made more so by the slightest hint of a smile. "How do you know how the cat spends his day when you're gone?"

"Call it blind faith," she said, incensed that Spencer would stoop to ragging her at a time like this. "The same way I know the refrigerator light goes off when the door is closed. But that's beside the point."

"Which is?"

"What started the fire?"

Spencer absently touched his slashed chest as he surveyed the smoldering rubble. "Could have been an electrical short. Whatever it was, I doubt a fire investigator could pin it down. A fire that hot most likely burned the evidence along with everything else."

Evidence. Sabrina slowly lowered her cheek to Quetzal's as an ugly seed of suspicion took root. It grew with the same unrestrained vigor with which the flames had consumed her humble abode of the past three months. But before she could voice the word "arson," an icy raindrop struck her face, temporarily altering her priorities.

"I guess I'd better get my things under cover before it starts pouring again," she said.

Great timing, she thought. The letup in the rain had come at a remarkably opportune time for the fire. That only enhanced her burgeoning notion that the conflagration hadn't been an accident of fate—someone had helped it along. She glanced at Spencer and caught him frowning at her pensively. He quickly averted his gaze, and she wondered uneasily if he could have been reading her mind.

Through the murky haze, Sabrina made out a tallish figure moving across the south edge of the clearing, near where Spencer had said he'd left the few items he had managed to rescue from the burning cottage. At first glance, she took it to be one of the firemen. Then a gust of wet wind lifted the haze enough for her to recognize Conrad Lafever.

She started toward him. In spite of her gratitude for his having rescued Quetzal, Sabrina wasn't pleased when Spencer fell in at her side. Experience had taught her that the combination of Spencer Bradley and Conrad Lafever was every bit as combustible as the cottage had proven to be. She didn't have the stomach to handle their war games right now. Not with the ruins of her own personal disaster still smoldering just yards away.

"You really should go have those cuts and burns tended to, Spencer," she said, hoping to head him off at the pass.

He, too, had spotted Conrad. "First things first."

She gave him an exasperated look. "You really get a kick out of getting in Conrad's face, don't you?"

"Wouldn't miss a chance for the world."

"Spencer . . . this isn't funny."

"I agree. It most definitely isn't funny."

Sabrina looked at him again and stumbled into a dip in the ground hidden among the shin-high weeds. His hand flashed out to steady her, then relaxed its firm grip and lingered on her upper arm a few seconds longer than necessary.

She stiffened and moved away, suddenly afraid of how easy it would be to fall into Spencer's arms at that moment and how much she needed to be held in the wake of this unexpected catastrophe. A thought flashed through her head. *Beware of considerate men.*

Why she had even fleetingly pictured herself turning to Spencer Bradley for consolation was beyond her. Taking into account all the doubts and suspicions that had been stirred up during her trip to Albany, her physical attraction to Spencer made no sense at all to her. If nothing else, she thought sardonically, the man had that in common with Darryl.

It's Quetzal.

From the moment Spencer had handed Quetzal to her, Sabrina's heart and mind had been thrown into hopeless disarray. Even now, though he had removed his hand from her arm, the feeling that they were somehow still in physical contact remained.

From the corner of her eye, Sabrina could see his tattered shirt stirring in the freshening breeze. She boosted Quetzal in her arms. "You're going to get pneumonia," she said, seizing on an obvious practicality. "Do you want your coat back?"

Spencer shook his head. "I dunked it in a puddle before I went into the cottage. Take it off the cat, and *he'll* get pneumonia."

"That's very thoughtful of you." She stole a glance at the claw marks on his chest. "Under the circumstances."

He grumbled something under his breath that she didn't quite catch, then added, "At least I'm not running around barefoot."

Sabrina looked down at her feet. She had actually forgotten that she'd lost her pumps during the mad dash up the gravel track from her smashed car. Her stockings were in shreds, but her feet were too cold to feel the damage.

She groaned. "What a beastly, awful day."

Spencer reached out and squeezed her shoulder, bringing an unanticipated surge of tears to her eyes. Sabrina hiccuped in surprise, her response to the simple gesture of encouragement way out of proportion to the act.

She pulled away from him again, afraid that she was about to let go and make a fool of herself. But he took her by the shoulder and turned her to face him. He didn't say anything. He just looked at her—into her—and she saw the hunger in his eyes.

Hunger... and a kind of animal triumph, because she knew he didn't hunger alone. And for a single, breathless moment, that was all that existed for Sabrina as she stood there, oblivious to the devastation, the cold, the heavy bundle in her arms.

Conrad saw them coming and met them halfway. He wore a spotless camel hair overcoat and carried a black umbrella tucked under one arm. Except for the mud on his shoes, he looked for all the world like a proper English gentleman out for an afternoon stroll.

Spencer looked him up and down with unconcealed disdain. "Where were you hiding out during the excitement, Connie?"

Conrad glowered at him. "I was working on the household books. Not that it's any of your business."

"Ah." Spencer looked at Sabrina as if she ought to find that significant. "While Rome burns, Connie fiddles with the books."

"Please," she said edgily, "this is hardly the time or the place."

"You're right, Sabrina." Spencer took in the smoldering remains of the cottage with narrowed eyes, nodded slowly, and returned his gaze to Conrad. "But there definitely will be a time...and a place."

"As should be expected from the likes of you," Conrad said acidly.

Sabrina's badly abraded nerves gave way. "I have better things to do than stand around watching you two children spit in each other's face."

She stalked past them as resolutely as she could manage in her stocking feet. Spotting her precious possessions piled haphazardly against a poplar at the edge of the clearing, she made a beeline in that direction.

The lingering smoky haze burned her eyes as she took stock. In the event of a fire, people were known to grab up the strangest things when fleeing the flames. From the looks of the selection Spencer had saved, he might have made a classic case study.

Propped against a gnarled tree root was the "notebook" that Spencer had mentioned. It was, in fact, the old leather-bound album containing every last family photo Sabrina owned. Her laptop computer rested atop the canvas duffel bag containing her dirty laundry. Next to that stood Quetzal's carpet-covered scratching pole. She smiled crookedly, her chin quivering, as she eyed this last item.

"Not much to show for thirty-five years, is it?" she whispered.

Quetzal freed a paw from the soggy tweed coat and began licking it. She shifted him to one arm and bent awkwardly to pick up the album, trying to blow away a soggy leaf stuck between the brittle pages.

A sooty hand reached past Quetzal and plucked the leaf free.

"Thank you, Spencer," she said in a tight voice. She didn't dare look at him.

"Here, let me have that," Conrad said from her other side. "It's going to get wet."

He relieved Sabrina of the album and tucked it under his coat. Then he opened his umbrella and held it over the two of them, leaving Spencer out in the cold rain beginning to fall. Trying to ignore their ridiculous little game of one-upmanship, she picked up the computer case and slung the strap over her shoulder.

"Had you brought any documents from Mr. Kellogg's files down here to the cottage?" Conrad asked.

Detecting an undertone of apprehension, Sabrina shook her head, unreasonably annoyed that he had felt it necessary to ask such a thing at just that moment. Couldn't he tell how much she was suffering? Granted, he had reason to be concerned. But she thought he at least could have waited until the smoke had cleared.

She glanced at Spencer, expecting him to ask if the fire had cremated *The End of the Line*. Fortunately, three months of research, along with the rough working draft that she had been preparing as she went along, were safely in the laptop's capacious storage. The backup diskettes were tucked away inside the computer's carrying case. Her personal life might be a complete disaster, she thought morosely, but the book project had survived intact.

Spencer was squinting up the sloping ground toward the mansion. Sabrina followed his gaze. She hadn't noticed Orrin Shaw standing in the deep shadows of a big cedar on the far side of the clearing, watching them. No—not *them*. She had a creepy feeling that he had been staring directly at her. Spencer motioned for Shaw to join them.

The old man hesitated, then started across the clearing. He took his own sweet time, the muddied hem of his long raincoat flapping around his rubber boots.

The rain was coming down in big erratic drops, peppering the ground like hail and washing the smoke haze out of the air. A new stench of wet ashes filled the clearing. The volunteer firemen conferred among themselves, then threw their shovels into the back of the fire truck and prepared to leave.

Sabrina wanted them to stay. There was work to be done, debris to be sifted through for . . . *evidence.* Spencer's word came back to haunt her.

The fire truck was lumbering down the gravel track by the time Shaw made it across the clearing. The handyman reminded Sabrina of a feral dog warily approaching a strange pack—he almost seemed to sidle up to them. Shaw clearly hadn't bothered to shave in several days. He had let himself go since Jeremiah Kellogg's death.

"Lend a hand with these things, *Mr. Shaw,*" Spencer said, indicating the duffel bag and scratching pole. "Miss Glade will be moving into the mansion."

Sabrina almost dropped Quetzal. The pressing issue of where she would live had remained magically at bay until now. She had been blindsided by Spencer's offer. Still, she was amazed that, even in her current state of desperation, she didn't simply acquiesce with the suggestion.

That's the problem, she thought. *It wasn't a suggestion. He's taking it for granted that you'll go along with the idea.*

Shaw threw Spencer a dark look, then trudged over to pick up the two remaining items. Sabrina's mind raced. Since the day he'd found out about his uncle's book, Spencer had made no bones about wanting her off the estate. Now he was suddenly doing a complete about-face, generously throwing open his door.

Beware of considerate men. The bitter lesson she had learned from Darryl seemed tailor-made for this situation. The issue of just how far Spencer Bradley was willing to go to kill *The End of the Line* had not yet been settled—at least not in Sabrina's mind. And this was the man who expected her to move under the same roof with him? She took a hard look at the blackened ruins of the cottage, and balked.

"I will not be moving into the mansion, Mr. Shaw," she said flatly.

Spencer hunched his shoulders against the rain and drove both hands deeply into his pockets. His exposed skin was reddening from the cold. She couldn't tell if his pained expression was in response to her statement or because he was freezing.

"Then what, pray tell, do you intend to do?" Spencer said through clenched teeth. "Live out of your car?"

She moved closer against Conrad. Her bare feet were going numb, and her only pair of shoes was lying somewhere back along the gravel track, getting soaked. Sabrina couldn't bring herself to mention that her car was at this moment firmly bashed against a tree near the entrance to the driveway. Right now, she didn't even have the luxury of loading up Quetzal and the material dregs of her life, and driving away.

"The cottage isn't...wasn't the only habitable structure on the estate besides the main house," she said stubbornly.

"Oh?" Rainwater dripped from Spencer's firmly set chin. "Please refresh my memory."

"How about the little gray stone building behind the mansion?"

Spencer snorted and walked away a few paces before whirling back to face her. "Dammit, Sabrina, that used to be a smokehouse about a hundred years ago. It isn't fit for your *cat* to live in."

She was taken aback by his biting sarcasm, which only served to harden her resolve. The more determined Spencer was that she move into the mansion with him, the more she distrusted his motives. The meeting with Noble Wetherbee had opened her eyes to a number of dark possibilities, chief among which was Spencer Bradley's solid motive for having wanted Jeremiah Kellogg dead.

He could be cold-blooded where his Uncle Jeremiah was concerned. The possibility that Spencer might have actually plotted and arranged Kellogg's "accidental" death raised its ugly head, sending a shudder through Sabrina. If Spencer was capable of murder, surely he wouldn't have shied from committing arson in order to sabotage *The End of the Line.*

Which begged yet another question: What was it that Spencer was afraid his uncle's book might reveal?

Afraid. There it was. She felt trapped between her own fear and Spencer Bradley's.

In one way or another, she thought, everyone in that clearing right now was afraid of something. She looked the three men over, one at a time, and realized that the common denominator was Spencer Bradley. She, Conrad Lafever and Orrin Shaw all had reason to feel threatened by him.

Spencer watched her stonily. Sabrina could sense the rage locked up inside him, even if she couldn't quite see it. And yet, there were his random acts of kindness, his unexpectedly gentle touches. And he had risked his life to rescue Quetzal from the flames... hadn't he?

Another shudder passed through her, this time with sickening force. Sabrina shook her head to clear it. There were too many contradictions. She needed time alone to sort this out.

"Mr. Shaw," she said, turning to the old man, "is the smokehouse really as bad as all that?"

Shaw slid his jaw from side to side as if he was preparing to spit. Instead he muttered, "Depends on what you're used to."

"The cottage, of course."

"No bathroom in the smokehouse."

That brought Sabrina up short. She glanced at Conrad, who had remained silent through all this. He looked oddly embarrassed.

"There are facilities just off the mudroom at the back entrance to the mansion," he said.

"That will do." Her mind was already made up. "How about heat and lights?"

Shaw stared sourly at the ground, clawed his grizzled sideburns, and finally nodded.

"Then the smokehouse it is."

Spencer cursed. "Of all the harebrained..."

Sabrina didn't wait for him to finish. She adjusted the strap on her shoulder and started walking, feeling like a refugee.

Spencer made it back from Albany without killing himself, which was some kind of minor miracle. He had been in no condition to be driving when he'd left the estate that afternoon. The return trip had been worse. He was so wound up that he damn near had the shakes.

After getting cleaned up following the fire, he had made the run down to Albany with the intention of having a serious talk with Noble Wetherbee. As it turned out, Spencer was glad he hadn't bothered to call ahead. If he had, he might have missed watching Conrad Lafever beating him to the punch.

He had been about to turn into Wetherbee's driveway when he'd spotted Lafever's car parked behind the attorney's vehicle. Lafever was striding up the sidewalk toward the front door, looking as self-satisfied as a cat with a canary between his teeth. The door had swung open right on cue as if it was operated by a sensor, and he had vanished inside. Unseen, Spencer had kept on going to the end of the cul-de-sac, turned around, and headed straight back to the estate.

As he passed between the big fieldstone gateposts now, the wash of Spencer's headlights caught the fresh gouge in the tree that Sabrina had slammed into just hours ago. With a grimace, he sped on toward the mansion, the thought that she could have been killed right then and there twisting in his gut like a knife. He remembered all too clearly how it had felt for a few hellish minutes that afternoon, when he'd feared she *had* been killed.

Spencer hadn't run into the burning cottage with the intention of saving her cat; he'd forgotten she even owned the ill-tempered tom. He slid a hand under his coat to gingerly finger the raw lacerations through his shirt. If he had it to do over again, he'd let the ungrateful beast fry.

Maybe.

Lights glowed in the third-floor windows as he pulled up just short of the portico. The rest of the mansion was cast in darkness. The Shaws had called it a day, he thought grimly, switching off the ignition key. Spencer sat there for a while, staring up at the lights through the grimy windshield, listening to the soft pinging of the cooling engine.

Thinking about her.

Sabrina suspected the cottage had been torched. He was certain of that. She had spurned his offer of quarters in the mansion as if he had invited her into a plague ward, as good an indication as any that she had pegged him as the arsonist.

He sighed, thinking she was a fool if she expected the smokehouse to be any safer. "Dammit, woman, what does it take to get your attention?"

Spencer wiped both hands down his face. His stomach was giving him more trouble, he had a headache he couldn't seem to shake, and he was so damned tired he couldn't think straight. So tired he didn't *want* to think. Tired of the whole damned show. If it wouldn't end up burning down the entire mansion, he would gladly torch the library and all its contents in order to get Sabrina Glade off the estate—and off that blasted book before it was too late.

That idiotic thought rattled around in his brain until the interior of the vehicle grew cold. With a heavy sigh, Spencer reached down to the floorboard in front of the passenger seat, retrieved the greasy paper debris of the fast-food supper he had grabbed on his way back from Albany, and got out.

CHAPTER EIGHT

A long black shoestring dangled from the cracked porcelain light socket in the ceiling. The twenty-five-watt bulb provided just enough illumination to reveal the windowless room in all its depressing glory.

Sabrina sat on the edge of the hard mattress, exhausted. Orrin Shaw had grudgingly set up the old iron bed after removing a truckload of junk, which appeared to have been accumulating in the smokehouse since as far back as the Spanish-American War.

From the looks of them, the dingy stone walls hadn't received a coat of whitewash in the past fifty years. A wobbly wooden chair doubled as a table near the head of the bed, holding her watch and photo album. Quetzal's scratching pole stood across the room by the heavy plank door. A few feet away, her laptop computer rested atop a metal milk crate containing the clothes she had washed and dried over at the mansion while Shaw worked to make the smokehouse barely habitable, muttering to himself and making no effort to paper over the fact that he hadn't appreciated being put to so much trouble.

Maybe Spencer had been right, she thought. Maybe this was a harebrained idea. She somehow hadn't expected it to be this bad. At least the place was warm, thanks to a squat electric heater in one corner. And if she closed her eyes and used her imagination, Sabrina could even convince herself that a faint aroma of smoked ham still lingered in the air. "Sure beats the smell of this old mattress."

She drew her knees up under her chin. At the far end of the thin pancake of a mattress, Quetzal lifted his head off

the faded quilt and perused Sabrina with slitted eyes. The
tip of his tail twitched peevishly. He looked slightly comi-
cal with his singed whiskers, but no one was laughing.

"I've managed to drag us down pretty low this time,
haven't I?" She leaned over and scratched behind his ear,
forcing a smile, trying to cheer them both up. "If I didn't
have you, my man, I think I'd be stone-blind crazy by
now."

Weird, she thought, that she could be so bushed, and still
feel as if she were about to jump out of her skin. The shock
of the fire had worn off while she was showering in the
minuscule bathroom that adjoined the mudroom just inside the back door of the mansion. By the time she had
pulled on a thick gray warm-up suit fresh from the dryer
and walked down the weedy stone path to the smokehouse, dusk had fallen—and Sabrina had made a disturbing discovery.

Fear came out and frolicked in the darkness.

There was a heavy metal hasp on the outside of the
smokehouse door—rusty, but still serviceable. But there
was no hasp on the inside. So even if she came up with a
padlock and she could lock someone out, she couldn't lock
herself in. Since the door opened out, she couldn't even
wedge the wooden chair under the doorknob for security.

"Be careful," she murmured, eyeing the door. "But
don't get paranoid. Stay in control." *And sleep with the
light on.*

Arson had done that to her. She was as convinced as a
frightened woman alone could be that the cottage fire had
been no accident. The very idea that anyone would want to
harm her—Sabrina Glade—had been a hard pill to swallow. The question of why—and whom—was no easier.

She took a deep breath and let it out through pursed lips.
Come to think of it, maybe the why was right under her
nose. Whether by accident or intent, Jeremiah Kellogg had
been stopped from completing his memoirs. Now someone real or imagined seemed to be trying to stop her. Sa-

brina couldn't afford to assume the threat would end with the burning of the cottage.

Sliding off the bed, she padded across the bare concrete floor, opened the door a crack, and peered out into the night.

The mansion loomed a hundred yards up the path leading from the smokehouse door. Lights still burned on the third floor where the Shaws lived. Off to the left, a small window glowed on the ground floor—Conrad Lafever's quarters. There were no lights visible on the second floor where, according to Conrad, Spencer Bradley had cavalierly taken over Jeremiah Kellogg's personal suite.

Her car was parked alongside the smokehouse where Conrad had driven it after reattaching the battery cable that had been knocked loose when she hit the tree. The left rear fender was badly crumpled, but the gas tank was almost full. She could pile Quetzal and her double armload of possessions into the back seat and head out. Right now.

And go where?

She closed the door, crept back to the old iron bed, and sat chewing on a thumbnail. The sad truth was, she had nowhere to go. No one to whom she could turn. Even Ira Sampson could hardly be expected to greet her with open arms if she was unable to fulfill the contract for *The End of the Line*. Not after she had already spent the book's initial advance. And once the tank of gas ran out, she would be just as stranded as she was now.

Sabrina weighed that against the cards she already held. Here, at least, Conrad Lafever could be counted on to help complete the book's research, thus enabling her to maintain a faint hope of financial salvation. The Shaws hadn't exactly gone out of their way to make her feel at home these past three months. But Maria had brought bedding down to the smokehouse while Sabrina was showering—a gesture that could be loosely interpreted as a positive sign, assuming that Maria wasn't simply following Conrad's instructions.

And then, there was Spencer Bradley.

The images, the sensations, lurked in the closest shadows of her mind, ready to leap out at the slightest provocation. They came now in an inescapable flurry of contradictions that caused her to pull up her legs and lower her forehead to her knees.

Deep-set eyes, like blue velvet bayonets. Bloody claw marks across an alluringly muscular chest. A scarred fist of steel, releasing her arm with the tantalizing whisper of a caress. The rage ... and the way he had looked at her that night in the cottage.

Sabrina moaned softly and shuddered with equal parts of fear and desire. The presence of Spencer Bradley was becoming a waking nightmare. He had worked his way into her flesh, haunting her into a flagrant awareness of sensual energies that she hadn't experienced since ... ever.

You must be losing your mind, to have those kinds of feelings for someone you have every reason to fear.

Logic warned her that Spencer had to be a prime suspect—but in what? The murder of an uncle from whom he stood to inherit a fortune that Spencer didn't need? Setting fire to what would soon be his own property?

She rolled her forehead back and forth on her knees. Greed alone couldn't account for the level of rage she had sensed in him. The headwaters for that must lie elsewhere, perhaps in the cottage itself. According to Spencer, he and his mother had lived there under Jeremiah's heel for seventeen years. More than enough time for a sore to fester, Sabrina thought.

Surprised by a sudden ache that rose within her, she shook her head vigorously—a mixture of denial and resignation. Spencer's contradictions were tainting her judgment, leaving her perilously open to deception.

True, the man was financially successful in his own right. And he had generously offered to move her into the mansion after the fire. But he was also the only person who was vehemently opposed to her work on *End of the Line.* Why? What is he afraid the book might reveal?

Sabrina raised her head. Her gaze drifted across the room to her computer atop the milk crate. She stared at it for several minutes, frowning quizzically, then slid off the end of the bed and went to kneel beside the crate.

Unzipping the laptop's case, she pushed back the cover and switched on the battery-powered computer. The screen lit up. She pulled up three or four random files in succession, just to reassure herself that the delicate electronics hadn't been damaged by exposure to the heat of the fire. Satisfied, she shut it off and drummed her fingers on the computer's plastic casing for a moment.

The backup disks were stored in a compartment inside the lid of the carrying case. She broke the watertight seal and pulled them out. Every bit of research and writing for *The End of the Line* that was contained in the computer's built-in data storage was backed up on those six disks, each in an individual protective sleeve.

She glanced around the room, telling herself that she wasn't being paranoid. She wasn't flipping out or constructing horror stories out of thin air. This was simply a matter of...insurance.

Quetzal's carpet-covered scratching pole stood by the door. Sabrina thought, *Yes,* and crawled over to it. The carpet smelled of smoke, and was still damp from the rain. But when she pried off the broad base, the hollow interior of the square wooden post was clean and dry. She placed the backup disks inside and hammered the base back on with the heel of her hand.

As she righted the post, another thought struck her. If Spencer had torched the cottage in order to scare her off, why would he have rescued her computer along with Quetzal?

"Contradictions," she muttered, sliding the post over against the wall.

Quetzal's curiosity finally got the better of him. He dropped down off the bed and slunk silently across the floor to inspect his personal property. After fastidiously sniffing the scratching pole, he gave the carpet covering a perfunctory swat without baring his claws. Then he went to stand by the door, his tail standing tall.

"No, Quetz. You can't go out tonight."

The tom looked back at her and rasped a protest.

Ordinarily he was allowed outside for a few minutes before bedtime. But Sabrina wasn't about to turn him loose this evening. His single-minded feline homing instincts would undoubtedly send him trotting down the hill to the charred ruins of the cottage, and she'd have to go chasing after him in the pitch dark.

"Come on, you have the bladder of an elephant," she said. "You can wait until morning."

He reared up and dug his claws into the plank door, loosing a yowl that made her wince. Sabrina continued to resist. She couldn't let him out on his own, and the naked truth was that she didn't want to set foot outside the smokehouse. Not tonight, with the cottage fire so freshly seared into her nerves.

Still, there was that other view of the situation—the one that said she would never be safer than she was tonight. The police were bound to be suspicious if she came to harm so soon after being burned out of the cottage. Surely no one would be stupid enough to risk that.

Quetzal went stock-still except for his lashing tail—a sure indication that impatience was curdling his attitude. Sabrina knew this cat; he would never give in. If she didn't let him out, she'd be climbing the walls right alongside him by morning.

"All right, but you aren't going alone, Bozo. You'll have to settle for a chaperone."

She got up and fished the stained and ragged sneakers that she had begged from Maria out from under the bed. They were a size too big. But the pumps she had run out of on the gravel track that afternoon wouldn't be dry until at least tomorrow, and even then might be too ruined to wear.

The spring-coiled auxiliary cord to the computer was the only substitute for a leash that she could find. Sabrina fastened it to Quetzal's bell collar, pulled on her coat, and opened the door a crack.

The cat shot through the opening.

A bone-chilling mist was falling as Sabrina climbed the sloping ground toward the smokehouse. Her feet were freezing in the wet canvas shoes. All the lights had gone out in the mansion, making the silent, tomblike darkness complete. She could barely see where she was walking.

At the moment, Quetzal's company was of little comfort to her. He walked at her side, more or less, advancing in short, resentful darts and jags. Sabrina had trained him to a leash when he was young. But it wasn't in a cat's nature to submit to boundaries, and three months on the Kellogg estate had brought out the primal beast in her city slicker.

They progressed slowly past her car with its forlornly crumpled rear end. When they reached the front of the smokehouse, she pulled open the door and backed inside, coaxing Quetzal to follow.

"I didn't know a cat would tolerate a leash."

Sabrina spun around in a panic at the voice, almost catching the tom's trailing tail as she jerked the door shut. Spencer Bradley sat on the foot of her bed, elbows on his knees, chin resting on his folded hands. The top hand was bandaged.

She dropped her end of the makeshift leash and sagged back against the plank door, trying to convince herself that she wasn't suffering from full cardiac arrest. It wasn't easy.

"Sorry." The iron bed creaked as Spencer rose. The top of his head almost touched the low, whitewashed plank ceiling. "I didn't mean to frighten you."

"Didn't you?" Sabrina scowled, her gaze locked with his. A warm, tingling sensation seemed to flow into her from his intense blue eyes. Then the spell broke, and she began noticing other things about Spencer. Things that killed the warmth like a dash of cold water. As she knelt to remove the cord from Quetzal's collar, her hands were trembling.

Spencer's wool coat was too damp for him to have just walked down from the mansion, and his shoes were as wet as hers. His cheeks were still flushed from the cold, so he must have entered the smokehouse just moments before she returned from walking Quetzal.

The thought that he might have been out there in the darkness stalking her, made Sabrina's heart act up again. Much to her consternation, she also felt a powerful surge of excitement.

After carefully stowing the auxiliary cord in the computer's carrying case, she went over to stand by the heater. That was about as far as she could get from her uninvited guest without going back outside.

A stainless steel thermos sat on the floor next to the heater. "What's this?" she asked.

"Hot cider and tea."

She took off her coat and backed up to the heater, holding her hands behind her. "How did you know how much I like that stuff?"

"I didn't." His eyebrows bounced once. "It seems we have something in common."

"Well . . . thank you. I'm sure I'll enjoy it."

He smiled, and took off his coat. "I thought we might share it."

"Oh." She had that walking-on-a-tightrope feeling that she sometimes got when she was around Spencer. And again, that exciting adrenaline rush of fear. "Well . . . there's only one cup."

"So there is." He pursed his lips, then shrugged. "Tell you what, you go ahead and help yourself, and I'll just dry my coat in front of the heater."

Sabrina picked up the thermos, he picked up the wooden chair beside the bed, and they swapped places. She unscrewed the stainless steel cap, then twisted off the cork, as he positioned the chair in front of the heater and draped his damp coat over the back. He paused to lift the cover of the photo album lying on the seat. After leafing through several pages, he turned and watched her pour a cup of steaming apple cider and tea.

"I hope it isn't too spicy for your taste," he said.

She took a whiff, and her eyes watered. "Just the way I like it."

He snorted up at the ceiling. "My God, Bradley—you actually did something to please her."

Sabrina looked at him sharply. He was smiling just a little, but seemed to be trying to keep it all to himself.

"Okay, I was upgraded from bastard to jerk," he said. "Then I saved your cat *and* brought you something hot to drink. What do I get promoted to now? Common scuzzball?"

"Are you trying to make fun of me?"

He shook his head slowly. "Just groping around in unfamiliar territory."

Quetzal had jumped up onto the bed. When he smelled the spicy concoction, he moseyed closer to make overtures, purring raucously. Sabrina set the thermos on the floor and held the cup out of his reach, waiting for the cider tea to cool enough to sip.

"He looks screwy with those messed-up whiskers," Spencer said.

"They'll grow back to normal." She sat on the edge of the bed and wrapped an arm around the big tom.

"The crossed eyes make him hard to look at, anyway."

"You get used to it." Talking about Quetzal made it easier to be in the same room with Spencer. *Tension dis-*

placement, she thought. "I can't thank you enough for saving him. And I'm sorry about your tweed coat."

"A total loss, was it?"

"Yes. I took the liberty of trashing it. Was that all right?"

He shrugged as if the expensive sport coat was of no consequence. "You're going to need some new clothes, you know."

She looked down at her gray warm-up suit and the oversize sneakers. The clothes she had worn that afternoon, a pair of jeans, two sweatshirts and a few articles of underwear represented the sum total of her remaining wardrobe. Back in New York, she had seen bag ladies pushing around more clothes than that in shopping carts. An alien-sounding burst of laughter escaped her. She was dangerously close to hysteria.

"Yeah," she said with false cheer, refusing to give in to raw emotions, "I'm thinking of hijacking a Goodwill truck."

Spencer eyed her somberly for an uncomfortable moment, then glanced around at the stark walls and furnishings. His gaze snagged on her computer just long enough to get Sabrina's attention. Then he came and sat down beside her on the bed, with Quetzal between them. The big tom started to jump down, but she held him firmly in place.

"This is even worse than I thought it would be." Elbows back on his knees, fingers entwined, Spencer stared down at her wet sneakers. "Sabrina, there are two entire suites of rooms at the back of the second floor—I checked. You could take your pick. Are you sure you won't change your mind?"

"Positive."

If Spencer hadn't sat down next to her just then, Sabrina might have given his offer more thought. She was that depressed. The smokehouse was worse than she, too, had imagined it would be. But his muscular thigh was pressed against the hand she had clamped around Quetzal's body,

and she couldn't hear herself think for all the alarms going
off in her head.

"Okay, it's up to you," he said. "But it's an open-ended
invitation."

Sabrina nodded. Her left hand was trembling. She leaned
over and placed the cup of cider tea on the floor, suddenly
unable to swallow.

"Listen—" he reached down and picked up her right
foot "—there's bound to have been property insurance on
the cottage. I'll check with Noble Wetherbee tomorrow.
You'll be compensated for your losses in the fire."

Insurance. Sabrina hadn't even thought of that. A tidal
wave of relief washed over her. She felt dizzy and idioti-
cally giddy like she'd just been snatched from the gallows.
It didn't last. He slid the sneaker off and started vigorously rubbing her damp foot.

Heat flashed up her leg. A second later, her heart gave a
major beat as if a surge of blood had just reached it. He
kept working on that foot, rubbing the sole, massaging the
toes. Every blood vessel in her body seemed to go turgid.
Sabrina was aghast. Spencer didn't seem to intend his ac-
tion to be construed as intimate—he was trying to help her
out. But how could he not be aware of the wildfires he was
setting?

When he picked up her left foot and that sneaker hit the
floor, she asked, "What if it was arson?"

Spencer blinked twice, then turned his head and looked
at her. "Arson?"

"The cottage." She cleared her throat, trying to get her
voice above a whisper. "Just a thought."

He nodded slowly. "Where do you suppose it came
from?"

She licked her lips. "Out of the blue, I guess."

"I see."

He nodded again, and turned his attention to her left
foot. Sabrina studied his face carefully, trying hard to see

through the expressionless mask he had donned and detect the slightest trace of guilt.

She didn't find what she was looking for, but was bothered by the fact that Spencer made no effort to pursue the subject of arson. She kept watching him, waiting, straining to keep her mind off her own feet. But her toes were tingling. A heavenly sense of relief from the numbness was transforming into new sensations that were even more difficult to ignore.

Spencer's face was losing its ruddiness from the cold. He didn't appear to be quite as pale as when he had visited the cottage, but there was still something not quite right about his color. And the tension was still evident in the pinched crow's-feet bracketing his eyes and in the knotted muscles of his jaw.

"I thought you were coming down with something," she said. He looked at her. "When you came to the cottage the other night," she explained, "you looked a little green around the gills."

He grunted. His gaze seemed to turn inward, and the movement of his hands on her bare feet slowed. She mentally kicked herself for having reminded him of that night. The skin of her breasts and abdomen went taut as if suddenly exposed to cold air, then flushed hotly at a too-vivid recollection of the way Spencer had looked at her when her robe had fallen open. She pulled her feet off his lap and tucked them under her.

"I, uh, just needed a little grease," he said, distractedly studying his empty hands.

Sabrina gave him a blank look, having lost the thread of conversation.

"My stomach had been bothering me for several days," he said. "I grabbed a bacon-cheeseburger and some greasy fries on the highway this afternoon. Fixed me right up."

"Oh. Good. Heal thy stomach. To hell with the arteries."

He grinned sheepishly. The transformation was so jarringly unexpected that Sabrina instinctively smiled back. Her grip relaxed, and Quetzal jumped down off the bed. The big tom headed straight for the crate containing her clothes. Bounding up onto the computer case atop the crate, he crouched with his tail coiled around his feet, eyeing Sabrina indifferently.

Spencer's smile didn't last long. But when it was gone, Sabrina no longer felt so on edge. Regardless of how torn she felt about the man, having his company at that moment was immeasurably better than sitting alone in the smokehouse, she told herself.

Better than worrying about whether he was lurking outside. The thought came and went without leaving much of an impression. The foot massage had set her up for the disarming grin. Sabrina was having trouble believing she had ever suspected him of stalking her.

"Is the hand as bad as it looked this afternoon?" she asked.

He plucked at the bandage, shaking his head. "Maria gave me some aloe vera goop to put on it. She's big on medicinal plant cures, it seems."

"Did it work?"

"I guess. It stopped the burning."

Sabrina hesitated. "How about the claw marks on your chest? A doctor should take a look at those."

"I've had a recent tetanus booster. I'm not in danger of rabies, am I?"

"No! I took him to the new vet in Schuylerville just last month for all his shots. I'm mortified that he did that to you."

Spencer shrugged it off. "He was terrified. Came unglued when I crawled on top of him under your bed."

"Under...?"

"I was making sure you hadn't gotten disoriented in the smoke and crawled under there to get away from the flames."

She stared at him. "You didn't know I was gone when you went inside."

He met Sabrina's gaze evenly, the unreadable shield sliding firmly into place. Nothing in his eyes mirrored the wild confusion of emotions that had suddenly overtaken her.

He thought you were in danger and he came for you. In the face of that new revelation, she couldn't let herself believe that Spencer had been the one who had torched the cottage. Not for now. She would deal with those conflicting inner voices later.

For now, Sabrina was more interested in learning about the man than about his actions. If she could find out what drove Spencer Bradley, she thought, she would have the answers to all the rest. But to know the man, she would first have to know the boy. And to do that, she would first have to get all the way around behind that protective shield.

She reached out and touched the sleeve of his flannel shirt. "Spencer," she said softly, "tell me . . . please. What was she like?"

"She?"

Sabrina nodded. "Zena."

CHAPTER NINE

Sabrina held her breath, waiting. The silence dragged on and on until she was afraid to break it. Spencer was looking straight at her, his face lined with tension in the wan light. But she could tell he wasn't seeing her.

Minutes passed, and still she waited. Finally he stirred himself, inhaled deeply, and said, "Proud."

He cleared his throat and started over. "My mother was proud—the proudest woman I've ever known. At least as tough-minded as Jeremiah. An unbending Kellogg to the core." His lips tightened. "That's what galls me about the title of his memoirs... *The End of the Line*. Because he isn't, you know—she hammered that much into my hard head. I'm as much of a Kellogg as he was."

Not in name, Sabrina thought. She steered clear of mentioning the traditional hereditary clause in Kellogg wills, which must have been made clear to him from earliest childhood.

"You remember Zena as being proud," she said. "And yet she put up with living down there in that mean little cottage all the while you were growing up. I'm sorry, Spencer, but that just doesn't make sense."

"Not to you, and maybe not entirely to me. But I can assure you, it made perfect sense to her."

He got up and stepped over to feel his coat, drying before the heater. Busywork, thought Sabrina. The room was too constricted to pace. When he returned to the bed, he sat farther from her than before.

"Jeremiah wouldn't allow Mother or me to as much as set foot in the mansion." His voice was low and tight. "He didn't want us on the property, period. But she would have fought him over that. So he bit the bullet and let us have the cottage.''

Sabrina straightened, recalling the way Spencer had surveyed the library on the day he moved into the big house as if he was seeing it for the first time. ''You mean you hadn't been inside the mansion until the day of your uncle's funeral?''

''Just once.'' He put his elbows on his knees, pressed his palms together, touched his fingertips to his lips, and stared at the far wall. ''He sent Orrin Shaw to fetch me one spring. I guess I must have been ten or so. Shaw always treated me as if I'd just been caught stealing, so by the time he had me hauled up in front of Uncle Jeremiah, I was shaking like a leaf, about to wet my pants.''

''You make that sound so vivid.''

His eyes narrowed. ''Right this second, it's a thousand times more vivid to me than that fire at the cottage this afternoon.''

Sabrina nodded in understanding. While he was speaking, she had, incredibly, forgotten all about the fire. ''What did Mr. Kellogg want to see you about that day?'' she asked.

''He *didn't* want to see me—that was the point. You see, my dog had disappeared, and I'd been roaming all over the place looking for him. That was verboten. I guess Jeremiah had looked out a window and spotted me. I was here on the estate, but he liked to pretend that I wasn't. It pissed him off to be reminded.''

Spencer's cheek muscles clenched as he dredged up the incident from thirty years ago. ''Jeremiah knew how to terrify a ten-year-old with a look. Even then, it struck me that he took pleasure in it. I must say, his method worked. After he finished dressing me down, I never made the mistake of crossing his path again.''

Sabrina felt a chill as if someone had opened a door to a dungeon. In a way, she decided, that was precisely what had happened. Spencer had opened a door to the buried past, giving her a look at the private Jeremiah Kellogg that the retired diplomat had kept hidden from her—and it left her cold.

She reminded herself that Spencer's recollections of his childhood were bound to be biased. But the physical evidence that he and Zena had eked out an existence in that grim little cottage for seventeen years added weight to his story. That, and his quiet tone of voice.

"How could you have lived that way?" she wondered aloud. "How could Zena have put you through that?"

"She had her reasons." He spread his hands, then pressed them back together. "Besides, most of the time, Mother and I were happy enough down there. At least, I thought we were at the time. Kids don't know what's normal and what isn't."

"What about adolescents? How did you feel about it when you reached the age of rebellion?"

Spencer stared mutely at the far wall. After a minute or so, Sabrina realized he wasn't going to touch that question. She backed out of the dead end and returned to a subject that he had introduced himself.

"What about your dog? Did you ever find him?"

His jaw muscles knotted. He shook his head slowly. "Jeremiah killed him."

"He *what?*"

"Well, probably not personally. He would have had Orrin Shaw do the honors. The morning after Jeremiah hauled me onto the carpet, I found Tinker's blood-soaked collar on the front stoop."

"Oh, God." Sabrina glanced at Quetzal, recalling the abject horror she had experienced that afternoon when she'd thought he had died horribly in the fire. But a ten-year-old...

The images Spencer had painted were too real, too intense. Coming so soon after her own traumatic afternoon, she felt almost as if she had relived his grisly childhood experience. Her hand went to her mouth. She closed her eyes, feeling physically sick.

The iron bed creaked as Spencer's weight shifted. He touched her cheek with the backs of his fingers. When her eyes popped open in surprise, he gently took her hand in both of his. "Hey, I didn't mean to upset you," he said softly. "You've been through a lot today. You don't need this kind of—"

Sabrina shook her head. "No, Spencer. It's just so hideous to think of someone killing a child's dog, and then doing that with the collar. That goes way beyond cruelty. What did Zena have to say about it?"

Spencer frowned in thought, still cradling her hand. Sabrina felt his hard palm on one side, and the smooth bandage on the other. But most of all, she was aware of his seemingly unconscious tenderness.

"That's odd," he said finally.

"You don't remember?"

"Oh, yes, I do." His frown turned quizzical. "Now that I think about it, though, it just seems kind of strange."

"Did she storm the mansion?" Sabrina would have. If she'd had a brother, and he had done something like that to her son, Sabrina would have made him eat that blood-soaked collar.

"No," he murmured. "She made me stop crying. Then she said, 'Remember, Spence ... remember.'"

"That's all?" Sabrina was incredulous. "I'd have thought she would have wanted you to put it out of your mind forever."

"Oh, no, Sabrina." He tightened his grip on her hand. "She wanted me never to lose sight of what kind of man Jeremiah Kellogg was. And I never did. Not for one moment."

Again, Sabrina felt a chill—like a gust from a graveyard. She shuddered. Spencer noticed, and moved closer. She didn't resist. Having him near, touching her, filled a need that seemed to keen from deep within her soul.

She glanced at Quetzal again, then at the computer case on which the big tom perched.

"Spencer, you despised your uncle."

"Still do. Always will."

"Then why did you save my computer from the fire this afternoon, when you'd like nothing better than to be able to kill his book?"

"I didn't give it a thought. Why? Do you have all your book research stored in it?"

"Come on, you must have guessed that I do."

He looked across the room at the computer, then straight into her eyes. "When I grabbed it, I wasn't making carefully examined judgment calls, Sabrina. It was pitch-dark in that smoke, and I had a twenty-pound tomcat stapled to my chest. I had one free arm and hand. When I started seeing daylight, I just grabbed hold of everything within reach."

She believed him. It was so easy to see the truth in those penetrating blue eyes. Too easy. Sabrina knew she ought to rely more on her power of reason than on her basest instincts. She carefully withdrew her hand from his, trying not to make it seem as if she was making some kind of statement, when all she was really after was a little objectivity.

Spencer clearly had instincts of his own. He backed off—just a few inches, but that was enough. She watched his expression solidify as the protective shield tried to come back up. But it didn't quite make it to his searching eyes. And so she was able to see Spencer Bradley for the paradox that he was.

It was written right there on his face. Steely impregnability trying to conceal a profound vulnerability that reached right out and stole something intangible from her. She felt that something leave her, realized what it was, and quickly turned away before he could see her own thin skin exposed by her missing shield.

"How did you like being a marine all those years?" she asked, flinging the question out of left field.

In the long silence that followed, Spencer's hand settled on her arm and slid in a feathery caress down to her wrist. The dim light in the smokehouse suddenly became dreamlike. The word "cozy" drifted into Sabrina's mind as his hand moved slowly back up her arm, taking the sleeve of her warm-up suit with it, baring her skin to his touch.

"I owe the Corps a good education," he said. "Among other things."

"What other things?"

"Oh, let's see." A smile had entered his voice. "How about honor, duty, self-discipline, how to kill a man with my bare hands?"

His hand—the one with the bandages—was moving back down her bare forearm, his fingertips exciting every nerve in their path. Sabrina couldn't look at him any more than she could pull away. She felt physically bound to the sensations, the way a victim is bound by the source of a powerful electrical shock. Only she didn't feel like a victim. She felt . . . immortal. *What?* She wrenched her mind back into gear.

"Self-discipline?" she said, shying away from that other disturbing talent of his bare hands. "That's interesting. How long have you been out of the marines?"

"Apparently too long."

His voice had turned gravelly. He took his hand from her arm and cupped her chin, gently turning her toward him. He was so close, his gaze boring into hers—*velvet bayonets*—slicing cleanly through to the elemental Sabrina Glade. She made one last desperate lunge for solid ground, thinking this was the perfect moment to take advantage of his pregnability and ask if he knew about his stillborn cousin, Jeremiah Kellogg II. But his thumb stroked across the sensitized curve of her lip, freezing the words on her tongue.

"We're alone, you and I," he whispered hoarsely. "We're the only two people in the universe."

Sabrina nodded. He kept talking, softly. She no longer heard what he said, only felt he was speaking to the very core of her being. All the grinding loneliness of the past months began to melt away and a pervasive warmth flowed into her, leaving her floating on a pillow of undulating air.

He lowered his head and tasted her lips, first the lower, then the upper. She sighed. Her jaw relaxed, and his tongue slid past her teeth as he groaned and drew her against him. She responded to his demanding kiss with another sigh, deeper and shuddering with passion. When their lips finally parted, Spencer nestled her face in the hollow of his neck and sat stroking her head and shoulders while they both tried to catch their breath.

"Spence, this is no good," Sabrina whispered, her fingers stirring the hair at his nape.

He swallowed, making a dry, clicking noise in his throat. "It's worse than no good. It's stupid."

"Insane." She squeezed her eyes tightly shut and forced out the rest. "I don't trust you."

His hands paused, then continued their gentle stroking. "Yes, you do."

They were both right. In her heart, Sabrina did trust him—he had saved Quetzal from the burning cottage—but common sense warned her that loneliness and desperation were blinding her to a clear and present danger. Because Spencer had all the motive a bitter man would need to have wanted Jeremiah Kellogg dead and to want her permanently off the book project.

He drew his fingertip in a slow circle around her ear. She couldn't think straight with him touching her like that, but she didn't want him to stop. Ever. Her lips parted against his neck, and she felt his skin quiver. He went stock-still as her hand drifted to the front of his shirt. She unfastened the top button. Then the next.

"Be sure," he murmured. "Be very sure."

When she released the button just above his belt buckle, Sabrina lifted her face to his, lips parted. But instead of plunging her into another hungry kiss, Spencer took her by the shoulders and shifted her back, forcing her to look him in the eye.

"Sabrina, you need to understand that I came here tonight wanting this," he said huskily. "I was fully prepared to leave still wanting you. But I was also prepared to stay...if that's what you wanted."

She nodded hesitantly, unsure what he was getting at. Of course she wanted him to stay. She thought she had made that rather obvious.

He brushed a thumb back and forth across her chin. "Then it isn't going to be a problem for you if, in a little while, I make a move for my wallet? You aren't going to think I was taking anything for granted?"

Sabrina still wasn't following his train of thought, but finally caught on before he had to spell it out. She slid a hand inside his open shirt, leaned forward, and pressed her lips to his bare chest.

He kissed her again, more urgently this time. Before Sabrina was ready for it to end, he tore himself free and stood. She looked up at him, startled, as he glanced around the room, frowning.

"What's the matter now?" she asked.

"You're the woman here. Isn't it obvious?"

"No." Sabrina hugged herself, beginning to feel self-conscious as she hovered on the verge of second thoughts. "Unless you're referring to a mood change that I'm contemplating."

Spencer shot her a worried look. "This shack," he said. "It's like making love in a toolshed."

He shoved the chair away from the electric heater, then reached over and tugged the light cord. The smokehouse went dark, except for the orange glow from the heater coils.

"It isn't candlelight," he said, "but it'll have to do."

It did quite well from Sabrina's standpoint, at least. "My God, you're a closet romantic."

Standing before her in the warm orange glow of the heater, Spencer stripped off his shirt, then kicked off his shoes. He seemed to move in slow motion. She sat spellbound, watching the play of light over the sharply defined muscles of his upper body.

He knelt in front of Sabrina and drew her feet from under her. His hands slid up her legs to her hips, his fingers hooking the elastic waistband of her sweatpants. She scooted back, and he slid them off. Then he was lying close against her on the narrow bed, pressing her head into the pillow with a kiss that drove all rational thought from her mind as Sabrina plunged into a realm of pure sensation.

The plastic zipper of her warm-up jacket smoothly opened. His lips traced the lacy outline of her bra as he found and released the front catch. When Spencer gently lifted her shoulders to remove these last garments, Sabrina wrapped her arms around his head, burying his face in her cleavage.

His hands roamed over her with exquisite tenderness, pausing often, like a blind man memorizing each hill and valley. She writhed shamelessly under his touch, gasping as his lips found and explored one erogenous zone after another. Every now and then, he would stop whatever he was doing and simply hold her, forcing her to rest for a moment before beginning the breathless climb to yet a higher peak.

Patience, she thought impatiently. Sabrina had never known such a patient lover, never experienced such heights of pleasure. They were already in the thinning, rarefied air far above the lonely jungle. And yet she sensed they were still so far from the summit that it frightened her a little...even as it drove her on. His belt scraped her hypersensitive skin. She reached for the buckle and felt his lips smile against hers. When she shifted her attention to his fly, his hand moved from her breast to his back pocket. He sat up.

It seemed like forever before he lay pressed against her once again, skin to skin. She could feel his desire pulsing through his body like a savage drumbeat, and still he held himself in check, until Sabrina dug her fingers into the hard muscles of his back and loosed the beast within him.

He rolled on top of her, growling into a bruising kiss as she curled her legs around him. She gasped his name as they joined. Together they lunged, lunged, and then leaped. Sabrina cried out—the sound of her voice lost in his—as they made the long, heart-stopping free-fall through space.

Sabrina squirmed slightly, unable to breathe. Spencer lethargically raised himself onto his elbows, his forehead still pressed into the thin pillow next to her head. Each found the other's face with a hand, tenderly, too stunned for words.

Her entire body tingled. Her lips felt swollen. She smiled wistfully into the near-darkness, her chin quivering as a tear escaped her eye and raced across her temple. He felt the tear, but not the smile.

"Are you okay?" he rasped. "I didn't—"

She pressed two fingers to his lips, shushing him. She didn't want to talk just yet. She just wanted to...float.

"I've never felt...that before," Sabrina said later, as they lay curled around each other beneath the quilt.

Spencer had been combing his fingers lightly through her hair. He stopped abruptly. His breathing skipped a beat, then resumed with a different rhythm.

After a while, she added, "I'm one of those who saved herself for marriage. Then, when fireworks didn't go off, I thought it was just me. After Darryl took a walk, I was sure of it."

He remained silent, but some minutes later, went back to raking his fingers slowly through her hair. Sabrina loved the feel of that. Along with the rage, she had discovered that

Spencer possessed a tremendous capacity for unselfish tenderness.

"I'm sorry, Spencer. That was lousy timing."

"For what?"

"Mentioning my defunct marriage."

He chuckled softly. "It was pretty good timing, actually."

"Really? You didn't seem to have anything to say about it."

"I've been lying here wondering if he was that bad—or if I was that good. I guess it's an ego thing."

Sabrina smiled, rose on one elbow, and gave him a long, lingering kiss. "I've misjudged you, Spencer. I didn't think you were the type who needed his ego propped up."

"When it comes down to the clinch, most men do." He pulled Sabrina on top of him, trusting her to avoid the sore claw marks on the left side of his chest. "Besides, since we're trotting out the confessions, I've spent the biggest part of my life grinding axes. You're something of a new experience for me, too."

"Is that a fact?" She stretched, then felt the hard planes of his body respond. "You aren't trying to tell me I'm the first woman you've known."

"I assume you mean in the biblical sense. No, you aren't. But you're the first I've wanted to know better." Spencer ran his hands down her smooth flanks. "A lot better."

She rested her head on his shoulder, thinking that this was a night of firsts. Spencer wrapped his arms around her lower back, anchoring her to him, and on a purely emotional level, Sabrina felt totally secure for the first time in her life.

Sabrina awoke groggily, then lay perfectly still, staring disorientedly across the room. A tall, dark figure stood in the open doorway, his head bent under the low door frame. He was watching her. Shivering in the frigid draft, she instinctively reached behind her to rouse Spencer. The door whined softly shut before she fully awakened to the realization that she was alone in the bed.

She drew the quilt around her, listening to the sound of heavy footsteps receding up the stone path toward the mansion. Then, once again, she reached back to the empty place behind her where he had been. And the confusion began to mount.

Spencer had to have taken great pains to ease out of bed without waking her. He must have sorted through their clothes with equal stealth, dressing in the near darkness, before stealing out of her life without so much as a goodbye. *Slam, bang, but not even a thank you, ma'am.*

Sabrina sat up and shook her head, dispelling the crude thought. She had just spent an incredible night with the man—or part of a night, at any rate. The least she could do would be to give Spencer credit for possessing simple human decency. There must be a thousand reasons why he might have felt it necessary to leave her bed—humble as it was—without saying goodbye. If she gave it some thought, she was bound to come up with one of them.

"Ask him in the morning," she whispered into the darkness, and settled back onto the thin pillow.

The bed seemed disturbingly empty without him. And cold. He had let in a terrible chill while leaving. She edged to the back of the bed—into *his* space—to make room.

"Quetz?" She made coaxing sounds and patted the bunk. "Come on, my man."

She didn't hear the tom so much as stir. Sabrina sat up slowly, straining to peer into the deep shadows beyond the glow of the electric heater. The chair was empty except for the album and her watch. So was the place she had last seen him—atop the computer case on the milk crate. She leaned out, squinting at the top of the scratching pole. No Quetzal.

Then it occurred to her that he must have bolted outside when the door was opened. Spencer might not have even noticed. "Oh, great." Sabrina flung back the quilt and threw her legs off the side of the bed.

And stepped right on top of him.

"For God's sake, Quetzal. What are you doing sleeping on the cold floor?"

He didn't even twitch. A cold lump, like an ice cube, settled in the pit of her stomach. Sabrina stood, arm flailing the darkness in search of the light cord.

The light came on and revealed Quetzal, sprawled on his side, half under the bed. His eyes opened a little when she placed a hand on his chest. His heart was racing alarmingly, but when she shook him gently, he didn't move. Instead, his stomach convulsed, and he vomited.

"Quetz!" Her voice broke on a high note of impending hysteria.

Sabrina took a deep breath to calm herself, then eased the cat's head out of the mess. As she was gathering him into her arms to lift him onto the bed, she noticed the thermos cap.

She had placed the stainless steel cup filled with heavily spiced cider tea on the floor earlier, untasted, while she and Spencer talked. It was empty now. Quetzal had licked it nearly dry.

Her hand shook as she picked up the container and held it under her nose. The cold dregs smelled strongly of cinnamon and cloves.

The thermos that Spencer had brought was on the floor next to the heater. Sabrina snatched it up, unscrewed the cork, and sniffed. The smell of cinnamon and cloves was stronger in the still-hot concoction. But beneath that, she thought she detected something else—an ever-so-slightly "off" odor.

She spun around and looked at the door, suddenly realizing her nakedness, suddenly feeling exposed and defenseless. In the stillness, she could hear her own panting, but was powerless to calm herself.

Spencer had made tender love to her. And he had poisoned her cat. Poisoned Quetzal with spiced cider tea he had brought for her.

A low, unearthly moan escaped Quetzal. The spine-chilling sound galvanized Sabrina. She quickly screwed the cork back into the thermos and began grabbing up her clothes and searching for her car keys.

Spencer tore off his coat and threw it as hard as he could against the armoire, then slammed the side of his fist into the hardwood monstrosity. Pain exploded from the bandaged hand, compounding his fury.

"How could you have been so *stupid?*" he hissed through clenched teeth.

Holding his burned hand against his chest, he strode into the sitting room. The room was dark, save for a shaft of light extending through the doorway from the bedroom. That was the way Spencer wanted it. The darkness suited his mood.

He went to the nearest window, jerked aside the lace panels, and stared out through the misted glass, wondering why Sabrina Glade couldn't just *leave*. Take her damned feline familiar, the infernal travesty of a book, her incredibly bewitching body, and just *go*.

"Get the hell out of here," he rasped loudly.

The soft flannel of his shirt chafed the inflamed claw marks on his chest. Spencer held the fabric away from the lacerations, aware that Sabrina had somehow managed to steer clear of them the entire time they had spent making love on that ridiculous iron bed that Shaw had taken down to the smokehouse. Either that, or he had been too intoxicated by her to feel any pain.

He leaned heavily against the window frame, his breath forming a pulsating circle of fog on the glass. The low clouds had broken momentarily, revealing a thin sliver of moon.

Through a ragged copse of cedars near the foot of the hill, Spencer imagined he could make out the charred ruins of the cottage in the predawn darkness. His lips drew back in a lupine grimace. Sabrina could have died there yesterday, just as his mother had twenty years ago—and just as part of him had.

Pushing away from the window, he paced the sitting room feverishly, trying to get past the simmering rage that he had lived with most of his life. It hadn't been so close to the surface in years. Not since he had enlisted in the Corps as a kid and learned to channel his emotions to work for him. But since his return to the estate, Spencer's visceral hatred for Jeremiah Kellogg had grown, turning into a suppurating wound that he'd begun to doubt would ever heal.

After a while, the feeling of being under great pressure eased without letting go entirely. He stopped pacing and wandered aimlessly toward the light in the bedroom, trying to imagine what it would be like to have the estate all to himself after he had gotten rid of Orrin and Maria Shaw, not to mention the conniving Conrad Lafever. To his surprise, Spencer sensed an unexpectedly confounding void.

He moved on into the bedroom and stood at the foot of his big bed, one hand absently curling around a lathed oak post. But he wasn't seeing the paisley velour cover on a thick down comforter. In its place, he saw a narrow iron bed, spread with a thin patchwork quilt that had seen better days. And when he imagined Sabrina gone, he felt a crushing, vacuumlike emptiness.

CHAPTER TEN

The brisk wind had shifted around to the north shortly before dawn. By the time Sabrina headed back to the estate from Schuylerville—alone—the pale blue winter sky had been swept clear of clouds. The brilliant morning sun hurt her eyes as she drove in through the front gate.

At the turnoff to the cottage, she automatically steered onto the gravel track. Braking sharply, she shifted into reverse, returned to the paved driveway, and continued on up the hill toward the mansion. She felt nothing. Her features remained frozen in an expression of numb fatigue.

The car's crumpled rear bumper rattled as she followed a muddy tractor path around the mansion. She parked next to the smokehouse and sat with the sun in her face, staring dumbly at Quetzal's narrow bell collar buckled around her wrist. Some time later, she remembered to get out of the car.

Up at the mansion, a light was still burning in the kitchen. She stopped and stared at it, trying to decide what to do next. When Conrad Lafever's pale face appeared at the window, she turned and scuffed up the path.

Conrad, decked out in his usual immaculate three-piece pin-striped suit, was nursing a cup of coffee at the kitchen worktable when she entered. Maria Shaw was at the sink, up to her elbows in dishwater. They both turned and looked at Sabrina. Conrad appeared concerned.

He got up and moved toward her, frowning. "What's happened, Sabrina? Where have you been so early?"

She let him take her hands and lead her back to the table. But she wouldn't sit. She had sat in the waiting room in Schuylerville for an eternity.

"I had to rush Quetzal to the veterinarian," she said. Talking was easier than she had expected. The sound of her own voice actually made her feel better.

"Quetzal? What happened to him?"

She fingered the bell collar on her wrist. "He was, um, poisoned."

Conrad looked at her as if he was waiting for Sabrina to tell him she was joking. Finally he said, "Dear God, Sabrina, I'm sorry. I know how much he meant to you."

"He isn't dead, Conrad. In fact, Dr. Neese thinks he has a pretty good chance of making it."

A fifty-fifty chance, tops, was what the young vet had told her. But that was immeasurably better than she had feared during the wild drive into town with Quetz sprawled across her lap. By the time she had roused the vet from his house next door to the clinic, she had been convinced that the tom was beyond help.

"There wasn't anything I could do," she added. "So Dr. Neese told me to come home. He said he'd call as soon as there was a change." For better—or worse.

"Good. You look out on your feet."

Conrad was finally able to coax Sabrina into a chair. Talk was eroding the numbness. She had begun to ache all over. Everything was hitting her at once—lack of sleep, the cottage fire, passionate lovemaking with the man who might have poisoned her cat. She wanted to curl up in a corner, close her eyes and shut out the world, just as she had seen Quetzal do so many times.

"How did it happen?" Conrad pulled a chair close to her. "Don't tell me Orrin left rat poison in the smokehouse."

"Orrin did no such thing." Maria shook her hands over the sink and dried them on a dish towel, the wrinkles in her face falling naturally into a waspish expression. "You have no call to suggest it, Conrad Lafever."

Sabrina gave the housekeeper a wide-eyed look. Conrad, too, seemed taken aback by the old woman's harsh tone.

"I wasn't suggesting negligence, Mrs. Shaw," he said evenly. "In all the excitement yesterday, it would be entirely understandable if a packet of rodent poison were overlooked."

"That wasn't what happened." Sabrina pressed her fingers to her lips, then dragged both hands down to her lap. "I think Quetzal drank some spiked tea."

"Spiked?" Conrad leaned back, unconsciously mirroring her pose.

"Mr. Bradley brought me a thermos of spiced cider tea last night," she explained. "I poured a cup, but never got around to drinking it. Quetzal did. I took the thermos to the vet. Dr. Neese is going to have a chemical analysis run on the contents."

"Spiked tea." Maria flung the dish towel down on the counter. "Well, we'll just have a look."

She marched across the kitchen, threw open the pantry door, and disappeared inside. In a moment, she could be heard rummaging through the tin tea canisters lining the back shelf, sounding like a foraging rat.

Conrad pulled at his chin, scowling. "Did the doctor indicate what kind of poison he suspected?"

"He said he had an idea what it might be from the smell, but he wants to be sure." Sabrina wrung her hands in her lap. "He also said that if the poison is what he thinks it is, there's a possibility that it found its way into the tea accidentally."

He looked doubtful. "Sabrina, are you prepared to go by the assumption that Spencer is that negligent?"

Her nerves were too shot to make that leap. And yet, not doing so would involve the loathsome admission that last night she had slept with a man who was trying to murder her. Sabrina had somehow managed to shut the possibility out of her mind during the tense hours at the animal clinic, sensing her sanity was at stake. She tried to keep it at bay even now.

"To tell you the truth, I'm so tired I can hardly think at all, let alone rationalize," she said. "I guess I should call the cops, shouldn't I?"

"That's an option, certainly."

"But what if it turns out to have been an accident, after all?" She got up and went to the window. "I'd feel paranoid accusing Spencer of trying to poison me."

"Better safe than sorry." Conrad came to stand beside her at the window. "You say he brought you the cider tea last night—after you were burned out of the cottage." He paused to let that soak in. "Did he offer to drink any of it himself?"

"Yes . . . no." She rubbed her forehead, trying to remember. "I'm not sure. I just remember pouring some for myself and not drinking it."

"Perhaps you had a premonition."

She shook her head, then felt herself flush. A premonition wasn't what had stopped her from tasting the hot drink. What had ultimately stopped her was Spencer himself. And once she had set aside the cup, he hadn't so much as mentioned it again. Of that much, Sabrina was certain.

"Oh, Conrad, I'm so confused." Emotional and physical exhaustion were both dragging her deeper and deeper into a vortex of mental chaos. She turned toward him and leaned into his concave chest.

He made little clucking sounds and patted her back, awkwardly trying to comfort her. She clamped her lower lip between her teeth, struggling to keep tears at bay. It was the fatigue that was getting to her, she told herself. She could cope with this. She would.

"It does seem a bit brazen of him," Conrad said acidly. "But I suppose we should have expected as much from the likes of Spencer Bradley. Mr. Kellogg always did."

Sabrina raised her head. "How so?"

"If Mr. Kellogg said it once, he said it a hundred times, 'The bastard—'"

"Oh, right," she interrupted, not wanting to belabor *that* subject again. "I know they hated each other, but Mr. Kellogg pretty much ended that feud by dying."

Conrad patted her back again. His hand felt wooden. "That would have been the case had you not chosen to complete Mr. Kellogg's book."

It all came back to the book, Sabrina thought. The book that she literally couldn't afford to walk away from. The book that, apparently, Spencer Bradley couldn't afford to let her finish.

With a groan, she returned her forehead to Conrad's chest. He hesitated, then put his arms around her stiffly. Nurturing wasn't in his nature. Maybe twenty-five years on Jeremiah Kellogg's payroll had burned it out of him, Sabrina thought. But she was in such need at the moment that even his clumsy efforts were enough to send her over the edge. Her breath hitched twice, and in spite of her best efforts, the tears came.

"Dammit all, Conrad," she choked, "I don't even know what there is about the book that anyone would want to hide."

Conrad shifted her aside and fumbled a crisp linen handkerchief from his inside coat pocket. Sabrina took it and pressed it against her eyes, trying to stanch the flow of tears.

"You can't continue like this, Sabrina. You really must go have another talk with Noble Wetherbee."

She started to protest that yesterday's meeting with Wetherbee had only made *The End of the Line* more complicated—but stopped herself. Conrad had said "another talk." The tears abruptly dried up as she tried to remember if, during the commotion to which she had returned yesterday afternoon, she'd had occasion to mention that she had been down to Albany for a meeting with Jeremiah Kellogg's attorney.

The door to the hallway swung open. They turned to find Spencer Bradley standing in the doorway, one knee bent as if he'd been frozen in midstride. He had on the same clothes that he'd been wearing when he'd left the smokehouse last night, minus the coat. Unshaven, he looked as ragged and frayed as Sabrina felt.

His gaze shifted from Conrad's face to hers before sliding down to Conrad's encircling arms. He looked startled.

"Speak of the devil," Conrad said, making no move to release her.

"What's that supposed to mean, Connie?"

Sabrina felt Conrad flinch at the hated nickname. She tried to step away from him, and he finally let her. Spencer slowly planted both feet squarely on the floor, but kept hold of the door with one hand.

"We were just discussing why anyone—specifically you—might find it necessary to poison Sabrina in order to keep her from completing Mr. Kellogg's book," Conrad said icily.

Spencer's eyes, as hard as nails, snapped in Sabrina's direction. She involuntarily sucked in her breath, then raised her chin defiantly. She wouldn't allow him to intimidate her with a look.

"Quetzal drank the cider tea you brought me," she said. "He nearly died. He still might."

He didn't so much as blink for what seemed like an impossibly long time. The shield was firmly in place. She hadn't a clue as to what was going on in Spencer's mind. When he turned his attention to Conrad, Sabrina had an instinctive urge to rush to the older man's defense, but didn't know how.

"We need to talk, Sabrina," Spencer said, still looking at Conrad.

He clearly wanted to get her alone. She couldn't agree to that. She was equally reluctant to continue what was rapidly beginning to feel like a three-way standoff.

"Not now, Spencer. I'm too tired. I have to get some sleep before I fall flat on my face."

He nodded slowly. Every move he made suddenly seemed measured, calculated.

"Let me take you upstairs," he said. "There's a comfortable room at the back—"

"No," she cut in, "I have a place."

He gave her that unblinking stare again. She stood it as long as she could, then glanced away, angry at her own weakness.

"You've made your point, Sabrina," he said. "You don't have to stay down there in that ridiculous shed on that damned old bed."

Something inside her ignited and flared. "That *damned old bed* was plenty good enough for you last night," she snapped.

Spencer's face went crimson, even as the knuckles of his hand clamped to the door turned white. His gaze flicked to one side, not quite reaching Conrad before returning to her. Sabrina couldn't look at Conrad, either. She couldn't believe she had blurted that out, leaving herself feeling more exposed than she had been while lying in Spencer's arms last night.

She knew without checking that Conrad was looking at her. She could feel him painting her with a tar brush of disapproval, and wanted out of that kitchen in the worst way. But she wouldn't let herself run. Not from Conrad— and certainly not from Spencer.

"Have it your way, Sabrina," Spencer said, forcing the words through clenched teeth. He whirled and stormed from the kitchen, slamming the door behind him.

Sabrina opened and closed her hands at her sides, listening to the sound of his receding footsteps, to the barbed silence from the pantry, to Conrad Lafever discreetly clearing

his throat. Then she crossed to the opposite side of the
kitchen and slammed out the back door.

The rage had taken over again, and there was nothing he
could do about it. Spencer took the stairs two at a time, ef-
fortlessly, the heat of anger pouring sweat from his body.
He tore off his flannel shirt, sending buttons flying, and
flung it half the length of the upstairs hallway.

"Connie Lafever, for God's sake."

He caught up with the shirt and kicked it viciously
through the open doorway into his sitting room. Kicked the
door shut. Paced in a tight circle.

"How could she let that weasel touch her?"

Catching Sabrina in Lafever's arms had, for the moment, hit Spencer harder than the fact that someone had
tried to poison her. He stopped pacing and looked down at
the claw marks on his chest.

Cat, hell, he thought. Who would have expected a cat to
drink spiced cider tea? Tea that Spencer had prepared with
his own hands and carried down to her.

His blood turned ice-cold. He crossed the room to the
window and stared down the hill in the direction of the
burned-up cottage. His jaw muscles spasmed and his breath
rasped in his lungs. He needed to think very clearly now, to
sort this out.

Spencer tried to relax. For the first time in his life, he
wanted the rage to let go, to leave him. But it wouldn't.
Maybe it couldn't, he thought. After all these years, maybe
the carefully fostered hatred had become too much a part
of him.

"Dammit, Jeremiah, you can't keep doing this to me.
Not from the grave." He hammered the side of a fist into
the window frame, rattling the glass.

Sabrina awoke to a cold draft on the back of her neck
and a creepy sense of déjà vu. Her nose was two inches

from the rough stone wall. She started to roll over, noticed she was incredibly warm, and realized she had somehow acquired a luxuriously thick paisley down comforter.

Yawning, she turned onto her right side. The door was ajar. A shaft of brilliant light stretched across the smoke-house floor almost to the bed. A long leg extended across the wedge of sunlight. She followed it into the shadows next to the doorway and found Spencer Bradley sitting on her wooden chair, freshly shaved and spruce in a leather bomber jacket and jeans.

He was opening a greasy wrapper. A greasy paper sack stood on the floor in front of him. A greasy French fry lay next to the sack in the shadow of two canned soft drinks.

"Cheeseburger?" He held one out to Sabrina.

Her mouth watered, but she drew back against the wall. "After the cider tea, you must take me for an absolute idiot."

"Oh, come on. Think of it as the poison du jour."

Sabrina glared at him. He physically withdrew the offer—and bit into the burger.

She sat up, pulling the comforter snugly around her neck. "Do I have you to thank for this?"

He glanced at the comforter. "Maria brought it down earlier."

"Oh." She bit back the expression of gratitude she'd been reluctantly about to offer. "You enjoy sitting there with the door wide open in the dead of winter?"

"Thought you might prefer to have it open, with me here." Spencer reached into the sack for fries.

"You have a point." Sabrina squinted at the angle of the light shining in. "What time is it?"

"Four-thirtyish."

"Good God. I didn't mean to sleep the whole day away." Her stomach growled.

Spencer picked up the sack and held it out to her. She gave it more than a knee-jerk thought this time, then shook her head.

"I'll take the one you're working on," she said.

"I didn't poison your cat, Sabrina."

"And you'd come right out and admit it if you had? Give me a break. You aren't that stupid."

"Thank you for saying so." He gazed out the door for a moment, chewing, then leaned over and handed her the partially eaten cheeseburger. "Since we're on the subject, I called the vet a few minutes ago. Quetzal's vital signs have improved some."

Her head sagged back against the wall. "You don't know how great it feels to have some good news for a change."

"True. I guess you're going to want the unopened can of soda."

"You got it."

"And no fries."

"Ditto."

He fished another burger from the greasy sack. "I'll bet you always stop by the local hospital on your way home to have your trick-or-treat candy x-rayed."

Sabrina let that pass and attacked the burger. "I wouldn't have believed grease could taste so good."

Spencer nodded. "You wouldn't believe how far I had to drive to get this terrific junk."

"Couldn't have been far. It's still warm."

"Had to zap it with the microwave when I got back."

They ate in silence. Spencer polished off two burgers while Sabrina finished her one, then they split the fourth—she did the dividing. While she cleaned the grease from her hands with a wad of paper napkins, he tilted the chair back against the wall, a can of soda on his thigh.

She leaned against the opposite wall, eyeing him from behind the comforter-draped ramparts of her raised knees. The sleep and the solid food had improved her frame of mind markedly. But she felt in serious need of a shower and shampoo.

"This was all very nice of you," she said.

He smiled ruefully. "You deserved breakfast in bed, after the way I behaved up there in the kitchen this morning."

"You're too generous." Sabrina meant it. After eight hours of sleep, the kitchen encounter seemed a week behind them, on the far side of a dense fog bank. All but a few seconds of it, anyway. "I didn't mean to lip off about, well, you know."

Spencer's gaze drifted down to the iron bed. Eventually he nodded. "Believe me, Sabrina, that old bed was good enough for me," he said softly. "I shouldn't have bad-mouthed it. I was just...steamed."

For some reason, the reminder of his volatile temper made it still more painful for Sabrina to think about last night. That, and the cider tea. "It must be difficult to eat, sleep and breathe such anger."

He raised his eyes and held her gaze for a dozen heart-beats. In spite of everything, she felt herself wanting to reach out to him, and wondered if she was out of her mind.

"I wasn't angry last night, Sabrina." He spoke barely above a whisper, the sound of his voice suddenly and devastatingly intimate. "Do you really believe I'm the kind of man who could torch the house you lived in, then turn right around and make love to you?"

Spencer lowered the chair onto all fours, placed the can of soda on the floor, and leaned toward her. She couldn't escape his eyes. They reached into her just as they had last night—demandingly—but with a mesmerizing tenderness that she was powerless to resist.

"You know me right now as well as any woman ever has," he said. "But how well do you know yourself?"

The questions kept coming, mercilessly on target. A small lump of anxiety grew into a mountain of fear as Sabrina watched him rise slowly...so slowly...and move toward the bed, his gaze never leaving her eyes. She pressed back against the hard stone wall, feeling like a deer frozen in the blinding headlights of an oncoming vehicle. Spencer leaned down and eased his hand beneath the comforter.

The zipper on the top of her warm-up suit slowly opened. His hand was warm, despite the chill in the room. And so gentle. Sabrina shivered.

"Think of last night, Sabrina," he whispered, leaning closer, closer. "Are you the kind of woman who could have given herself so completely, so joyously—" his lips sealed hers with a long, probing kiss to which she couldn't help responding "—to a killer?"

Sabrina gasped at the word. Spencer withdrew his hand and lips, without haste. By the time her head had cleared, he had returned to the wooden chair next to the door. They stared at each other across the abyss of her confusion. Her lips and the places he had touched with his hand felt cold and abandoned. And she felt betrayed by her own arousal.

"That wasn't fair," she said finally.

"Not much is these days."

"It doesn't change anything."

"You're right." Spencer nodded somberly. "But I think it's going to be a little harder now for you to pretend that you can separate what you think about me from how you feel about me."

That shook her. "You're convinced that you know me pretty well, aren't you?"

He cocked his head. Nodded. "You're stuck here, Sabrina. Flat broke, is my guess. Not a soul you can turn to for—"

"You don't know that."

Spencer picked up the can of soda, drained it, and pitched it into the sack. "Last night, you asked what it was like for me as an adolescent, living down there in the cottage. Let's just say that I know 'cornered' when I see it. Like it or not, we have that shared experience."

She arched a brow, trying not to show how close to home he had hit. "Therefore, you know what makes me tick."

"If you insist on hanging a cliché on it."

"Well, then, if we're such kindred spirits, why don't I have you figured out yet?"

He shrugged. "Maybe you're trying too hard to find what isn't there."

"Or maybe you're trying too hard to hide what is," she retorted.

"What's there to hide?" Spencer smiled easily, leaned back, and crossed his arms over his thick chest.

Observing this, Sabrina said, "You'd make a lousy trial lawyer, Spencer."

"I can live with that."

But what can't you live with? she wondered. *What do you keep locked up in that pressure cooker of rage that you carry around inside you?* She didn't know what it was—wasn't even sure she had the stomach left to find out. But maybe Spencer was right about one thing. Maybe she had been looking too hard.

Sabrina consciously broadened her sights. And there it was, staring her in the face. If she was correct, she realized, the release valve had been right there in front of her all along. Her mistake had been in assuming that it was named Jeremiah Kellogg. She couldn't resist giving her theory a test.

"Your mother died very young," she said.

Slam. Spencer kept smiling, but the shield came up with dispatch. Sabrina could almost feel the pressure building behind that smile. The small thrill of discovery was dwarfed by a discomfiting sense that she had just kicked a defenseless dog. She started to back off, then remembered Quetzal heaving up on the car seat during the mad drive down to Schuylerville, and pressed again.

"Do you still miss her?"

Spencer plucked at the bandage on his hand for a moment. "You're operating on the misconception that I once did."

That knocked Sabrina down a peg. "You're right. I thought—"

His snort of laughter cut her off like a hatchet blade. "You just can't let sleeping tigers lie, can you?"

He wadded up the greasy hamburger sack, cans and all, shaking his head. Then he reached under the chair and hauled out a heavy-duty paper sack bearing the logo of a hardware-store chain. He tossed this across the room at her. It landed on the foot of the bed with a loud clank of metal.

Ducking his head, Spencer stepped outside and glanced around. Then he leaned back in and looked at her, all pretense of a smile gone.

"I'm not going to waste my breath offering you the means to leave, Sabrina." He raised a hand when she opened her mouth. "If your circumstances are as bad as I think they are, I can't force you out, either—not until after the will is read. Unfortunately you know that."

She nodded.

"So, at least let me give you some friendly advice." He made a pistol with a thumb and forefinger and aimed it at her. "Watch your back at all times." He pulled the trigger.

Sabrina pressed a fist against her galloping heart as she watched him walk away up the stone path toward the mansion. When he moved out of sight beyond an overgrown privet hedge, she tore open the sack he'd thrown. It contained an assortment of hand tools, a big tempered-steel hasp and a large padlock—certified bulletproof.

Clutching the heavy padlock, she crawled out from under the down comforter, shivering as the cold air hit her. As she stood in the doorway, staring up the stone path at the gloomy back of the mansion, two huge possibilities presented themselves to her.

The first was that she could be crazy—lusting after an irresistible enigma who might not be above murdering her to prevent the completion of a book that he feared. The second was that Spencer was outright psychotic—playing deadly games with her mind *and* her emotions.

Her teeth chattered.

Sabrina pulled the door closed and turned up the electric heater full blast. One advantage to the small dimensions of the smokehouse was that it didn't take long to heat.

Climbing onto the bed, she shook the tools and hasp out of the sack onto the comforter then smiled grimly as she paused to stroke the warm covering. She wasn't quite as alone as Spencer thought. She hadn't expected such a kind gesture from Maria, which led her to suspect that Conrad Lafever might have been behind it.

Weighing the heavy padlock in one hand, she frowned pensively at the thick plank door. The fast-food meal could have been simply an excuse for Spencer to come down to the smokehouse and toy with her mind. Had the padlock been more of the same? A physical reminder of his implied threat?

"You have from now until the will is read at the end of the month," she murmured aloud. "Use your brain instead of your hormones. Now that you know what you're up against, you can watch your back that long. You'll do just fine."

She had no choice. With Conrad's help, Sabrina was determined to make the risk worthwhile. And now she was more certain than ever how she could go about doing that. If Ira Sampson needed a powerful incentive to extend her delivery deadline for *The End of the Line,* she had a feeling she could find more than enough reason in Spencer Bradley . . . and Zena.

CHAPTER ELEVEN

The thick paisley comforter was four times too big for the bed. But by doubling it, then tucking one side up over two fat bolsters against the wall, Sabrina was able to convert the narrow iron bed into a surprisingly handsome daybed, set off by a braided oval rug in matching hues. A large South Seas travel poster was taped to the rough wall behind the bed. Across the cramped room, the poster was reflected in the beveled-glass mirror of a small antique vanity. In one corner, her new wardrobe hung from a short length of pipe suspended from a pair of bicycle hooks screwed into the low ceiling.

The smokehouse was beginning to feel almost cozy, she thought, as she perched on a velvet-cushioned vanity stool to pull on her dress boots. Every day or so for the past two weeks, she'd returned from working in the mansion's library to find yet another item added to the furnishings of the makeshift dwelling. Among the first had been the small microwave oven on the floor at the foot of the bed, along with an assortment of microwavable pasta meals in pull-tab cans.

Maria had brought down dinner trays several times, but Sabrina had stuck with the microwaved ravioli. It was easier than wondering, worrying. And she hadn't had a sip of hot tea in two weeks.

Sabrina stood and shook out her long, wool tartan skirt. Two dove gray business cards wafted off the edge of the vanity and fluttered to the floor. She picked them up and tucked them securely into the mirror frame. She had returned from walks twice to find Noble Wetherbee's cards

tucked into the door frame of the smokehouse. Maybe
she'd be lucky enough not to be out the next time he
dropped in.

Leaning over to check her makeup in the vanity mirror,
she smiled at the reflection of the wall behind her. The
South Seas poster had shown up yesterday—the only totally incongruous addition to the decor. Two nearly nude
sunbathers on a stretch of sun-washed Tahitian beach
didn't strike her as being Conrad Lafever's style. But then,
maybe that was why he had relegated it to her wall and not
to his own.

The smile died as her gaze fixed on the bronzed sunbathers. She wondered what Conrad would think if he had
any inkling of what went through her mind every time she
looked at the pair, their legs suggestively entwined on the
pristine sand. The poster was the last thing Sabrina had
looked at before falling asleep last night. She had dreamed
of Spencer Bradley's warm hands, and awakened with a
frustrating hunger.

Her heavy winter coat still smelled new as she pulled it
from its wooden hanger. She had found a stack of mail-
order catalogs on the worktable in the mansion's library the
second morning after the fire, along with a more-than-
generous check from an insurance company to cover her
losses. Thanks to telephone ordering and express delivery,
she wasn't hurting for decent warm clothes.

That had somehow provided a much-needed boost to her
self-confidence. After two weeks of working almost around
the clock, she was beginning to believe she just might be
able to finish researching *The End of the Line* before being forced to leave the estate following the reading of Jeremiah Kellogg's will next week.

She removed the padlock from the hasp on the inside of
the plank door and peeked outside. Early dawn was barely
discernible under a dark canopy of low clouds. A light
snow had fallen during the night. She could smell the threat
of more in the air.

Leaving the warmth of the smokehouse, Sabrina pushed the door shut and snapped her new padlock onto the outside hasp. She had entrusted the spare key to Conrad two weeks ago. Every day since then, he had asked if she wanted it back. Odd, considering what a good time he seemed to be having "decorating" the smokehouse in her absence.

The thin crust of snow crunched underfoot as she made her way up the stone path to the back of the house. Halfway there, she realized she was walking over fresh footprints, barely visible in the dim light. Someone had already been down the path from the mansion since the snow had fallen. Sabrina backtracked a few paces to where the earlier footprints stopped near the overgrown privet hedge, within sight of the smokehouse.

She measured the sole of her boot against the larger footprints. They obviously belonged to a man. Bending close, she could just make out a treaded pattern. She pulled her collar higher around her ears and continued up the path to the mansion.

After wiping her boots on a mat in the mudroom, she opened the door to the kitchen. To her surprise, Conrad Lafever stood at the stove with his back to her, a butcher's apron over his suit, tending a copper skillet of bacon. He looked around as she closed the door.

Sabrina glanced at his shoes. They were dry. Besides, she had never seen him in anything even approximating work boots.

"Conrad, what on earth are you doing up at this ungodly hour?"

"The same might be asked of you," he said with a vague smile.

"You know why. I'm busting my buns trying to beat an impossible deadline."

"Precisely why you should start the day with a substantial breakfast." He stabbed a fork at the bacon.

"I've already eaten down at the smokehouse," she lied automatically, not without regret.

The bacon smelled outrageously delicious. But she hadn't eaten anything from the mansion's kitchen since the day the cottage burned. In spite of Dr. Neese's opinion that Quetzal's poisoning had been an accident, the incident was still like an open wound to Sabrina. She was in no hurry for that wound to heal. During the ensuing weeks, it had served as a constant warning to her. She ate endless cans of ravioli down at the smokehouse. On the alternate days that she visited Quetzal at the animal clinic in Schuylerville, she sometimes splurged for a more substantial meal at a nearby café.

Conrad kept his back to her, doing a pretty clumsy job of hiding his disappointment. He had clearly gone to a lot of trouble to rise early and start breakfast for her. But Sabrina wouldn't give in. It wasn't that she didn't trust Conrad. After all, she had given him her spare key. But he had fed her distrust of the mansion's kitchen by quietly supplying her with the microwave oven and tamperproof victuals. In a way, he had himself to blame when Sabrina took the view that there was no telling who else had had access to those breakfast fixings before him.

To salve her own sense of guilt, she considered thanking Conrad for the South Seas poster, but then sidestepped that temptation, as well. When she had expressed her appreciation of the paisley comforter two weeks ago, he had seemed more embarrassed than pleased. Since then, Sabrina had allowed him to make his phantom contributions to her comfort without comment, although she intended to find some way to repay his many kindnesses before she left the estate.

"I take it that Maria isn't up yet," she said, crossing to the hallway door.

She wouldn't have minded running into Maria just to have another woman with whom to talk for a change. Lately, the housekeeper had been making awkward little gestures toward her, as if she didn't quite know how to be friendly. Sabrina tried to meet her halfway, sensing how difficult it was for the old woman to shake the mood of the place.

"I don't believe either of the Shaws has stirred."

"Oh." That told her all she needed to know about who belonged to the boot tracks in the snow. "I'd hoped to get to work in the library before Mr. Bradley started prowling around."

Conrad poked silently at the bacon. She watched his back for a moment, then asked, "I don't suppose you know his schedule for the day?"

"Yesterday, Orrin mentioned they were to begin clearing away the debris from the cottage. I quite imagine that will occupy both of them for the remainder of the week." Conrad glanced at her over his shoulder. "You do seem to go out of your way to avoid Bradley these days."

Conrad was a master of understatement, Sabrina thought. Over the past couple of weeks, she had tried desperately to convince herself that she couldn't bear the sight of Spencer Bradley. She'd failed miserably, just as she had with equally hard-fought attempts to ignore the insane ache of knowing there would never be anything between the two of them besides that one explosively sensual night in the smokehouse.

"Yes," she said, suddenly feeling bleak. "As you well know, the man can be pretty distracting."

She ran her hand up and down the door frame, thinking about Spencer poking around in the cottage ruins. Suddenly this seemed like the perfect time to air the question that had been nagging at her for weeks.

"Conrad, why did you go out of your way to keep me from learning that Zena and Spencer Bradley had lived in the cottage all those years?"

He reached down slowly and turned off the burner under the skillet. "I was following Mr. Kellogg's instructions."

She nodded to his back. Sabrina had always suspected that Conrad's loyalty to Jeremiah Kellogg had known no limits. Now she knew. Such blind loyalty alone, she thought, would have put him at odds with the tenants in the cottage.

"Do you know why Mr. Kellogg didn't want me to know?" she asked.

He kept poking at the bacon. There was something testy about his movements now. Her questions were irritating him. He wasn't going to answer this one. She smelled another deception-by-omission.

"Sabrina, I—" Conrad hesitated, then slid the skillet off the burner and turned toward her. "I must insist that you take this back." He held out the spare key to her padlock.

She stared at it for a moment, recalling the time Spencer had held out a key to her under very different circumstances. In this case, she was both puzzled and exasperated.

"Conrad, at least tell me why it bothers you so much to have it."

"Please, Sabrina."

He looked profoundly discomfited as she continued to hesitate, then relieved when she finally felt sorry for him and took the key. His hand felt cool and clammy to her touch. Not unlike a fish, she decided. The grossly uncharitable thought filled her with shame.

"Well, I'd better get to work."

He nodded. "If you should need me for anything at all, I'll be working in my rooms."

She ducked out of the kitchen, listened briefly for the sound of footsteps in the still-dark mansion, then stole quickly along the corridor to the library. After quietly closing the door, she wandered across the shadowed room to the mullioned windows and stared out at a heavy flurry of snow drifting past the glass.

The padlock key felt oily as she rubbed it between her fingers. She slid it into the deep slit pocket of her skirt, wondering what had driven Conrad to insist on returning the key to her. When the answer proved to be hopelessly elusive, she gave up and switched on the library lights.

Half an hour later, she was so deeply engrossed in her work that she didn't even notice the sunlight burst through the clouds.

Late in the afternoon, Sabrina leaned back and rolled her shoulders, trying to shake off a crick in her neck. She was making a lot of headway on the book's working draft. But her eyes ached, and her head felt as if it were stuffed with cotton batting. If she didn't take a break, she might as well write off the rest of the day.

Her joints protested as she pried herself out of the hard library chair. She stretched elaborately, tucked her blouse back into her skirt, and blinked at the bright light outside the windows. The snow had all melted, except for a few thin patches in the shade beneath the windows.

A breath of fresh air would be just the ticket, she thought. Taking a brisk walk in the sun would surely help clear the cobwebs out of her brain. Sabrina put on her coat, turned up the collar, and headed for the door.

The sunlight hurt her eyes as she loped down the steps and emerged from the dank shade of the portico. She glanced at her watch, a game plan beginning to take shape. Thirty minutes of vigorous walking, then a quick drive down to the Schuylerville animal clinic to cheer up Quetzal. Maybe she'd stop at the café on her way back to grab a decent meal for a change. After that, she would be primed to work like a demon until midnight or later. She struck out across the sloping, weed-infested lawn.

As she left the protection of the mansion, a gust of frigid wind snatched at her coat. Sabrina turned her back to the assault and moved briskly downwind, holding her collar snugly around her ears until she reached the shelter of a dense copse of cedars. She followed the tree line downhill, hoping to stay out of the wind.

The charred smell reached her even before the intermittent thudding sounds, coming from somewhere off to her left on the other side of the copse. She slowed as she came to a narrow break in the trees—possibly an old deer trail—that cut back sharply through the overhanging boughs. Realizing that she had stumbled onto a shortcut to the one place she had least intended to go, Sabrina nevertheless veered left.

The deep humus was spongy underfoot. She followed the trail thirty or forty yards before coming out on the west edge of the clearing at the base of the hill. Her stomach did a slow roll at her first sight of the gutted shell of the cottage since the day it had burned.

Orrin Shaw's pickup truck was backed up to what had been the front stoop, its wide bed piled high with charred lumber, twisted sheet metal and the blackened remains of a refrigerator. As Sabrina watched, an oven door sailed up onto the heap.

"That'll do it, Shaw." Spencer Bradley's gruff voice drifted from the far side of the truck. "Haul this last load to the dump, and we'll have another go at it tomorrow. And next time, see if you can't get down here before half past ten."

Orrin Shaw's floppy-brimmed work hat came into view through the truck windows. The handyman climbed in behind the wheel, started the truck's throaty engine, and went lumbering off toward the gravel track that led around to the main driveway.

Spencer stripped off heavy leather work gloves and tucked them under his belt as he watched the truck drive out of sight. He was reaching into a carton at his feet when he spotted Sabrina standing at the edge of the clearing. He froze, only his hair stirred into motion by the wind, until she started toward him. By the time she got close enough to read the label on the carton, he was popping the tab on a can of beer. Watching her.

Charcoal dust coated his faded jeans and the outer of two plaid flannel shirts. Both shirts were open at the collar. He seemed too lightly dressed for such a raw day. But as Sabrina drew nearer, she noticed that he was actually sweating. He tipped up the can and appeared to drink down half of its contents before pausing for breath.

She stopped several feet away and surveyed the ruins of the cottage. Something had drawn her here as surely as a powerful magnet attracts iron filings. But it hadn't been this charred heap of wood and stone, she thought. Sabrina remembered something Spencer had said a couple of weeks ago, and thought, *I can't help it. I've come to give the sleeping tigers another nudge.* After a minute or two, she felt the weight of Spencer's intense gaze slide off her face.

"It's really a mess, isn't it?" Her voice was hushed. She hadn't expected to feel so awed by the destructive powers of fire.

"Not as bad as it was this morning." Spencer leaned down and plucked another beer from the carton. "Shaw just left with the fourth load."

He offered the second can to Sabrina. When she shook her head, he drained the first one, pitched it into a sack next to the carton, and popped the tab on the second.

"Isn't Shaw a little long in the tooth for you to be pushing so hard?" she asked, toeing a big daggerlike knife imbedded in the ground next to a coil of hemp rope. The initials U.S.M.C. were engraved on a small metal plate on the knife handle.

Spencer snorted. "Don't waste your time worrying about that old hellhound. He has a way of setting his own pace."

Sabrina glanced at the dark hair plastered to Spencer's forehead. "So, it seems, do you. I would have thought you'd have hired someone else to do this filthy work."

"Because I can afford to?" He smiled mirthlessly and wandered over to stand close to her. "No, this is a labor of love. I wouldn't miss personally making a clean sweep of this place for the world."

She moved away, hoping Spencer hadn't noticed her shudder. For just a moment there, he had sounded and looked bitter enough to torch the cottage all over again. Assuming, of course, that he'd been the one who had burned his childhood home to the ground.

She stopped, hands in her coat pockets, and peered into the sack. From the looks of all those empties, he appeared to have been making a concerted effort to turn the job into a gala occasion.

"You can lose a lot of body heat, drinking in this kind of weather," she said. "Hypothermia, and all that."

He toasted her comment, then pivoted to scowl at the ruins. "I assure you, I have plenty of body heat to spare."

She took another look at the sack. "Well, I'm surprised you can still stand up." As far as she could tell, he was as sober as a judge.

"Ah, Sabrina, your puritanical streak is showing." He took a long draw on the can in his fist. "Besides, a generous application of suds takes some of the edge off—" he fanned a hand toward the rubble "—this."

His tone had changed, slipping from merely acerbic into something darker. There was more to this than bitterness, she thought uneasily.

"When I first got here, I thought you were just cleaning up a mess," she said. "But it's beginning to sound more like you're lancing a boil."

He gave her an odd look, then snorted again, this time halfheartedly. Lowering himself onto his haunches, he sighed heavily, the beer can cradled between his fingertips.

The burn on the back of his hand had mostly healed, but the oblong patch of skin was inflamed where the coarse leather gloves had rubbed. Otherwise, his hands looked hard and rough. Sabrina knew better. Thrusting from her mind a too-vivid image of warm hands skimming over hypersensitive flesh, she moved farther on around the corner of the ruins.

"Watch out for stud nails over there," Spencer warned. "They're scattered all over the place."

She kept picking her way along, eyes on the ground now. Spencer had grown up hating this place—hating it because of his uncle, she thought. But Jeremiah Kellogg hadn't been the only player here twenty years ago. As tigers went, she was beginning to flirt with the intriguing possibility that Kellogg might not even have been the biggest.

Sabrina stopped on the far side of the rubble to mentally review her talk with Noble Wetherbee two weeks ago. In retrospect, the interview seemed sloppy and incomplete. Whether by chance or by design, the aged lawyer had left her with a multitude of blank spaces to fill in—holes big enough for a large tigress to stroll through. She picked one, and nudged.

"I went down to Albany to see Noble Wetherbee, the day the cottage was set on fire," she said.

Spencer showed no reaction to the revelation that she had been consulting his uncle's longtime personal attorney. Nor did he make any effort to contradict her flat contention that the fire had been a case of arson. He just squatted there, turning the beer can slowly between his fingertips, and stared into the charred ruins as if mesmerized by invisible flames.

"He claims he doesn't know how your mother died," she added.

"How convenient."

"Wait a minute. Let me get out my notebook. I want to get every word of this down." She waited in vain for her sarcasm to stir up something, then looked up at the hazy winter sky. "Jeez, I can't believe how little I've been able to turn up about your mother, Spencer. Zena Bradley must have made Greta Garbo seem like a raving publicity addict."

His eyes snapped up. "Bradley?"

The setting sun was behind Spencer, leaving his face in shadows. But she could swear he had gone pale. He carefully placed the beer can on the ground and came to his feet slowly, gracefully.

Tigerlike, Sabrina thought. *Powerful, dangerous, and . . . awakening.* And she was glad the ruins stood between them, because she couldn't stop herself. She had to keep nudging.

"What is there about your mother's death that no one wants to touch?" she asked.

"You really don't know, do you?" His hands hung at his sides like spades. "You don't get it at all."

While Sabrina was still trying to figure out what he was talking about, he started moving around the ruins. Her heart skipped a beat, then resumed its normal rhythm but at a quickened pace. She felt an urgent impulse to turn and run, but sensed that if she so much as twitched, Spencer would cut straight across the gutted remains of the cottage and be on top of her before she'd gone ten feet. Besides, where was she to run? She watched his approach with growing trepidation, feeling like an animal staked out as bait.

A cacophony of warring voices suddenly clamored inside her head. *He won't dare hurt you—not here, not now. But you can't be sure. Spencer has never hurt you. Two weeks ago, he gave you the most incredible physical pleasure you've ever known. For just a little while, you felt totally safe with him,* she reminded herself as she came under the spell of his penetrating gaze. Then a sharp pain skewered her. *That was before Quetzal was poisoned. Remember Quetzal.*

His shadow descended on her. With the winter sun out of her eyes, she could see his face clearly now. It looked shuttered and glacial.

"You're afraid of me, Sabrina."

She had a wild urge to bob her head, like one of those stupid spring-necked dogs that people stuck in the rear windows of their cars. But she managed to meet his gaze evenly.

"That's what you want," she said.

"No, it isn't."

"Then what *do* you want, Spencer?" Her voice rose, squeezed through a tightening throat. To her horror, Sabrina realized that she was suddenly very close to tears. He had that power. He could send her emotions off on crazy tangents at the drop of a hat.

"I want you away from this damned place," he said coldly.

"Why? Because of the book? Or just so you can come into your own as high-muck-a-muck of the manor without having to deal with the ghost of one of your one-night stands?"

Spencer grabbed the collar of her coat before she realized he had even moved. Sabrina clawed her nails into the backs of his hands and into the still-tender flesh where he had been burned. He seemed oblivious to the pain as he pulled her into a bruising kiss.

When his lips released hers, she suddenly knew exactly how Spencer felt when the rage took hold. It shot through her with a blinding flash of heat.

"Damn you!" she cried, still clawing at his hands. "You were willing to do anything to get rid of me, weren't you? If you couldn't burn me out, you'd—"

He pulled her to him again, growling, the taste of her own tears salting the beer-flavored tang of his mouth. This time, his lips and tongue probed demandingly, unrelentingly, until they finally broke through her fury to reach something deeper, more primal.

Sabrina stopped struggling. Her hands slid from his. She swayed. Gradually his lips softened, grew less demanding, more coaxing. And—God help her—Sabrina felt herself responding.

"Damn you," she whispered when their lips finally parted.

"I'll not tell you this again, Sabrina," he said hoarsely. "I did not poison your cat." He let go of her collar and traced a finger down the side of her neck. "And one more thing—any time you want to get off the one-night-stand block, just give a whistle."

"You arrogant..." She whirled away, dragging a sleeve across her lips.

"I just know what I want. And I know what you want. Or have you forgotten who unbuttoned my shirt that night?"

She turned to face him again. His invasive gaze hammered right into her. Sabrina fought it.

"Deny it, and you'll be lying through your teeth," he went on, driving deeper, deeper. "That goes for just now, too. You argued the point on principle at first, stubborn thing that you are, but you finally had to admit that you wanted that kiss."

He stepped closer, the hard bore of his blue eyes as once sensual and menacing. "You still want it, Sabrina," he said harshly. "But you just can't let yourself believe that what you want isn't going to turn on you. Well, let me give you a news flash. Every man on the face of this planet isn't a carbon copy of that piece of crud you married."

"You don't know a thing about Darryl." Sabrina realized she was skating perilously close to defending her ex, if only to keep from conceding the rightness of what Spencer was saying.

He laughed brutally and again stroked a finger down Sabrina's neck with devastating effect. "Don't I, Sabrina? Don't I?"

She backed away on rubbery legs, wondering how she had come to be so quickly and hopelessly in the thrall of this man. She couldn't allow him to control her mind, as Darryl once had. The thought of permitting that history to repeat itself filled her with a fear that bordered on phobic.

"Why should I believe a thing you say?" Her voice rose again. She pointed at the cottage rubble. "How do I know you aren't clearing away this mess just to get rid of the evidence?"

"Evidence of what? Arson?"

"There you go," she snapped.

Spencer kicked at a blackened fieldstone. "You really think I have it in for your cat, don't you? If I can't fry him, poison him. That's why you've left him at the clinic all this time, isn't it? You're afraid I'll go *completely* crazy and try to pitch him off the roof of the mansion!" He finished at the top of his lungs, his voice reverberating across the clearing.

"That isn't the least bit funny."

He jabbed a finger in her face. "There *you* go, lady."

He leaned toward her, flushed with anger. Sabrina forced herself to return his unblinking gaze.

"I'm fed up with being called a bastard behind my back and a would-be killer to my face," he said with sudden, deadly calm. "I'm not as incompetent as you must believe. If I wanted to kill someone, I think I could manage it in one try. I'd have made sure you were home—preferably asleep—when I torched the cottage. And I sure as hell wouldn't have put nicotine in the cider tea. The stuff smells like dead fish when it's hot."

"Not if it's covered up with enough cinnamon and cloves to choke a horse," she flung back. Then her jaw dropped. She had told only Conrad about the results of the lab tests on the thermos of cider tea. "How do you know?"

"My mother used to spray nicotine on her roses when I was a kid. It's an old-fashioned remedy for aphids."

Sabrina shook her head, searching his expression. "No. I mean, how do you know the cider tea was spiked with nicotine?"

"I asked the vet, of course."

"Oh, I see. And while you were at it, you just happened to mention to Dr. Neese how easy it would have been for the tea to be *accidentally* contaminated with pesticide."

"I did nothing of the kind," he said. "If that had been my intent, I'd have pointed a finger at the locally pressed cider. It conceivably could have been bottled in a jug that had once been used for mixing nicotine.''

''Then I suppose you've rushed right over and had the jug tested?''

''What makes you think that isn't being done?''

She eyed him sharply. For some reason, she was tempted to give Spencer the benefit of the doubt on that one. But even if he was having the cider jug tested for traces of the pesticide, that didn't necessarily prove anything.

''It would be easy enough to create evidence of a so-called accidental poisoning by contaminating a cider jug with nicotine before having it tested.'' Sabrina glanced at the gutted cottage. ''And not nearly as much work as clearing every trace of this cottage off the estate—maybe to get rid of evidence of something worse.''

Spencer bared his teeth. For a second or two, he looked as if he was about to grab hold of her again. Instead, he raked both hands back through his tousled hair and cursed.

Sabrina noticed the claw marks of her fingernails across the backs of his palms, so much like the ugly wounds that Quetzal had slashed across Spencer's chest. She was reminded of something he had said that evening in the smokehouse. Something about the Marine Corps having taught him *duty...honor...how to kill a man with my bare hands.*

She jammed her fists into her coat pockets as a bone-deep chill stole into her. Was Spencer playing deadly cat-and-mouse games with her mind? Or were she and Quetzal both guilty of fighting for their salvation?

''I just don't know, Spencer,'' she said wearily. ''I don't know if you rescued Quetzal from the fire just to cover for yourself. I don't know if you're trying to kill me, or frighten me off, or just drive me insane to get the book stopped. I don't even know if I'm already out of my mind for thinking those terrible things about you.''

Spencer's anger, too, seemed to have spent itself. The color had left his face. He suddenly looked pale, haggard and years older than his age.

Sabrina took a deep breath and glanced up the hill toward the mansion. "You were right the other day about one thing—my back is against the wall. I'm flat out of alternatives. So I'm going to stick it out here on the estate until you have the legal power to boot me off next week. And between now and then, I'm going to give everything I've got to *The End of the Line,* because it's the end of *my* line."

Spencer turned and squinted straight into the sun for a long moment. "I've never known a more pigheaded woman."

"Stubbornness plays no part in this. It's just the only choice I have."

"So you're going to spend the rest of your time here—"

"Watching my back."

He said nothing more. He didn't even look at her. For a moment, Spencer appeared almost calm. But then something seemed to swell inside his chest. He spat one last curse into the freshening wind and drove a work boot viciously into a charred snag. Before the crumbly chunks of debris had settled, he was striding off across the clearing.

The sun had set by the time Sabrina emerged from the animal clinic in Schuylerville, still plucking cat hairs from her wool skirt. Following his back-to-back near-death experiences with the fire and the poisoning, Quetzal had settled into the clinic's kennel with feline aplomb. Sabrina couldn't make up her mind whether to be relieved that he was adapting so well to being boarded, or disappointed that he found life so bearable without her.

She glanced up at the sky as she climbed into her battered car. Clouds had rolled back in, matching her mood. Low. Gray. Unpromising. She turned up the car heater full blast, and headed back to the Kellogg estate.

The Roadside Café was just that—a squat frame building set close to the side of the highway about a quarter of a mile north of the clinic. A string of ragged plastic pennants fluttered in the wind, marking the edge of the parking lot. Sabrina started to drive on past, too depressed to have an appetite. She changed her mind at the last second and whipped into the lot, scattering pea gravel. Parking in the wash of light around the front door, she got out.

Inside, the café was warm, cheery and unusually empty, the air redolent with the aromas of home-cooked food. The small square tables were covered with plain white paper torn from a big roll behind the lunch counter. The centerpiece of each was a coffee mug containing an assortment of crayons. The Roadside Café took seriously the "family friendly" promo at the bottom of its sign.

Sabrina was just settling in at a table when a matronly bleached blonde in a brown-and-white checked uniform banged through the louvered swinging doors from the kitchen. Her round face lit up when she spotted Sabrina.

"Thought I heard someone come in." She whipped a dog-eared menu from beside the cash register at the end of the lunch counter. "I was back in the storeroom watching the tube."

"Kind of quiet, isn't it, Eloise?"

"Yeah. Just one of those nights. I sent the cook home an hour ago."

Sabrina glanced up from the menu. "I didn't know you managed the café."

Eloise laughed gustily. "Honey, I *own* the danged place. And that old gorilla who slings hash in the kitchen is my dear, sweet husband, Frankie."

"Really?" Sabrina grinned and handed back the menu. "So what do you have on the back burner?"

"You name it. Being my only customer entitles you to special treatment."

"Then bring us each a cup of coffee and surprise me with the rest."

"Sounds like a blue-ribbon winner to me. I always enjoy having a good sit-down with one of my regulars. You've never hung around long enough before."

Eloise bustled around behind the counter to fill an insulated plastic carafe with coffee and hook a finger through the handles of two mugs. She deposited these on the table, along with a handful of powdered-cream packets from an apron pocket, before disappearing into the kitchen.

Sabrina was pouring herself a second cup when the swinging doors flew open again, and Eloise reappeared with a large serving tray. Sabrina glanced at the two heaped platters.

"Ravioli?"

"Yep. This is Italian night." Eloise slid the hot platters onto the table, along with a basket of warm Italian bread. "You should have been here last night. Frankie went Mexican. Whipped up the best batch of Tex-Mex enchies I ever sunk my teeth into. Folks were lined up out the door."

"Sorry I missed that," she murmured, eyeing her platter. One of the reasons she had changed her mind and pulled off at the café was that she hadn't been able to stomach the idea of popping yet another can of ravioli into her microwave. "Your cuisine has amazing ethnic diversity, Eloise."

"For just a dinky little burp in the road? Well, as Frankie likes to say, 'The quickest way to broaden your mind is to let out a notch on your belt.'" Eloise plopped into the chair across from Sabrina, helped herself to a slab of bread, and dug in.

There was a quantum leap between the canned ravioli and what Frankie had left on the back burner of the Roadside Café. The company might have had something to do with it. Eloise's nonstop chatter about everything from the annual tourist count at the General Philip Schuyler House down on Route 4 to the trendy cut of Sabrina's new coat was like a soothing balm. Sabrina ate until she thought she would burst, then smiled happily as the older woman trotted out generous slices of homemade apple crumb pie.

The pleasant respite from the ever-present tension and gloom of the Kellogg estate came to a disheartening end when Eloise poured them each one last cup of coffee and asked, "How's the book coming?"

Sabrina dropped a packet of powdered creamer into her coffee. Eloise handed her a spoon with which to fish it out.

"Didn't mean to startle you."

"That's okay." Sabrina tapped down a fresh packet and tore it open. "I guess I didn't know the project was common knowledge around here."

"Honey, everything that goes on between Glens Falls and Saratoga Springs gets talked about over these tables. Folks have known why you're here since a week after you showed up."

"Is that a fact?" She took a sip of coffee and waited for it to find a place for itself in a stomach already filled to capacity. "What else about me has made it down the grapevine?"

"Let's see. You're divorced, no kids. You lived in that old cottage on the estate until it burned down, so everyone figures you must have moved up into the mansion." Eloise chuckled. "Let me tell you, that's set a few tongues wagging, now that young Spence is living there, too. He must be quite a change, after all those months of putting up with the likes of Jeremiah Kellogg."

"Spencer is . . . different." She put down her mug. "You didn't like Mr. Kellogg?"

"What was there to like?"

"He was once a nominee for the Nobel Peace Prize, Eloise. I'd have thought people around here would have been proud of a native son of that caliber."

Eloise sniffed. "Jeremiah Kellogg always was good at pulling the wool over folks' eyes. Good thing the Nobel committee came to their senses in time and didn't give it to him."

Sabrina looked across the dining room at the fogged windows, wondering how much she had allowed her own perspective to be skewed by that Nobel Prize nomination.

"Eloise, you wouldn't have had a bone to pick with Mr. Kellogg, would you?"

"Personally?" Eloise shook her head. "I never met the man. He was too highfalutin to set foot in a place like this."

"That's his loss."

"Don't get me wrong," Eloise continued. "I'm not down on the whole family. Take young Spence. He did all right for himself, even though he had such a rough row to hoe, being a bastard and all."

"Whoa!"

Eloise flapped a hand. "I know, honey. It isn't nice to call Spence that just because his daddy ran off without marrying Zena."

"Double whoa!" Sabrina sat back and stared at her. "Are you telling me that Spencer Bradley is illegitimate?"

The woman's sharp brown eyes opened wide, then narrowed conspiratorially. "You mean to tell me you didn't know?"

"Had no idea." In retrospect she realized that Conrad Lafever had been perfectly clear about it on the day of Jeremiah Kellogg's funeral. But Sabrina had been too quick to chalk up his comments as profanity. "Mr. Kellogg barely mentioned his sister. While he was alive, I was under the impression that he was never able to come to terms with her premature death."

Eloise laughed and slapped a hand on the table. "You've sure been looking at that all cockeyed, honey. Why, the old coot never forgave Zena for having a love child. You have to understand, that sort of thing was a 'dirty little secret' back in those days. Sometimes, he'd go so far as to pretend his sister was a widow, but we all knew better. Anyway, he made her live in that cottage right there on the estate all those years just so he could look down on her."

"I have it from another source that Zena insisted on living there."

"No fooling?" Eloise seemed to give that some serious thought, which caused Sabrina to put more stock in her assessment of that long ago situation. "Well, that doesn't shake out, when you put it with the way Zena died."

Sabrina's purse was hanging from the back of her chair. She reached back into it without looking, took out her pocket tape recorder, switched it on, and eased it onto the table between them. To her relief, Eloise barely glanced at it.

"Eloise, this might be very important. Can you tell me for certain how Zena died?"

"Sure. She got so blasted depressed over the way she was treated by that high-and-mighty brother of hers that she up and slashed her wrists. Poor Spence was just seventeen, as I recall."

"Zena committed suicide?" Sabrina caught herself shaking her head, and wondered what had triggered the automatic denial.

"Bled to death right there on the cottage floor. I heard that straight from my brother-in-law. Henry worked at the funeral home in those days. He was sent for, to pick up the body."

"Bled to death?" She started as if someone had emptied a bucket of ice water down her back. "That's how Mr. Kellogg died."

"That's right, I forgot. But Jeremiah had that stroke, or accident, or whatever it was."

"Yes...whatever." Sabrina tapped a finger absently against her lips. "First, his mother kills herself. Then Spencer joins the marines and learns how to kill a man with his bare hands."

Eloise nodded. "It's a good thing he didn't learn that before. I heard he went up to the mansion the day Zena was buried. Wanted to give his uncle an earful for driving Zena to kill herself, I suppose, but that dried-up Lafever fellow wouldn't let him in. Spence blew his top. He has kind of a temper, you know."

"Yes . . . I know."

"Well, Spence got his tail run back down the hill with a shotgun. Couple of months later, he turned eighteen, and that was the last any of us set eyes on him until this month."

Bled to death . . . bled to death. Sabrina couldn't get the words to shut off. She could see the thick, dark pools of blood spreading over the cottage floor, dripping down the back staircase at the mansion. *Nothing is as it seems.* And Spencer, his face bloodred with rage. Her dinner tried to back up into her throat.

As Eloise began clearing the table, Sabrina reached out and switched off the tape recorder. After a while, she got up, paid for her dinner, and left. She somehow made it back to the Kellogg estate on automatic pilot, too preoccupied to give driving much conscious attention. She pulled in next to the smokehouse and sat in the car with the engine and heater running. Feeling cold.

Zena Bradley had bled to death. Twenty years later, Jeremiah Kellogg had met a disturbingly similar fate, albeit under very different circumstances. He'd suffered a stroke while carrying a tray of dirty dishes down the back staircase, and had fallen on a piece of broken china.

"What the devil was he doing carrying those dishes downstairs, when he paid Maria to clean up after him?"

Sabrina drummed her fingers on the steering wheel. Zena had bled to death. Jeremiah had bled to death. In her mind's eye, a bloodred trail of rage—Spencer's rage—connected the two.

"Oh, God," she moaned, a wave of sickness washing over her.

Surely, if the birth of an illegitimate son had driven Jeremiah Kellogg to treat his own sister so abysmally, he would never have named Spencer as his sole heir. That didn't make sense—unless Spencer wasn't the whole story.

She shut off the engine, found the key to the smoke-house padlock, and dragged herself out of the car. The cold blanket of darkness closed in around her as she made her way to the door. Sabrina glanced back at the mansion. The top two floors were dark.

A pale light shone in one of Conrad Lafever's windows on the ground floor. She stared at it for a moment, imagining a younger Conrad chasing a raging, adolescent Spencer away with a shotgun.

Sabrina turned away and felt for the padlock. Her fingers were already cold enough to cause her to fumble with the heavy chunk of steel. She tilted it up to insert the key—and realized the shackle hadn't been engaged.

With a confused gasp, she dropped the padlock and stepped back from the door, her heart suddenly racing. She stood there for a moment, panting, her fear focused blindly on the unsecured lock. Then, gradually, her sense of reason began to seep back into control.

The lock wasn't engaged, but the shackle was passed through the hasp on the outside of the door. Therefore it was unreasonable to assume that someone might be lying in wait for her inside. She must have failed to engage the shackle herself, after bringing her laptop computer back to the smokehouse late that afternoon.

She knew she hadn't.

But she must have.

Pocketing her key, Sabrina stepped up to the door and removed the heavy padlock from the hasp, slipping the shackle through the hasp ring in the door frame. Taking hold of the wooden pull, she eased the door open a foot . . . two feet.

Whack.

She threw up her left hand and ducked back as something hissed toward her out of the pitch darkness. Her hand and arm were snapped back, and the momentum spun her hard into the side of the building, knocking the wind from her. Sabrina slumped to the frozen ground, unable to move—unable to breathe—a terrified scream locked inside her.

CHAPTER TWELVE

The pain came slowly at first—a vague stinging sensation across the palm of her hand. Sabrina reflexively closed her fist. An excruciating nerve pain shot up her wrist and forearm, exploding into her elbow and triggering her first lung-filling breath since she opened the smokehouse door.

She grabbed her left hand. It was wet, and something wasn't quite right with the palm. She was bleeding badly, from the feel of it, and now the pain was coming in great galloping thrusts. She gritted her teeth to chop off a whimper and managed to wriggle shakily to her knees.

"Calm down." Even whispered, the words sounded too high-pitched, teetering on the raw edge of panic. Sabrina took a couple of deep breaths and tried to assess her situation. She literally couldn't see her hands in front of her face. Someone could be standing over her right this second, reaching out for her throat with a—

"Stupid!" Holding her bleeding hand out in front of her, she struggled to her feet, took the panic shutters off her eyes, and looked around. There was nothing within spitting distance but her own fear.

Sabrina edged over to the smokehouse door, kicked it wide open, and waited. She wasn't sure for what—maybe a saber-toothed tiger. At any rate, something monstrous and lunging. When nothing came out, she finally gathered up her courage and went in.

For some reason, the hardest part of all was feeling around in the darkness for the light cord. She tried to keep her mind blank as she swept her hand from side to side, side to side, trying not to think of what she might touch besides the dangling brown shoelace. And then, there it was, and she jerked it hard, and the room was flooded with glorious, miraculous light.

She rushed back across the room, retrieved the padlock from the outside hasp ring, pulled the door shut, and slipped the padlock shackle over the inside hasp, dripping blood everywhere. Her coat was already ruined. She sank onto the edge of the braided rug and gently, tremulously eased open her left hand. Dabbing at it with the hem of her coat, she carefully examined her palm, expecting the worst.

The laceration was long and deep, but nowhere near as bad as she had feared. She was bleeding like a stuck hog, but all of her fingers still worked. Sabrina pressed her coat hard against the slash, held it to a count of ten, then took another look. The bleeding had slowed considerably, but when she waggled her fingers experimentally, the flow welled up again as vigorously as ever.

The gash would need stitches, she decided. In time, maybe the worst she would end up with would be a second lifeline on her left hand.

"Jeez, you're a hurting little sucker." Talking to herself made her feel less alone. As her voice grew steadier, so did she.

Sabrina wadded a clean patch of coat hem against her palm, and gently closed her fingers. Her heart was still pumping as if she'd been in a footrace, but she was getting a grip on herself. She was hurt, but not too badly. And she was safe, at least for now.

Then she saw *the thing*. Sabrina actually thought of it as *the thing* at first, because she couldn't immediately figure out what the devil it was.

The elaborate combination of steel cable and wood— vaguely resembling a sprung crossbow—was secured to the backrest of her wooden chair with yards and yards of hemp rope. The seat of the chair itself had been weighted with a heavy flat rock. A thin wire stretched from *the thing* to a small pulley wired to the iron frame of her bunk, then on to a nail near the bottom of the plank door.

The chair had been positioned directly in front of the door. *Aimed at it,* she thought. Sabrina reached out slowly, as if confronting a live snake, and tugged very lightly at the wire. *The thing* attached to the chair danced wildly. She felt some of her hard-won control slip away.

"Booby trap."

The apparatus had been rigged to fire some sort of projectile when the door was pulled open. But she was the only person who had a key to the padlock. Wasn't she? Then again, she had gone off and left the outside padlock's shackle disengaged. Hadn't she? Doubts flew at her from every direction.

Tearing her attention away from the wicked contraption, Sabrina received yet another shock. Her laptop computer, still in its case, sat on the floor next to the vanity where she had left it. But the case had been bashed in with something heavy—most likely the chunk of granite weighing down the chair. The drawers of the vanity hung open, their contents strewn over the stool and floor.

She scrambled over to Quetzal's scratching pole, and tilted it onto its side. The concealed diskettes rattled inside the rectangular wooden tube. That was some small relief. At least the book was still safe.

"Which probably means you're still a target."

Sabrina took another look at her wounded hand. A few inches higher, and she would have had a slashed wrist—just like Zena. Her stomach spasmed. Zena had bled to death. So had her brother, Jeremiah. Had one really been suicide, and the other purely an accident?

More doubts.

Jeremiah might have hated Zena enough to go beyond mental torture. But that didn't make a lot of sense to Sabrina. Not over an accidental pregnancy—not even back then. Still, if Spencer had found out about it, that might have driven him to have murdered his uncle.

"And you. Let's not forget about you," she said under her breath, eyeing the smashed case containing the computer.

A hard knot filled her throat. For a moment, it hurt more than the gash in her hand. She desperately wanted to deny to herself that Spencer had had anything to do with this. But he was the one who wanted the book stopped. He was the one who had brought her the new padlock. Even if he hadn't done the simple thing and kept a key for himself, he was a security systems expert. Surely, getting past a simple padlock would have been a piece of cake for him.

Her hand was aching all the way to her shoulder now. Sabrina was finding it difficult to think through the pain. She needed to get to a doctor, but there was no way she could drive. If she could make it to the mansion, she could call a doctor—and the police. And maybe Noble Wetherbee.

She bit down hard on her lip, eyeing the padlock. Compared to venturing back outside, the smokehouse felt safe, but she knew that was an illusion. Stone walls. Wood ceiling, roof and door. Lots of wood and cloth inside. With a little help, the place would burn every bit as merrily as had the cottage.

Before she could chicken out, Sabrina felt under the thin mattress on the bed for her flashlight, then gave the light cord a decisive tug. After giving her eyes a moment to adjust to the darkness, she quietly removed the padlock and opened the door a crack.

A biting wind shook the denuded tree branches, sounding like dry bones rattling in a basket. Her teeth chattered, although she was too pumped up with adrenaline to feel the cold.

The mansion was still dark, save for the pale glow in Conrad's first-floor window. That small square of light gave Sabrina the courage to step outside. A gust of wind tore the door from her grasp and slammed it back against the outer wall. She cried out. Fumbling madly with the flashlight, she finally got it switched on and swept the surrounding area with the wide beam.

The nearby trees and shrubs whipped wildly in the shifting halo of light—skeletal demons caught in a frenzied devil-dance. The halo began to jig, she was shaking so hard. Sabrina turned and hurried up the stone path toward the back door to the mansion.

A dozen yards along, the outer edge of the flashlight beam glinted off something. With a gasp, she flicked the light in that direction, and stopped as it settled on a familiar daggerlike knife imbedded head high in the trunk of a gnarled oak. Sabrina stared at the letters engraved on the shiny metal plate on the handle. *U.S.M.C.*

Standing directly in front of the knife, she turned and aimed the flashlight straight back at the smokehouse doorway. The beam landed smack on the chair—and *the thing*.

She realized she had stopped shaking. But as she tucked the flashlight under her left arm so she could work the knife blade out of the tree, Sabrina had a strong desire to throw up. First the fire. Then poison. Now a knife. At least the third time hadn't been a charm for Spencer.

The knife came free. She examined the ugly weapon—the kind of blade a pirate might clamp between his yellowed teeth. The kind of blade, she thought, that would make quick work of a jugular vein. The hair on the back of her neck prickled even as she experienced a visceral sense of sorrow.

As she hurried up the path, Sabrina flicked the flashlight beam toward the converted stables. One of the garage-bay doors was open—the bay in which Spencer usually kept his Cherokee. The space was empty. She almost tripped but kept on going.

So you didn't want to be caught on the premises at the time of the crime, she thought. *But if you were that smart, why would you have used your own knife?*

The chilly mudroom smelled of damp boots and musty bags of potatoes. Without turning on a light, Sabrina ducked quietly into the adjoining bathroom just long enough to grab a clean towel off the rack and wrap it around her disabled hand.

She knew the kitchen was empty before she opened the door and peeked inside. There was a stillness to the mansion that seemed to communicate itself through her nerve endings. The comforting aroma of fresh gingerbread permeated the air.

Sabrina crept across the linoleum floor to the door leading into the hallway and stopped, listening. She had a creepy feeling that someone was on the opposite side of the door, also listening, and had to force herself to move on through.

The dark hallway eerily reminded her of a New York subway tunnel with the lights out. She experienced that same unnerving sense of an impending explosion. With the towel wrapped around one hand, the flashlight and knife firmly gripped in the other, she slid an elbow along the wall next to the door and flicked the light switch.

As a series of tarnished brass wall sconces blossomed wan light from small candle-flame bulbs, no ghosts slipped furtively back into the woodwork. She stole a glance down the short stretch of hallway that angled off into deep shadows to her left, and spotted a band of bright light beneath the door to Conrad Lafever's rooms.

She smiled. Her face felt as taut as the banjo string of hysteria that threatened to snap and send her into gales of maniacal laughter. She couldn't let herself give way to that—not quite yet. With one last wary look down the hallway, she turned left and moved toward the safe haven of Conrad's quarters.

At the end of the hallway, she rapped lightly on the paneled door. When there was no response, she repeated the knock and called softly, "Conrad?"

In the utter stillness of the house, surely he couldn't have missed hearing her. She could only conclude that he must have stepped out, perhaps down to the library. Sabrina

knocked one more time, just to be sure, her earlier sense of
near security suddenly feeling dangerously premature.

She worked the knife and flashlight into her coat pocket
and tried the doorknob. The door eased open on silent
hinges. She had never been in Conrad's private rooms. Had
circumstances been different, she wouldn't have dreamed
of entering them uninvited now. But she wasn't about to go
traipsing all over the mansion looking for him. Nor was she
inclined to climb up to the third floor to rouse the Shaws—
not with Spencer Bradley's quarters between here and
there. For all she knew, his car was parked out front, and
he was upstairs now . . . waiting.

No. She would go inside, lock the door if she was lucky
enough to find the key handy, and then make a beeline for
Conrad's phone. He would understand. And if he didn't—
well, at this point, Sabrina didn't much care. Because, she
figured, Conrad Lafever's private quarters were probably
the last place Spencer Bradley would expect to find her.

She opened the door wider, slipped inside, and eased it
shut behind her. The small sitting room was warm and fastidiously, fussily, neat. Perhaps that was what made Conrad appear so out of place.

Sabrina stared at the carefully pressed navy cotton pajamas and the lint-free navy wool robe, both of them with
bright crimson piping that almost exactly matched the color
of his blood.

Suddenly, nothing seemed to work anymore. Not her
mind . . . not her legs . . . not her vocal cords. Nothing at all.

Spencer slumped against the car door, a loose fist on the
steering wheel, his foot heavy on the accelerator. The radio was tuned to an all-night talk show, but he wasn't listening. He felt rotten.

The misery was his own damned fault. He deserved it for
having stayed semitanked on beer all day, trying to drown
the ground swell of grim emotions, which had engulfed him
while he was working to clear away the cottage. Seeking the

easy way out of a bad situation had never been in his nature. He should have known better than to think for one moment that a painless course might be available to him now, of all times.

Sabrina had been right, as hard as that was for him to admit—the work *had* been like lancing a boil. The sad part was that Spencer was no longer sure that scraping the cottage off the face of the earth was going to cure what ailed him. Thanks to Miss Sabrina Glade, he was no longer sure of a lot of things these days.

Slowing just enough to turn in at the front gate of the estate, Spencer thought he glimpsed a rare flicker of winter lightning beyond the top of the hill. As he wound his way up the long driveway, the flashes grew more regular, then distinctly rhythmic. He straightened as they ultimately defined themselves as a collection of rapidly repetitive blips in red and blue.

At the head of the driveway, Spencer pulled in behind a dark Volvo station wagon and two police cars—one belonging to the Saratoga County sheriff's office, and the other to the state police. A young man talking on the two-way radio in the state police cruiser eyed him curiously as Spencer walked past. His gut seized up when he saw a hearse parked under the portico and at least two more police cars in the shadowed driveway beyond it.

The front door of the mansion stood open. Spencer entered, feeling oddly as if he were sleepwalking. A uniformed sheriff's deputy ordered him to stand aside as two men in dark suits pushed a squeaky gurney across the foyer toward the door. An opaque body bag was strapped to the gurney.

Spencer's brain registered only one thing. *Fire, poison, now this.* His knees almost went out from under him.

A moment later, with the gurney outside and the door closed, the hard-eyed deputy turned his attention to Spencer, who identified himself in a voice that had gone cold and flat with shock. The deputy looked mildly surprised.

"What happened?" Spencer asked, staring numbly at the door through which the body bag had just been wheeled.

The deputy responded by motioning for Spencer to follow him. The sound of their footsteps reverberated hollowly in the high-ceilinged foyer. Spencer somehow knew they were headed for the library. A steel band tightened around his chest as they approached the door. The deputy stood aside, waving him through the doorway first.

Spencer hesitated, a terrible sense of dread tightening the band around his chest nearly to the point of suffocation. When he finally entered and glanced around, his knees threatened to collapse for the second time in as many minutes.

Cops. The room was crawling with cops, some in uniform, others in plainclothes with badges hanging from their breast pockets. Additional chairs had been brought in and positioned around the library table. At one end, the Shaws were seated together, holding hands, of all things. Pale and downcast, the brother and sister appeared to be giving a statement to an officer across the table from them, and took no notice of Spencer's arrival.

A quite different tableau was arranged at the other end of the table. A burly officer in a black overcoat sat with one leg propped on the corner of the table, tapping a spiral notebook on the tips of his fingers. An older man in a baggy warm-up suit stood a couple of feet away. Between the two, Spencer caught a glimpse of sable hair. He took a dreamlike step to the side, to get a look between the cop and the warm-up suit. And then, he had to put out a hand to brace himself against the wall.

Sabrina. Alive. She looked as if some rude giant had tossed her bodily into her usual chair at the end of the library table. Her skirt and blouse, besides being in disarray, were streaked with drying blood. One arm was draped over the side of the armrest. Her left hand, heavily bandaged, lay limp in her lap. Her head lolled at an angle against the high backrest, her eyelids were drooping, and she was as white as a sheet. But she was alive.

Spencer pushed himself away from the wall and moved toward her, his actions feeling jerky and uncoordinated. The deputy beat him to the officer in the black overcoat, but he barely noticed. The man in the warm-up suit stepped aside, busying himself with the contents of a black leather medical bag. When he reached the chair, Spencer planted his hands on the wooden arms and leaned close, peering into Sabrina's blanched face as if he was seeking the meaning of the universe.

Obviously she had been drugged. She was so whacked-out that he doubted if she even knew he was standing there. He touched her ghostly cheek.

After what seemed like forever, her eyes shifted, and then focused on him. A frown line deepened between her brows. The tip of her tongue appeared, making the rounds of her parched lips. She seemed to be about to say something, when Spencer felt a firm tap on his shoulder. He glanced around in time to glimpse a spiral notebook gripped in a big-knuckled fist.

"I said we'd better have a talk, Mr. Bradley."

Spencer straightened. The cop's tone had been soft, almost pleasant. Even so, Spencer felt suspect.

"What the hell's happened?" He nodded toward the library door. "Who was on the gurney?"

"We'll get to that, sir. My name's Montroy... Lieutenant Montroy." He held up a plastic evidence bag. "Can you identify this, sir?"

Spencer stared at his old commando knife. The sense of being suspect mushroomed. Instinctively he made every effort not to let it show.

"The knife is mine," he said evenly.

Montroy nodded. "Mr. Bradley, can you explain how *your* knife came to be used in a booby trap that injured Miss Glade, here?"

"Booby trap?" Spencer's hand settled on Sabrina's shoulder. She trembled at his touch and then went limp again. He wondered what she had told the police before going off to the land of fog and gentle mists. "I couldn't begin to explain that."

"Sir, we have reason to believe the same weapon was used earlier to kill—" he consulted his notebook "—Conrad Lafever."

"Connie?" Spencer shook his head in part disbelief, part denial, part sheer awe at the impact of it.

"You know nothing about Mr. Lafever's death, I take it, sir?"

Spencer shook his head again. He wasn't fooled by Montroy's politeness. The beefy investigator's quick, watchful eyes told quite a different story.

"Am I under suspicion, Lieutenant?"

Montroy arched a brow. "Should you be?"

Spencer hated people who answered questions with questions. He caught his fingers digging into Sabrina's shoulder, and relaxed his grip.

"It's no secret that Conrad Lafever wasn't on my Christmas card list," he said.

"No, it isn't."

Spencer glanced down at Sabrina while Montroy made a brief notation in his notebook. "I don't have a clue as to who killed him, Lieutenant. Or why. Or for that matter, where it happened."

"In his sitting room at the back of the house."

"How, uh, bad was it?"

"My guess is you'll have to get rid of the rug. Miss Glade found the body, by the way, right after her own encounter with the booby trap."

A barely audible curse slid past Spencer's lips. He could only imagine what Sabrina must have gone through. It shouldn't have happened that way, he thought. None of this should have happened at all.

After more than half a lifetime of long-distance hate, it already seemed strange that Connie Lafever had been so abruptly and permanently taken out of the picture. Spencer felt something very close to regret.

Montroy flipped a page in the notebook, scanning his notes. "The Shaws had retired early this evening and heard nothing." Another page flipped. "Miss Glade was in Schuylerville when the killing occurred. She returned in time to almost make this a double homicide." He turned to a fresh page. "And what about you, Mr. Bradley? Where were you this evening?"

Spencer glanced at his commando knife, encased in the evidence bag. "Mostly on the road. I went down to Albany to meet a client at the airport." He patted down his coat pockets until he finally retrieved the client's business card and handed it to the cop. "An ice storm in Chicago canceled his flight, so the meeting turned out to be a no-show."

Montroy lowered his chin and peered at Spencer over the tops of nonexistent glasses. Spencer had never been in trouble with the law, but he was beginning to see some pretty ugly writing on the wall.

"Look, Lieutenant, has anyone bothered to contact Noble Wetherbee, down in Albany? He was my late uncle's—"

"I'm aware of who Mr. Wetherbee is, sir. Miss Glade has already tried to call him. The gentleman seems to be out for the evening."

Damned convenient of him, Spencer thought grimly, recalling the time he'd caught Lafever sneaking down to Albany for a clandestine meeting with the old man. He mentally stepped back to take another look at that, trying hard to be objective. Maybe the meeting hadn't been as under-the-counter as it had seemed to him at the time, Spencer decided. Then again, maybe it had been worse. Maybe Connie Lafever had badly underestimated Noble Wetherbee.

Maybe I have, too.

A phone rang in another room and was picked up at once. The fact that no one who lived in the house had done the honors left Spencer with an itchy sense that the situation was more than ever out of his control. Quickly examining his immediate options, he wondered if insisting on calling one of his own attorneys down in Hartford would only further darken the lieutenant's suspicions about him. He decided it might be better to go along as they were for a while longer.

With a heavy sigh, Sabrina slid lower in the chair. Spencer took hold of her good hand. It felt oddly stiff.

"What about Sabrina?" he asked. The blood on her skirt and blouse had dried into patches of dark, stiff rust.

"Her hand required suturing," said the man in the warm-up suit. He hefted the medical bag off the library table and extended a hand to Spencer. "Dr. Blakely."

"Is she going to be all right, Doctor?"

"Perfectly. I've given the young lady some fairly potent analgesics for the pain." He handed Spencer a small envelope containing what felt like three large capsules. "In case she requires more. If she has any problems during the night, I'm in the book."

Spencer watched the doctor stride out of the library, then turned back to Sabrina. Her eyes were wide open—startlingly so. She was staring at the doorway through which the doctor had just departed, her lips twitching fitfully.

"Blake..." she said thickly. "He said...about J.K."

Spencer leaned closer, irritatedly aware that Montroy was hovering over his shoulder.

"That's right," Montroy said. "I heard Blakely say he was Mr. Kellogg's doctor."

"Something..." Sabrina shook her head drunkenly. "Can't remember."

"You two really had your heads together when I got here, before Blakely gave you those pills," Montroy said. "But don't sweat it. It'll probably all come back to you when the medication wears off.''

''Well, she isn't going to sit here until it does,'' Spencer said.

''I'm not finished with you, Mr. Bradley.''

''Give me ten minutes.''

Spencer scooped Sabrina out of the chair. She gave a little gasp, but was too groggy to protest further. He was grateful for that. However, every eye in the room followed them across the library and out the door—and none of them looked friendly.

The gurney bearing Conrad Lafever's body had left black wheel marks across the floor of the foyer. Spencer unconsciously sidestepped them and headed up the staircase. On the second-floor landing, he turned left toward his own rooms without hesitation. Getting the door opened required the juggling of some body parts.

''Didn't need a knife,'' Sabrina whispered.

''What?'' He raised a knee under her legs to free his hand enough to work the doorknob.

''Thought you could kill a man with...with bare hands.''

''In theory, yes.'' The painkiller was causing her to ramble. At least, Spencer hoped that was the case. If not, he didn't much like the direction her thoughts were taking.

Sabrina was watching him, her face not six inches from his. She never took her eyes off his as he kicked the door shut and carried her through to his bedroom.

''How're you doing?'' he asked, throwing back the covers and fluffing a pillow before stretching her out on the big bed.

''Something about adoption.'' She said it with absolute clarity.

Surprised, Spencer switched on the bedside lamp, checked her eyes, and recognized an anomaly when he heard one.

''You're out of it,'' he murmured.

She let him haul off her boots, then the skirt and blouse. Blood had soaked through to her skin. He went into the bathroom and returned with a wet washcloth. With great care, he wiped away darkly crusted streaks of blood on her left thigh, across her abdomen, above the bandaged hand to the elbow.

She never stopped watching him.

Spencer covered her with the sheet and blanket, then traced the tip of a finger across her parched lips. "Thirsty?"

Sabrina nodded.

He took the stained washcloth back to the bathroom and returned with a glass of water. But when he leaned over to help her drink, he found her sound asleep. He watched her for several minutes, monitoring the slow rise and fall of her chest. Then he placed the glass on the nightstand and switched off the lamp, leaving the bathroom light on in case she awoke in the strange place. Backing out of the room, he eased the door silently shut, though he was quite sure he could have slammed it without waking her.

It was just past midnight when the last of the authorities finally cleared out. Orrin and Maria Shaw had retreated to the third floor an hour or so earlier. Spencer stood in the suddenly empty foyer for a few minutes, thinking he could use a drink, but having no desire whatever to go find one.

He felt much the same way about moseying back to Conrad Lafever's quarters. He thought he ought to have a look at the killing ground for himself, but it was an easy thing to put off. Instead, he took the stairs slowly, pulling at his tie, feeling like an old man.

When he reached the end of the second-floor hallway and pushed open the door, the sitting room seemed...different. Spencer didn't turn on the light to see what had changed, because he already knew what it was. He wasn't walking into an empty suite. He shrugged out of his suit coat before quietly opening his bedroom door.

"They didn't arrest you?"

Spencer stopped. The bathroom door was still open, but the light was out. The only illumination was a greenish glow from the light on his electric shaver, recharging on the lavatory counter. It took a moment for his eyes to adjust enough to make her out. Sabrina was sitting at the foot of the bed.

"You're awake." He tossed his coat onto a chair.

"They didn't arrest you," she said again. Her voice sounded clear, alert.

"I'm not sure why," he said. "I have to go in for more questioning in the morning—on their turf. Maybe they'll put me behind bars yet."

"You don't sound worried."

"Too tired. How's the hand?"

"I won't be kneading bread for a while. But that isn't your fault. You didn't burn the cottage, poison my cat, or booby trap my door. I don't think."

"It's nice to know you're so clear about all that." He smiled sardonically. "How did you get so awake?"

"Had to work at it. I took a long shower in your funky bathtub." She plucked at her attire. "I hope you don't mind my borrowing."

Spencer moved closer and saw that she was wearing his old chamois robe. Six extra inches lay puddled around her feet. He sat down beside her at the foot of the bed. Then, with a groan, he leaned forward and rubbed his face.

"You did it, didn't you?" she asked quietly.

He turned his head and looked at her vaguely defined shape in the murky darkness. "You really must think I'm a cold-blooded bastard."

"Don't use that word, Spence—literally, or otherwise." She laid a hand on the bed next to his leg. "And as for the cold-blooded part, well, someone like that wouldn't have done what you did."

Spencer thought about this last statement for a moment. "Are you sure we're on the same wavelength here?"

"I woke up awhile ago, and the first thing I noticed was the paisley pillowcase and the matching trim on the sheets." Her hand moved up to his shoulder. Then, tentatively, to the side of his face. "They match the down comforter on my bed in the smokehouse. And that carved wooden statue on the dresser—you've been to Tahiti. You're the one who brought all those things to the smokehouse while I wasn't looking."

Her fingers lightly brushed his cheek. Spencer felt a stirring. "Was that a crime?" His voice had thickened.

"No. That was not a crime."

He put a hand on the soft chamois material covering her knee. When she neither tensed nor drew away, he traced the outline of her thigh all the way up to her hip. Turning, he fingered back her silky hair and cradled her face in his hands. His thumbs slid over wet cheeks.

"Oh, God, you're crying again," he murmured.

She nodded almost imperceptibly. "I guess that means you're going to make love to me again."

Spencer's breath caught in his throat. His pulse quickened, a dull ache of rising desire swiftly overriding his fatigue.

"Do you always cry when you're made love to?"

"This makes twice." She tilted back her head, closing her eyes as he pressed his warm lips into the soft hollow of her neck beneath her left earlobe. His lips parted, and the tip of his tongue blazed a fiery trail down to her collarbone.

"Why?" he whispered.

"You're—so generous."

"Just because I gave you a comforter?"

"Because you didn't tell me you did."

Spencer's lips began an unhurried circumnavigation of her face, his breath hot on her skin. She floated, awash in sensations, anticipation building to an exquisite pain. With it came the same sense of being in a safe haven that she had experienced that last time he held her in his arms.

"You can be so blasted pigheaded," he said. "I didn't think you'd accept anything if you knew it came directly from me."

"You thought right." The robe seemed to fall away from her shoulders of its own accord. She leaned into him, demanding what he was so ready to give.

Spencer at last pulled her into his arms, crushing her to him, feeling his own heart pounding against her breasts. Her lips were sweet and maddeningly soft. He needed softness now—needed it as much as he had ever needed anything in his life. Spencer plunged into it, body and soul. And Sabrina welcomed him with a murmuring sigh as if her need was as great as his.

Her bandaged hand brushed his chest as he worked out of his shirt. He paused and kissed her fingers one at a time, ever so gently, and by the time he had finished, she had his belt unbuckled. Spencer laid her back on the bed, hardly aware of what he was doing now, every move a reflection of his desire.

Sabrina waited for him to shed the last of his clothes, then pressed her good hand against his shoulder. As though in perfect harmony with her intent, Spencer rolled onto his back, taking her with him. She stretched out the length of his hard body, aware of the surging of his heart and the rise and fall of his powerful chest. She drank deeply from the molten fountain of his mouth, giving back as much as she received, a part of her heart and mind and soul poignantly conscious of the tenderness with which he cradled her bandaged hand.

"It must have been horrible for you," he breathed into her lips, drunk with passion.

She shushed him with a kiss that carried them both beyond just passion, into a state that was almost a reaffirmation of life itself in the face of a death that had struck so close to both of them.

Later, as Sabrina lay across his chest beneath the paisley-trimmed sheet, Spencer stroked her arm and stared into the darkness in a kind of daze. In his mind, their lovemaking in the smokehouse two weeks ago had gradually transformed itself into something akin to a fantasy. There were times, he realized now, when he had actually doubted that any of their passionate embraces had taken place at all in the way he'd remembered.

In contrast, he knew there would never be a moment of doubt in his mind as to what he had just experienced with Sabrina, if only because he already remembered so incredibly little of what had transpired. He couldn't remember having slipped the robe from her shoulders, couldn't even recall having shed his own clothes. None of that seemed to matter.

What did matter was that he had just shared a sense of total physical and emotional harmony with another human being for the first time in his life. And it scared the hell out of him. It laid bare a part of him that, for nearly forty years, he hadn't known existed.

Sabrina stirred, moaning softly in her sleep. He shifted carefully, and she slid off his chest. Spencer gently slipped his pillow under her bandaged hand before easing out of bed.

The cool air of the room quickly dispelled the lingering warmth her body had left on his. He kicked through the clothes scattered on the floor until he found the robe Sabrina had borrowed and slipped into it. She had showered in his bathroom, using his soap. There was none of her own fragrance in the chamois fabric, he noted, disappointed as he went over to stand at the window.

The glass was fogged. He left it that way. There was nothing out there in the bleak winter night that he wanted to see. What he needed to look at—hard and brutally—was inside himself. But he wasn't sure how to go about doing that.

"I thought you'd gone."

Spencer turned at the sound of Sabrina's drowsy voice. "And I thought you were asleep."

"Just dozed for a second." She moved toward the center of the bed to make room as he came and sat on the edge of the mattress.

"How's the hand?" he asked. She hadn't moved it on the pillow.

"Mmm."

"Want another painkiller?"

"What? And waste all this afterglow?"

He chuckled softly and bent to kiss her forehead. They sat without talking for a while, Spencer fingering her silky tresses, while Sabrina lightly traced circles on the back of his hand with a fingernail.

Finally she cleared her throat and took hold of his hand. "I don't want to be afraid of you, Spence."

He didn't know what to say. So in the end, he resorted to the hopelessly inane. "My employees say my bark is worse than my bite."

"When I found that knife—"

It had to come up. "Do you really believe I'd have been stupid enough to use my own knife in a booby trap?"

She was silent for several beats, then, "You kept a key to that padlock you gave me, didn't you?"

In the dark, their silences grew telling. "No. I didn't need one."

"It was bulletproof, but not pickproof?"

"If you have the right tools. And locks are a part of my business."

Sabrina withdrew her hand from his. "You broke into the smokehouse to leave presents?"

"I thought of them as bare necessities, Sabrina. I won't apologize."

"A Tahitian travel poster can hardly be classed as a necessity of life, Spencer. But that's beside the point. I guess it all comes down to trust—and it's hard to trust someone who plays his cards so close to his vest." She sighed. "I guess what I'm trying to say is that the only way to get skeletons out of the family closet is to throw the door wide open.''

''Pretty radical idea. I suppose you've tried it your-self?''

Silence. Then, ''My husband was a psychological sadist who tried his level best to destroy my sanity. He succeeded in alienating every friend I had to my name. The best thing he ever did for me was to run off with a barmaid—the poor woman. I was careful with the check from the insurance company after the cottage fire, so I still have about two hundred bucks in the bank—and a veterinary bill that will run several times that. On a one-to-ten scale, my future prospects don't even register on the meter.''

''Interesting'' was all Spencer could manage.

Silence. ''I don't hear the door to your closet slamming back against the wall.''

''I don't know where to start.''

''Men rarely do.'' Sabrina took his hand again, a disturbing tension creeping into her voice. ''How about if I help you out? You know, crack the door a little.''

Spencer wasn't sure he was ready for this. But she didn't give him a chance to approve or disapprove.

''I know some things about your mother, Spence.'' She squeezed his hand as if reassuring him. ''I know Zena gave birth to you out of wedlock, which is no big deal these days.''

''No—not these days.'' But it had been a very big deal when Spencer was a kid, as he recalled.

''And I know now that she . . . took her own life.''

He frowned into the darkness. ''Know *now*? Then you didn't find out from old Jeremiah?'' Spencer had suspected as much, the confirmation shouldn't have come as such a surprise. ''I guess it just never occurred to me that he and I were guarding the same closet for different reasons.''

Sabrina pulled his hand against her cheek. He felt her eyelashes flutter closed. ''Did you love her, Spence?''

He didn't think he should have had to think about it as long as he did. "Sure."

"Like her?"

"Sometimes."

She suppressed a yawn. The painkiller that Dr. Blakely had given her hours ago was coming back on her, Spencer thought. He stroked her temple with the backs of his fingers, hoping it would put her out.

"That's what gets me, I guess." Her lashes popped back up. "The way I understand it, Zena kind of got in your uncle's face, forced him to let you two live down there in the cottage. I just can't see her as, well, a weak person—like I was."

"She could be as hard as nails with Jeremiah. And with me. Sometimes, it was as if she had a master plan for everything."

"Wetherbee thinks Jeremiah might have been afraid of her," she said.

Spencer frowned into the darkness. "Wetherbee told you that?"

She nodded. "Isn't that strange? Why should a man like that be afraid of his own sister?"

"Because Zena was Zena. And he hated her for it."

"Yes. Zena was wild, like a Kellogg, Wetherbee said. But then she went and slashed her wrists." Sabrina tensed. "God, I'm sorry. I forgot, Spence—we're talking about your mother."

"That's why I don't want her in that book," he said quietly. "It makes such a pathetic picture—the esteemed Jeremiah Kellogg's fallen sister living in that ramshackle cottage. It would be like letting him give her one last kick from the grave. That's all the tabloids will see. But Zena wasn't a pathetic figure at all. Even at her worst, she was more than that."

"And yet she took her own life?"

He grunted and kept stroking her temple, although he'd given up hope of tipping Sabrina over the edge into sleep.

"Okay, we've chased her out of the family closet. Now what?"

She resettled her shoulders on the pillow and sighed restlessly. Spencer could almost sense the workings in her brain overheating.

"You're going to think I'm crazy," she said, "but I think I'm beginning to see a pattern."

"I'll try to keep an open mind. Fire away."

"Your mother bled to death. After his stroke, after his fall down the stairs, your uncle ended up bleeding to death. Tonight, someone tried to do me in with a knife. And from the looks of his... remains, I wouldn't be surprised if Conrad died of blood loss. Spencer, what if Jeremiah's death wasn't an accident? And what if your mother's was no suicide?"

His mind took fully half a minute to swim up to the surface. When it finally did, Spencer realized he had stopped breathing and sucked in a great gulp of air.

Her hand groped for his again. But he got up and returned to the window, staring blindly at the misted glass, feeling sick at heart. The pieces appeared to fit perfectly. Spencer wondered how Sabrina had managed to make all those connections—and worried about how much she'd had to stretch her imagination to keep him out of the equation. Assuming that she had.

"Spencer, would you mind holding me for a while?"

"Mind?" He turned, eyeing the dark hulk of the four-poster speculatively. She was lost in the shadows, except for the pale splash of white bandage resting on the dark paisley pillow. "Of course, I won't mind. But let me get you another painkiller first."

Spencer went around to the other side of the bed. As he raked the floor for his suit coat, then fished for the small packet of capsules in the pocket, his mind was working furiously.

CHAPTER THIRTEEN

Sabrina awoke several times before she finally managed to pry her eyelids open. A bright shaft of sunlight glared through a window across the room, making her eyes water. She squinted at it groggily, her tongue feeling like a thick wad of cotton.

All right, my friend, she thought sluggishly, *where are you...and when will you know it?*

Her left hand was throbbing like a son of a gun. She raised it in front of her face. Stared blank-faced at the bandage. *Click.* All the pieces dropped neatly into place.

She checked the other half of the bed to her right. Empty. Disappointment rushed in. The last thing she remembered about last night was lying in Spencer Bradley's arms. It would have been nice to have awakened in the same secure embrace and to have lingered for just a little while before innocence fled from the cold light of day like an emotional vampire.

"Maybe he wouldn't find it so special," she murmured, clawing tangled hair out of her eyes.

Spencer had left his robe thrown across the foot of the bed. Sabrina pulled it on, slid off the high bed, and padded barefoot to the bathroom. She avoided the mirror over the lavatory until after she gave her face a quick one-handed rinse, finger brushed her teeth with some of Spencer's toothpaste, and made good use of his comb.

Even then, her first look at herself was something of a shock. Her face was so pale that the creases around her nostrils appeared blue.

"Terrific," she murmured. "When he woke up and got a look at you in broad daylight, he must've thought he'd gone to bed with a corpse."

The thought—joining as it did with her memory of the last time she had set eyes on Conrad Lafever—sent an icy chill through Sabrina. She remembered exactly the heft and perfect balance of Spencer's knife, the way the double-edged blade had been honed to razorlike sharpness.

When she had discovered last night that Spencer was the one who'd been stealthily furnishing the smokehouse, Sabrina had been deeply moved by his kindness. Now she feared that her gratitude might be symptomatic of a return to her old mind-set—her fatal weakness for considerate men. *Darryl redux.*

A haunted expression spread across her face and she couldn't seem to get rid of it. She thought of the knife and the horror in the room behind the pantry.

"Oh, Conrad," she moaned, quickly turning away from the mirror before the tears brimming in her eyes had a chance to spill down her cheeks.

The bloodied skirt and blouse she had worn yesterday were gone. In their place, someone had laid out a full set of clean clothes on a chair in the bedroom. Jeans, a heavy turtlenecked sweater, socks for her boots. Everything she needed, right down to the underwear.

A folded slip of paper protruded from the pocket of the jeans. She pulled it out and opened it.

You make me sorry I'm not a poet. Spence

A pained smile forced its way onto her lips. Doubt couldn't expunge what she had come to feel for Spencer. Having spent the night in his arms, she wasn't sure she could ever fear him again. Bringing herself to trust him was the hard part. She still couldn't decide if that inability to trust was a weakness within her, or a strength.

With only the use of one hand, it took forever for her to pull the snug almost-new jeans up over her hips and get them buttoned. By the time she stepped out into the second-floor hallway, the downstairs clock was tolling the hour of nine and her bad hand was screaming.

She descended the stairs slowly, listening. After last evening's deadly violence and turmoil, the mansion seemed preternaturally quiet. Sabrina crossed the foyer and moved down the shadowed hallway toward the kitchen at the back.

At the intersection with the short corridor leading to Conrad's rooms, she couldn't help glancing to the right. His door stood open. From inside came sounds of movement and the distinctive squish of a sponge mop being squeezed over a bucket of water. With a shudder, Sabrina moved on to the kitchen, leaving Maria to her grisly work.

Upstairs in Spencer's bathroom, she had pocketed the envelope of painkilling capsules that he'd left on a shelf over the lavatory. She filled a glass with tap water and took out the envelope. There were two capsules left. Sabrina shook one out and eyed it ambivalently. Her hand hurt fiercely but she knew the drug would have her sound asleep again within an hour.

She had left the kitchen door to the hallway open. The disturbing splashing, squishing noises were still coming from Conrad's rooms beyond the pantry. *Mopping up blood.* Sabrina had a quick vision of Conrad propped in a chair, his head—

"Jeez!" She shook off the image.

No, she decided, she definitely did not want to go back to sleep. Sleep was the ultimate state of vulnerability.

Carefully breaking the seal and pulling the two ends of the capsule apart, she leaned over the sink and emptied half the contents down the drain. Then she fitted the capsule back together, popped the remaining painkiller into her mouth, and washed it down with water.

Before pocketing the last pain capsule, Sabrina ran her thumbnail back and forth under the name printed on the envelope. Theodore Blakely, M.D. Blakely. The name triggered hazy flashes of memory.

While suturing her hand last night, Blakely had done a creditable job of distracting her attention from the operation with a more or less constant stream of gab. All things considered, she seemed to recall having done a fairly respectable job herself of pumping the doctor for anecdotes about Jeremiah Kellogg—the kind of human interest trivia that Blakely could draw upon without violating the rules of doctor-patient confidentiality. Unfortunately, Sabrina had been too traumatized to even think of trotting out her tape recorder. So most of what Blakely had said probably would remain lost in the fog forever.

She did vaguely recall having brought Spencer and Zena into the conversation. And maybe that was when Blakely had said something about adoption. She rubbed her temple, straining to remember. Could he have told her that Spencer wasn't Zena's illegitimate son? That she had *adopted* him?

Granted, her research had only managed to scratch the surface where Zena and Spencer were concerned. But nothing in it so far had indicated that Spencer might have been adopted. Still, she found the possibility discomfiting. If Spencer wasn't actually descended from the Kellogg line—and Zena had somehow kept that from her brother's knowledge—it seemed likely to her that the traditional bloodline clause in Jeremiah Kellogg's will would block Spencer from inheriting the family fortune.

"Murder motive number ten thousand eight hundred and forty-two," she said dully.

Sabrina leaned against the drain board, cradling her bad hand, feeling guilty for trying so hard to keep her mind off blood. Conrad had died horribly just a dozen or so hours ago. But as horrifying as that was to her now, Sabrina had a feeling that she still had not yet felt its full impact. Before she could even begin to, she felt a mild buzz as the painkiller found its way into her bloodstream.

The sharp throbbing in her hand dropped back to a tolerable level. That was good. But her thought processes lost what cogency they'd had just a moment earlier, like a gear wheel intermittently slipping from its cogs, and that was bad. She left the kitchen and the mansion through the mudroom, hoping the cold outdoor air would clear her head.

The slate-colored winter sky was almost cloudless. Last night's blustery wind had gentled to a steady breeze backing around to the southeast. With the hulking walls of the mansion serving as a windbreak, the sunshine felt deceptively warm.

Feathery drifts of ice crystals and snow had collected between the flat stones of the path leading down to the smokehouse. Passing the unkempt privet, she automatically looked toward the converted stable. The garage bay where Spencer kept his car was empty again. Sabrina dimly recalled his mentioning last night that he had to undergo further questioning by the police concerning Conrad's murder. Frowning, wondering if he would succeed in dodging the arrest bullet one more time, she moved on down the path.

The smokehouse door stood open. After the seemingly endless locks and secrets of the past months, the sudden profusion of open doors this morning was actually making Sabrina uncomfortable. She crept up and looked inside.

"What are you doing in there, Mr. Shaw?"

The old man dropped the slab of granite he had just lifted off the wooden chair in the center of the room. It hit the floor with a loud crack, chipping a fist-size chunk out of the concrete. Shaw looked at her. Sabrina looked at the granite.

"It's a good thing you didn't drop that on your foot," she said, then repeated, "what are you doing in there?"

"Getting rid of this." Sullenly he waved a hand at the chair, still draped in the tangled remains of the booby trap.

"Shouldn't you leave that for the police?" She noticed that Shaw had already removed the elaborate trip wire.

"Bradley said they took plenty of pictures. Said I was to get rid of this. Burn it."

He squatted down and lifted the granite. Sabrina stepped aside. Shaw leaned out the door and heaved it as far as he could. The slab went about three feet before thudding onto the frozen ground.

"Maybe we should talk to Mr. Wetherbee before you disturb anything else," she said.

"Orders is orders." Shaw spat out the door in the general direction of the rock. "And Wetherbee ain't running this show."

Sabrina frowned again, confused now. Dammit, her mind wasn't processing all of this. She sensed that something was badly amiss, but like a half-remembered dream, she couldn't seem to pull it all together.

"Mr. Wetherbee is the executor of the will," she said. *And he was visiting the estate the evening that Jeremiah Kellogg had his accident.*

Shaw smiled. It was the first time Sabrina had ever seen him do that. He didn't appear to be very good at it.

"There's some that say he's got more than just a lawyer's interest in how things turn out." Shaw wiped his hands on the front of his insulated coveralls and picked up the chair with its sprung booby trap.

"Wait, wait, wait." Sabrina held up a hand, trying to skim one clear thought from the surface of the painkiller-induced soup that her mind had become. "Are you saying Mr. Wetherbee doesn't want Spencer Bradley to inherit—"

Shaw spat out the door again. *Wrong turn,* Sabrina thought.

"Oh. Mr. Wetherbee *does* want Spencer to inherit it all." She took a deep breath of cold air, hoping for its restorative powers, wishing she'd just gritted her teeth and put up with the pain. She couldn't *think.* "Well, he was Mr. Kellogg's attorney. Isn't it natural for Mr. Wetherbee to want what his client wanted?"

Shaw stood in the doorway with the wooden chair held in front of him, one eye almost shut as he scowled up at the mansion. There was something important she needed to ask him. Sabrina felt it in the deep recesses of her mind, but couldn't quite make it surface.

"What is it, Mr. Shaw?" she asked softly. "Help me out here. Please."

The handyman sucked on an eyetooth for a moment. "Zena never married her pup's sire," he said finally.

"I know." Sabrina couldn't help noticing how Shaw had reduced the statement to kennel terms.

"There's some that say the pup looks a lot like Noble Wetherbee."

"Whoa!" Sabrina wasn't sure if she'd said it out loud. But she had darn well thought it.

She stared at Orrin Shaw. He took no notice. Hefting the chair higher in his arms, he turned his back to her and lumbered off in the direction of the garage.

As she watched him walk away, Sabrina realized she was slowly shaking her head. The serpentine road of discovery had just taken one too many hairpin twists, she thought. The jarring concept of Noble Wetherbee as Spencer Bradley's father simply would not compute.

She gazed up at the mansion. The high, dark walls looked every bit as forbidding in brilliant sunshine as they did in gloom. Her skin crawled and then flushed. She suddenly felt like a house divided.

In Conrad Lafever's sitting room last evening, she had viewed what she fully expected to be the single most horrifying sight of her lifetime. But just hours later, she had gone on to experience moments of pure ecstasy interspersed with periods of incomparable peace—all of them in a room on the second floor—in Spencer Bradley's arms. Were terror and passion such closely related emotions that they could coexist in the same night?

Sabrina rubbed her temples, trying to focus on the central issue—trying, for God's sake, just to *find* it. Noble

Wetherbee, she thought. The aged attorney had been at the estate, but had gone out to look for something in his car, when Jeremiah Kellogg had had his fatal accident. How convenient, as Spencer would say. Wetherbee had stated he was in Miami when Zena died. And he had been with Sabrina when the cottage burned. And last night, she'd been unable to reach Wetherbee—the second phone call she'd made after finding Conrad's body.

She was sure he would have a perfectly good alibi for last night, as well. But when did an alibi, or a collection of them, become just a shade too pat?

Before Sabrina could follow through with that speculation, her thought processes slipped again, freewheeling for a minute or so before she managed to get them back in gear. But then she couldn't quite find the trail she had been following.

It had something to do with Noble Wetherbee. Yes. Did he really bear a physical resemblance to Spencer? She had never had that impression, not even during the only time she had seen the two men together at Jeremiah Kellogg's funeral. But that was the last thing she would have been looking for.

She glanced up at the mansion again, at the windows on the second floor, and sighed. What she needed between herself and Spencer now was time and distance. Time to sort out her feelings, and enough distance to be assured that her mind was her own. That her delicate emotional instrumentation wasn't being thrown off by the magnetic field that seemed to surround him.

She was so tired. Too tired to think of the book anymore. Too tired to fight reality. It was over. She had reached the end of the line.

The sun was hurting her eyes, making them tear up. Making her chin quiver. Making her breath catch. "One too many twists," she whispered. "Time to get off the race track while you still can."

Sabrina wasn't completely finished. She would go down to Albany that morning and arrange for a meeting with Noble Wetherbee, if only to satisfy her own curiosity. But she would stop in Schuylerville along the way to pick up Quetzal. She hoped Dr. Neese would agree to some kind of payment plan for the bill. Because she wouldn't be coming back.

Her car was backed up in front of the door to the smokehouse, the trunk lid gaping. All her earthly belongings had filled the vehicle to the roof when Sabrina had arrived at the Kellogg estate early last fall. As she loaded her meager assets now, just about everything stowed easily in the none-too-spacious trunk. *The End of the Line* was supposed to have been her financial salvation, she thought morosely. As it turned out, she had lost considerable ground and gained absolutely nothing.

She kept casting wary glances toward the empty bay in the garage. Spencer still hadn't returned. Sabrina hoped to be long gone before he did.

Stepping back into the smokehouse, she took one final look around to make sure she hadn't missed anything. Her gaze drifted from the braided rug, to the paisley comforter, to the Tahitian travel poster with its two sunbathers entwined on the beach. Just looking at it hurt.

She was tempted to roll up the poster and take it with her. As bad as this place had been, a part of her wanted to stay almost as badly as she wanted to flee. She didn't need a reminder of the all-too-brief moments of pleasure she had known here. If she took the sensuous poster, the feeling that she was being torn in two might never go away.

Something on the floor, just peeking from under the rug, caught her eye. Sabrina toed aside the rug and picked up the key to the smokehouse padlock. She lightly tapped her jeans pocket and felt the outline of her other key. The one in her hand had to be the key that Conrad had returned to her yesterday morning. It must have fallen from her coat pocket after her encounter with the booby trap last night.

She stood rubbing it between her fingers, recalling how strangely eager Conrad had been to return it to her. A frown line deepened between her shadowed eyes. The key felt oily. She remembered that, too.

Sabrina raised it to her nose. It smelled faintly like—what?—clay. Maybe clay. That was odd. She examined it more closely. She would need a magnifying glass to be sure, but she thought she could see faint traces of a greenish substance in the grooves. Green clay?

She sat staring at it for a moment. She had seen enough spy movies to know you could make a copy of a key if you had a clay impression. It took her sluggish brain awhile to take the next step. Maybe Conrad had been anxious for her to have the key back because he suspected someone had made an impression of it, and he wanted to give her a chance to notice that herself.

Of course. Someone had to have gotten into the smoke-house to rig the booby trap. She had locked the padlock that night before she left. She *had*. So, why wouldn't Conrad have just told her what he suspected?

It wouldn't have been the first time he'd left her in the dark. There had been that little omission about the Bradleys having lived down in the cottage for seventeen years. But he'd deceived her then out of loyalty to Jeremiah Kellogg. Kellogg was dead. Whom would Conrad have been protecting as recently as yesterday? Certainly not Spencer whom he despised. Then who else? And why?

There was only one person toward whom she could imagine Conrad Lafever might have felt a sense of loyalty-by-association. That was Jeremiah Kellogg's longtime attorney, Noble Wetherbee. Conrad and Wetherbee had shared secrets—of that she was certain. Only now, they weren't shared any longer. They belonged entirely to Wetherbee, lock, stock, and barrel.

The flywheel spun loose again. Sabrina rubbed her temples furiously. She only had to take this one step further. But dammit, her mind wouldn't *work!*

Rest. If only she had time, distance, and some rest, she'd be able to think.

Pocketing the key, she knelt beside Quetzal's scratching pole, jiggled the base free, and retrieved the backup disks she had concealed there. Then she reset the base and looped an arm around the post.

Maria Shaw was waiting next to Sabrina's car, bundled in a warm coat, eyeing the clothes piled loosely in the trunk. The housekeeper looked up as Sabrina emerged from the smokehouse, her attention shifting to the scratching pole and the stack of disks clutched in Sabrina's good hand.

"You're leaving." There was an element of surprise in Maria's tone, though it wasn't duplicated in her expression.

Sabrina nodded. She stowed the scratching pole in the space she had left for it in the trunk, alongside her precious photo album, and slammed the lid. Her purse was on the front passenger seat. She went around, leaned in through the open window, and tucked the disks in next to her checkbook.

Her eyes blurred slightly out of focus, and a wave of dizziness seized her as she straightened. She grabbed hold of the window frame, waiting for it to pass, once again wishing she hadn't taken the blasted painkiller. Even in its diminished form, the drug was going to make her an unsafe driver.

"Let me do something for you."

Sabrina turned, nonplussed by Maria Shaw's totally unexpected offer. The old woman moved closer and placed a liver-spotted hand on her arm. Sabrina suppressed an instinctive urge to pull away from her, telling herself the feeling was irrational. Maria was only trying to be kind.

"I don't want you to go away thinking badly of us," Maria said, patting Sabrina's sleeve. "Let me fix you a good breakfast."

"I, um, don't have much of an appetite, Maria." She raised her bandaged hand. "My stomach is upset because of the pain medication."

"That's because you took it on an empty stomach. You'll feel better once you start eating." Maria tugged on her arm. "You'll see."

Sabrina glanced toward the empty bay in the garage. She was eager to be gone before Spencer returned, whenever that might be. But her reflexes were still impaired by the painkiller. A cup of coffee might help keep her alert. She wouldn't help her situation if she ended up driving into a ditch within sight of the estate.

"You win. But just a bite." She smiled, loath to discourage the old woman's efforts to be civil. Maria really had been trying lately. "I do have to get on the road."

Maria simply nodded. But as Sabrina shouldered her purse and they headed up the stone walkway to the mansion, she sensed that the housekeeper was pleased by the capitulation.

The kitchen smelled of coffee. A thick slice of ham sizzled in a skillet on the back burner of the stove. The oven light was on, and Sabrina could see what appeared to be homemade baking-powder biscuits browning on the rack. Her stomach rumbled. Sabrina found Maria's all-out effort somehow saddening.

"I'll fix you an omelet." Maria swapped her coat for an apron. "That'll set nicely on a bad stomach."

Sabrina looped the strap of her purse over the back of a chair at the kitchen table and sat down, a bit overwhelmed by the woman's sudden display of nurturing domesticity. The old saying about a leopard never changing its spots definitely didn't seem to apply here. But on a certain level, Sabrina understood what had transpired. In the wake of

Conrad Lafever's brutal murder last evening, she, too, had been experiencing that nothing-will-ever-be-the-same-again feeling.

Maria dumped beaten eggs into a copper skillet on the range. After pouring a big mug of coffee for Sabrina, she picked up a bowl from the counter and tilted it over the sink to drain liquid from its contents.

"You like mushrooms, don't you?" she asked.

Sabrina's attention was distracted by thudding, scraping sounds coming from beyond the door to the basement. By the time she belatedly latched on to the question and opened her mouth to protest, Maria had already upended the bowl over the skillet. Sliced mushrooms plopped onto the simmering omelet.

Sabrina sampled the coffee. It was hot, but a little on the weak side. Fine. She had lost her taste for strong, spicy drinks.

Minutes later, Sabrina was staring at a heated platter heaped with sufficient biscuits, eggs and ham to feed a lumberjack. *No way,* she thought. To her chagrin, Maria poured herself a mug of coffee and settled onto the chair across the table to watch.

"This is awfully sweet of you, Maria," she said, knowing she couldn't make a dent in it, but feeling obligated now to give it her best shot.

She concentrated on the omelet, preparing herself for a long haul. Maria had been right—her stomach did find the eggs acceptable. And the mushrooms weren't all that bad, once she got used to them. But after just a few bites, she quickly discovered that she could think—or she could eat. But thanks to the mind-dulling effects of the painkiller, she was temporarily lacking in the mental agility required to do both at the same time.

She ate. And gradually the movement of her fork from platter to mouth took up an unconscious rhythm with the faint thudding, scraping sounds beyond the basement door. Sounds that Maria didn't seem to notice.

Time slipped away, becoming less and less of a consideration. Sabrina continued her dogged nibbling, pausing frequently to slug down more coffee, hoping the caffeine would somehow gain the upper hand. By her second mug of coffee, however, that strategy had begun to backfire. Instead of becoming increasingly alert, she began to feel sluggish, light-headed and slightly nauseated.

She had alternated the coffee with a surprising amount of the mushroom omelet before she realized Maria had been talking to her, possibly for some time. Sabrina paused with her mug raised halfway to her mouth, aware that an alarm had gone off somewhere in her fogbound consciousness.

"What did you say?" she asked.

Maria sat with her bony hands folded on the table, gazing at Sabrina with equanimity. "You came back earlier than expected last night—almost caught Orrin booby-trapping the smokehouse door. Messed up his aiming of the knife."

Sabrina slowly returned the mug to the table. Her heart lurched in her chest, skipping a beat. Her hands and feet felt cold, but she realized she was perspiring profusely. Fear, she thought, meeting Maria's steady, unblinking gaze. In an oddly distant sort of way, Sabrina was scared to death. She mindlessly forked another bite of omelet into her mouth.

"We warned Jeremiah you'd nose around until you found out he was adopted." Maria spoke evenly as though she was merely commenting on the weather.

The fork slipped from Sabrina's hand and clattered to the floor. A bead of sweat ran swiftly down the side of her face to her jaw. She could feel her heart beating, but slowly...so slowly.

Serious wrong turn, she thought, dragging her gaze down to the platter. She had made a bad mistake with the omelet—the last of a long line of fatal errors, dating all the way back to the day she had agreed to ghostwrite Jeremiah Kellogg's memoirs. And that didn't even include Darryl.

"Mr. Kellogg was adopted?" she heard herself ask. *Not Spencer. Jeremiah.*

Maria interrupted something she'd been saying, and nodded. "Old Layton always made out that Jeremiah was his blood son, on account of that clause in the Kellogg will. But he never gave up hope. Remarried four more times, trying for the real thing, but only came up with Zena. It took her to have a real Kellogg."

Another bead of sweat stole down the side of Sabrina's face. Her mind had begun to clear, possibly from the shock of what she was hearing. But something else was going badly wrong. Something to do with her body.

Her hand seemed to find its way back into her purse of its own accord, her fingers finding and curling around the pocket recorder. "Layton Kellogg didn't have a direct biological male descendant?"

Maria laughed without smiling, sending a chill racing up Sabrina's spine. "Close to being sterile as a mule. We always thought it was fitting, in a way, that Layton's adopted son turned out to be just like him in that."

"How do you know?"

Maria took a biscuit from Sabrina's platter, and sat crumbling it on the table. "Jeremiah never could manage a child of his own. That's why he hated Zena so. She up and popped out that bastard of hers by *accident.*"

Sabrina concentrated on easing the tape recorder out of her purse onto her lap, telling herself that she was doing this for Spencer. She had to leave him something, if it was the last thing she did in this life. Some small something to atone for her distrust of him. Her thumb searched along the row of controls. She cleared her throat to cover the faint clicking sound as she compressed the Play/Record buttons.

"Maria, did Jeremiah kill his sister?"

The housekeeper sneered. Sabrina forgot about the recorder for a moment, forgot about the alarming distress signals arising within her own body, and riveted on that profoundly disturbing expression.

"He didn't have the nerve." Maria put down the biscuit, dusted the crumbs from her hands, and peered hard at Sabrina. "But somebody had to do it, after Zena began to suspect Jeremiah wasn't a real Kellogg."

Sabrina had trouble swallowing. "How do you suppose she got wind of that?"

Maria pressed one finger to a shallow depression in her chin. "Zena finally noticed that Jeremiah, Orrin and I all had the same cleft. Can you imagine, after all those years? Then she started picking up on other things. You know, sometimes brothers and sisters don't look so much alike when they're young. But as they get older, the bone structure starts showing through."

"Brother and..."

Jeremiah Kellogg had been a sibling of the Shaws? Sabrina's jaw went slack. She desperately wanted to check the tape, to make sure the recorder was working properly. But she dared not draw attention to it by dropping her gaze to her lap.

"Zena wasn't dumb. Once she had it figured out, she threatened to see a lawyer about getting her and her kid a share of the estate—maybe even get Jeremiah robbed of his inheritance altogether. There's this clause in the Kellogg will, you know."

Sabrina leaned forward, trying to roll with a sudden muscle spasm. Sweat was pouring out of her, drenching her jeans and sweater. "But...Mr. Kellogg was your... *brother?*"

Maria nodded. "Didn't know it until Orrin and I looked him up right after he got out of college." Her withered lips twitched sourly. "Didn't seem pleased to see us at all. We got suspicious when Jeremiah right away started making us all kinds of offers, saying he'd look out for us if we'd just keep it quiet. Finally got him to own up about that inheritance clause. You see, he was adopted off the black mar-

ket—old Layton and his first wife never told a living soul.
If the lawyers had found out he wasn't a real Kellogg, they
might have taken everything away.''

"So...*you* killed Zena.''

"Me and Orrin. Had to. She'd have ruined it all for us.''

"You made it look like a suicide. And Mr. Kellogg...
went along.''

Maria's fingers stirred through the crumbs on the table,
her thin lips curling downward. *Wrong turn,* Sabrina
thought.

She stared at the bandage on her hand. A thin line of
blood had seeped through across the palm. Despite her
pain, despite her wrenching sickness, Sabrina felt her own
anger rising.

"He couldn't stomach it," Maria said. "He curled up
like a pill bug...let the guilt fester inside.''

Sabrina lowered her forehead onto her arm. God, she
was scared. She wanted to get up and make a try for the
door. But she would just be wasting what little strength she
had left for no gain. At least if she bided her time for a few
precious minutes more, she might get enough on tape to
help Spencer.

"That's what the book was all about." She raised her
head as the thought came to her with the clarity of a crystal bell. Jeremiah Kellogg had never intended the book as
a self-tribute to his stellar diplomatic achievements. The
private-school application for his stillborn son, so conve-
niently left in that last carton of documents, had been a
kind of cornerstone. *The End of the Line* was going to end
up as a confession. "So you killed your own brother...just
so you could hide the other killing?''

"Had to.''

"He wasn't carrying a tray downstairs.''

"No.''

"You pushed him?''

"Orrin did.''

Being pushed down a flight of stairs by your own brother would be enough to give about any old man a stroke, Sabrina thought. Tears were streaming down her cheeks, but she wasn't crying. She was too weak. She could feel her heart struggling for each beat.

"So Orrin broke the dishes. Made it look like a fall. Slit Kellogg's jugular."

"Well, I did that part."

"And you killed Conrad," Sabrina stated.

"Had to," Maria responded.

A wave of searing nausea lifted Sabrina's stomach into her throat. She fought it down, clinging to the tape recorder as if it were a life preserver. And it was . . . for Spencer. With the tape, he couldn't be accused of having the blood of two men on his hands.

"Now me." Sabrina closed her eyes.

This was some kind of macabre coffee klatch. Tell her everything, because blind little Sabrina Glade isn't going to be around much longer to tell tales. She got scared of all the wrong people, and then swallowed her poison like a good girl.

So sick. So full of pain. Every square inch of her skin was drenched with sweat.

"What are you waiting for?" Sabrina whispered.

"Waiting for Orrin to finish."

Sabrina realized the thudding, scratching sounds coming from beyond the basement door had stopped. She heard heavy footsteps climbing the stairs. Then the door behind her opened and closed.

She turned slowly. Orrin Shaw stood sucking his eyetooth. For a moment, she thought he was going to haul off and spit on the floor. He was holding a roll of dirty green canvas tarp.

"You aren't gonna *die*," he said, glowering at Sabrina. "You're just gonna turn up permanently missing. And maybe some of your hair will be found in the back of Bradley's car."

Without taking her bleary eyes off him, Sabrina doubled over with another spasm. As it slowly passed, she managed to ease the tape recorder into the sweat-soaked waistband of her jeans and cover it with her sweater. Her skin was slick with sweat and she prayed that the recorder wouldn't slip out.

Her hands and feet were so cold. Everything seemed to have slowed down to three-quarter time. She propped both arms on the table, her head drooping over the platter. The smell of fried ham wafting into her face triggered another staggering wave of nausea.

When it passed, Sabrina looked up, first at Maria, then at Orrin. "The mushrooms?"

Maria nodded. "Dried panthers. Tried them on Jeremiah, but he caught on real quick. After that, he wouldn't eat anything that didn't come fresh out of a can."

"You poisoned . . . my cat, damn you."

"Tried the nicotine on Bradley, too. Just a little poison to slow him down, you know. But he started eating out."

And he brought me cans of food and a microwave oven, Sabrina thought. Maybe he hadn't known for sure. Maybe he'd thought she wouldn't believe him if he told her about his suspicions. And maybe he'd have been right.

"I'm going to die." She said it with a curious lack of fear. Maria reached out and touched her hand. Sabrina pulled away in revulsion. "You're psycho. Both of you."

Orrin Shaw looked at his harpy-faced sister. And then, he shook out the tarp.

CHAPTER FOURTEEN

Spencer skidded the Cherokee to a stop in front of the garage, jerked the key from the ignition, and started to hop out. But on a second thought, he leaned over, unlocked the glove compartment, and grabbed the licensed .38 that he kept there.

He eyed the weapon for a few quick seconds, but long enough to wonder if he could be misreading this whole situation. Then he clipped the holster to the back of his belt under his coat and slid out of the vehicle. He hadn't meant to be gone so long. Considering what he'd found out down in Albany that morning, he wished to hell he hadn't left at all.

Pocketing his car keys, he hurried up the stone walkway that led from the garage around to the back entrance to the mansion. He had a bad feeling—a very bad feeling. He could be wrong. Sabrina could be still sound asleep in his bed where he had left her.

Sound asleep.

Not dead.

The heat of anger was in him again. Somebody should have told him about all this a long time ago. He shouldn't have had to beard Noble Wetherbee in his den, stupidly accuse him of murder, then pull the real story out of him one sordid fragment at a time.

After a totally senseless shouting match that had left both of them wrung out, the old man had finally spilled the truth about Jeremiah Kellogg's origins. Wetherbee claimed to have known about the adoption for only the past several months, Jeremiah having confided in his longtime attorney at about the same time he had signed the contract with Sampson Books. Still, Wetherbee hadn't found out about the critical Shaw connection until early this very morning.

"Connie—Conrad, I'll owe you that one for the rest of my life," Spencer muttered, breaking into a trot.

The walkway turned up a steep grade toward the mudroom. Spencer automatically glanced back to his right, toward the smokehouse—and staggered to a halt.

Sabrina's battered car was backed up to the smokehouse door. He stared at the vehicle . . . at the open plank door. Then he took off, sprinting down the sloping path.

Her briefcase was on the front passenger seat of the car. Spencer quickly strode to the smokehouse doorway. Before leaving the estate at dawn, he had slipped the padlock onto the hasp. Now the door stood wide open.

Calm down. There's a simple explanation for this. Sabrina got up and came down here to get something. He rubbed a hand across his mouth as he glanced at her car parked at the door, as if readied for loading.

Spencer stepped inside the smokehouse. Sabrina's clothes were gone from the rod suspended from hooks in the low ceiling. The wooden chair with its sprung booby trap rig was gone, after he had left specific instructions with Orrin Shaw to leave it alone. The scratching pole that had always stood next to the door—gone. Her trashed laptop computer had been left in its case next to the vanity. Spencer checked the vanity drawers. Empty.

He was panting, his heart hammering wildly. *Calm down, dammit! So she's packing up to leave. Isn't that what you've been trying to make her do since the day you got here?*

His head snapped around. Spencer looked at the place where the booby trap chair had stood in the middle of the floor. His breath rasped painfully.

He looked again at the smashed laptop. Then at the empty space where the chair had stood. If she intended to leave behind the worthless laptop, it didn't seem reasonable that she would have gone to the trouble of getting rid of that chair. So maybe she hadn't been here alone.

Cursing under his breath, Spencer bolted out the door, caromed off the crumpled rear flank of her car, and went sprinting up the stone walkway, arms pumping hard, heart trying to hammer itself out of his chest.

I won't die.

The steep wooden stairs pounded into Sabrina's back, one after another after another. She tried to sit up in the hammocked tarp. A rough hand shoved her back down. Then the tarp resumed its punishing descent into the musty bowels of the mansion.

She might have been able to walk. But the Shaws had insisted on dumping her into the oily tarp and dragging her down the stairs. Said it would be faster. Said for her to shut up. Said it would soon be all over.

Sabrina was afraid, but not terrified. And the fear kept coming and going. She was growing too disoriented to focus on any single emotion. Instead, she was in the grip of the childish, but all too human, belief in immortality, which promised her that this really wasn't happening. She wasn't going to die, couldn't die, not here, like this. Part of her reaction stemmed from the poison, the painkillers, simple hysteria. But there was also the elemental animal instinct for survival.

Even so, there were worse things than dying when you hurt as badly as she did. Her clothes were drenched with sweat as if she'd been dragged from a cold pond. Her heartbeats were so slow, she could feel each one swell and collapse like a big bubble behind her breastbone. The stomach spasms kept coming—a sort of gratuitous violence on top of all the rest. She was becoming weaker and weaker from the sweating, from fighting the spasms, from struggling so hard just to keep her mind from fading out completely.

A crazy thought came spinning at her out of left field—she felt worse than death. She would have to get better before she could die.

That notion almost drove her into a fit of hysterical laughter. Almost. But the bottom step caught her in the kidney, the shoulder, the head, *boom boom boom* in rapid succession. After that, Sabrina was in no condition for even the blackest of black humor.

The tarp scraped across a flat surface. Not concrete, but damp, packed earth. Sour smelling. She put out a hand. The floor of the basement felt slimy. A bulb hung from the bare ceiling joists, glowing like a small pale moon an unimaginable distance away.

They're going to leave me here to die.

The realization came to her through the vicious savagery of another spasm that rolled Sabrina into a tight ball and squeezed every last molecule of air from her lungs. She pressed a hand against the rectangular bulge under her sweater.

Just so long as they don't find the tape recorder. Spencer...or someone...will find me. And when they find me, there will be this gift—from me to him.

Then they dropped the edges of the tarp.

And she saw the open grave.

Her eyes widened. They were tugging at the tarp, sliding her toward the gaping hole. *Can't do that,* she thought. *No one will ever find me.*

A large spider skittered up the side of the grave toward her face. And then the reality of what was happening struck home like a steel fist in the solar plexus. Something unlocked inside her.

Sabrina opened her mouth, filled her lungs, and screamed, *"No!"*

They yanked the tarp from under her, sending Sabrina tumbling into the grave. Seconds later, a fistful of computer disks rained down on her. Then came the dirt.

She kicked and flailed, screaming again, this time with a desperate fury as she was hit by another spadeful of loose dirt, then another. But she was too weak. The dirt kept coming faster than she could throw it off.

Dirt in her mouth. In her eyes. She was blind, choking.

A shout suddenly halted the barrage of dirt. She heard loud cursing. Then the sound of something metal clanging against wood, followed by the explosion of a single gunshot.

Something enormous landed in the grave with her. Sabrina covered her face and felt herself sinking, sinking into the eternal night of the damp earth.

Purring.

No. Snoring. She had been awakened by snoring, very close by.

Sabrina felt utterly horrid. This was worse than the flu. Worse than being hit by a speeding freight train. She felt far too rotten to be so rudely awakened, much less to risk opening her eyes. A soft moan escaped her lips. The snoring shut off abruptly as something tightened around her right hand.

"Sugar...?" A hoarse whisper, to her right.

Sugar? In what? She was thirsty—bone-dry. A glass of juice would be a godsend.

"Come on, sugar. Come on. Please, wake up."

The pressure on her hand intensified. Sabrina cracked her eyelids just a little and squinted at the small, sparsely furnished room. A plastic IV bag hung from a stand next to the bed. She took that to mean she was in a hospital, and was at the same time comforted and alarmed—because she had no recollection whatsoever of how she had gotten there.

"That's my girl."

An encouraging pat on the arm. Feathery stroking on her cheek. Sabrina rolled her head toward the raspy voice, blinking. Spencer was sitting in a metal chair pulled up close to the bed, holding her hand, watching her like a hawk. His hair was uncombed, he had purple shadows under his eyes, and he badly needed a shave. But when he broke into a wide grin, she thought he was without doubt the most beautiful thing she had ever set eyes on.

She smiled crookedly at him, and his dark eyes brimmed with tears.

"What...?" Her voice rasped. She winced at the soreness in her throat.

"Easy now. You've had tubes down your throat." He let go of her hand and lifted the lid on a plastic pitcher on the nearby tray table. He fished out a sliver of ice and placed it gently between her lips. "You had a close call."

"Doesn't feel like it's over," she managed around the ice.

"It is." Spencer smoothed her hair. Stroked her arm. Fetched her another sliver of ice. "You're still pretty sedated. But you're going to make it, sugar. I know that... now."

He sounded as if he was trying hard to convince himself as well as her, which told Sabrina just how bad her situation must have been—and maybe still was, considering how rotten she felt.

"Tell me," she said.

"Later. You need to rest."

She shook her head. "Now."

Spencer sighed. But when she kept staring at him, waiting, he finally relented. "You already know most of it. We found your tape recorder."

Sabrina nodded. "Payment for not trusting you."

"Payment for..." He lowered his head for a moment. When he looked at her again, his cheeks were wet. He made no move to dry them. "Lady, if you're going to start trying to balance our debts to each other, I can tell you right up front that I'm never going to be able to dig myself out of hock."

Her eyes stung. She raised a hand to his cheek, surprised by how much effort it took. Beard stubble prickled her fingers. "The gunshot. That was you?"

He shook his head. "Actually it was Lieutenant Montroy. I'd agreed to meet with him again yesterday morning."

Yesterday? Sabrina realized she had lost at least an entire day.

"I figured I could pay an early call on Noble Wetherbee, then get to Montroy's office in plenty of time. But the Wetherbee thing turned into something more than I'd expected, and I ended up tearing hell-bent back to the estate. When I didn't show up at his office, Montroy got a warrant and came after me."

"You were arrested?"

"Not quite. He caught up with me just as I was charging to the rescue of a fair damsel. I was just reaching for my gun—"

"Didn't know you carried a gun."

"I don't usually. Which is probably why I was just getting around to reaching for it, going down the basement stairs, when Orrin Shaw threw a spade at my head, then came at me with a pick." She saw his jaw muscle clench. "Montroy pegged a shot past my right ear—barely past. Orrin is recovering from a bullet hole in the leg. Maria's in the slammer." His voice softened. "And you're here."

"You robbed my grave," she said.

Spencer looked startled. "Well, yeah. That's one way of putting it."

Sabrina rested, her eyes closed. She might have dozed briefly. But when she opened her eyes again, he was still sitting there, watching her intently.

"Why Conrad?" she asked.

He shook his head slowly. "According to Noble Wetherbee, Conrad had suspected for years that the Shaws were holding something over Jeremiah's head. Then he really got suspicious of their behavior following Jeremiah's death.

But he was too loyal to risk stirring up even a posthumous scandal by going to the police, so he went to Wetherbee, instead. And Wetherbee hired a private investigator to trace the Shaws' background.''

Spencer paused to get her another piece of ice and stroke her forehead. ''The report came back this morning. The Shaws' parents had lengthy police records. They'd given up their first child for adoption—sold him, would be more accurate.''

''Jeremiah.''

He nodded, then shook his head. ''The sad part was, Wetherbee says Conrad thought I was somehow in league with the Shaws.''

Sabrina crunched up the last of the ice. The cold liquid was making her a little more alert and easing the discomfort in her throat. ''What did Wetherbee think?''

''About me?'' An odd expression crossed Spencer's face. ''He said I didn't always make it easy, but he always tried to think the best of me . . . since I was his only son.''

She choked on nothing. Spencer patted her on the back until she got control of herself, then held her for a moment, rocking her gently.

''It hit me the same way,'' he said.

''Old man Wetherbee . . . and Zena?'' she said into his shoulder.

He chuckled dryly and laid her back on the pillow. ''He wasn't old nearly forty years ago. And he was married to a woman he loved very much.''

''Then why . . . ?''

''I didn't ask. He'd probably have said it was just one of those things.'' Spencer pressed the backs of her fingers to his lips for a moment, thinking. ''I have no illusions about my mother, Sabrina. I loved her, but she was no candidate for sainthood. Whatever happened back then was probably as much her fault as Wetherbee's, maybe more. But when she found out she was pregnant, she told him, because she said he had a right to know. But she never breathed a word about it again, and refused to take a dime from him."

"Pride."

"That's the way she was."

They were silent for a while. Spencer sat stroking her hand. Sabrina lay trying to remain awake long enough to convince herself that she wasn't dreaming all this.

"By the way," he said after a while, "the news media are packed like a bunch of sardines into the waiting room down the hall."

He grinned wryly at her expression. "Enough of the tawdry Jeremiah Kellogg story has leaked out to have sent the media into a feeding frenzy. And your publisher has called three times."

"Ira Sampson?"

"Yes. An American original." He made a face that could have meant a lot of things. "Sampson is ready to offer you a new book contract—not a ghost job, but one with Sabrina Glade splashed across the cover."

She stared at him.

"For now, you'll be happy to hear that Sampson Books plans to rush Jeremiah's story into production—" Spencer reached into his pocket and pulled out a stack of computer disks "—just as soon as you're up to adding a lengthy epilogue dealing with Zena Kellogg and yours truly."

Sabrina stared at him in disbelief. "I wouldn't do that to you, Spence." She paused, swallowing painfully as he placed the disks on the tray table and reached for more ice. "Not after you saved my life."

"Of course you'll do it, sweetheart." He slipped another sliver between her teeth. "Granted, I was against seeing my mother's name dragged through the tabloids just because she'd made one mistake when she was nineteen years old. Especially when that mistake was me. But she didn't commit suicide—she was murdered. And if there's one person in this whole mess who deserves to have the record set straight, it's Zena Kellogg." He leaned over and kissed the corner of her mouth. "Besides, I trust you."

Sabrina sucked in a deep breath.

He stared into space across the room, his lips clenching and unclenching. Then he smiled at her. "I hope you don't mind, but I did a little negotiating with Sampson. There will be a slight change in the title. A question mark will be tacked on."

"The End of the Line?"

"That's it. You see, since my mother couldn't marry my father, my legal name is Spencer Bradley Kellogg. I've just always used my middle name as my last so people wouldn't think the obvious about my mother." His smile twisted ruefully. "I'm still getting used to the fact that I'm more of a Kellogg by blood than old Jeremiah ever was."

She frowned and tried to sit up. He pressed lightly on her shoulder. Sabrina settled her head back against the pillow, alarmed by what the small effort had taken out of her. When she had the strength, she said, "You're as much a Kellogg as old Layton was, Spence. But don't forget, you're still as much Wetherbee as you are Kellogg."

She rested for a moment, then continued. "It must have taken a lot of courage for Wetherbee to finally tell you. He didn't have to, you know."

Spencer nodded. "Maybe it's confession time for all the old salts."

"And maybe it's time to end the war and begin the peace."

His fingers entwined firmly but gently with hers. Sabrina rested with her eyes closed for a few minutes, then opened them to study the lines of fatigue in his face. Something in his expression had altered. The savage darkness behind the sapphire blue eyes had begun to fade.

"You really are going to be all right," he murmured.

Sabrina nodded, still feeling like death, but willing to give him the benefit of the doubt as long as he held on to her.

"I love you," she murmured. "Can't remember what it was like when I didn't."

Maybe that was how it was, she thought groggily, when the right man came along. You stopped looking back—stopped being afraid—and turned your face toward the sunrise.

Spencer let out a deep sigh.

"Those are the sweetest words I've ever heard," he said. "I've waited so long for you, Sabrina. You're the first and last woman I've ever really loved."

"Don't let go," she whispered through a half smile, unable to keep sleep at bay. "Because I intend to do everything in my power to make sure you aren't the end of the line. All our children will be Kelloggs."

* * * * *

SILHOUETTE Shadows®

Welcome To The Dark Side Of Love...

AVAILABLE THIS MONTH

#43 DARK, DARK MY LOVER'S EYES—Barbara Faith

When tutor Juliana Fleming accepted an assignment in Mexico, she had no idea the turn her life would take. Kico Vega—her solemn, needy student—immediately warmed to her presence, but Kico's father, Rafael, showed her nothing but contempt. Until he took Julie as his bride, ravishing her with his all-consuming desire—yet setting in motion Julie's worst nightmare.

#44 SLEEPING TIGERS—Sandra Dark

Someone didn't want Sabrina Glade to finish the biography she was ghostwriting—ever. First her subject mysteriously died. Then would-be heir Spencer Bradley emerged from obscurity, demanding that the book be stopped. Sabrina felt strangely attracted to the secretive Spencer, but then she began to wonder how far he would go to ensure that his family skeletons remained forever in the closet.

COMING NEXT MONTH

#45 FALSE FAMILY—Mary Anne Wilson

It was the part of a lifetime. And actress Mallory King jumped at the chance to "play" long-lost daughter to millionaire Saxon Mills. For her, it represented family and acceptance, while for someone else she signified a threat that needed immediate removal. Brooding Tony Carella had a strong interest in the Mills family fortune—and especially its newest heir. And soon Mallory feared that Tony's ardent advances would end with her final curtain call.

#46 SHADED LEAVES OF DESTINY—Sally Carleen

After a vicious attack, Amanda Parrish remembered almost nothing of her present life, yet memories of a distant time—and a tragic love affair—invaded her senses. Then next-door neighbor Dylan Hunter came to her aid, evoking a passion as timeless as the attraction between them. Theirs was a bond that had ended once in death—and now seemed destined for the same fate.

Award-winning author

BARBARA BRETTON

Dares you to take a trip through time this November with

Tomorrow & Always

How fast can an eighteenth-century man torn with duty and heartache run? Will he find the freedom and passion he craves in another century? Do the arms of a woman from another time hold the secret to happiness? And can the power of their love defeat the mysterious forces that threaten to tear them apart?

…Stay tuned.

And you thought loving a man from the twentieth century was tough.

Reach for the brightest star in women's fiction with

MIRA™

MBBTA

Now what's going on in

?

Guilty! That was what everyone thought of Sandy Keller's client, including Texas Ranger—and American Hero—Garrett Hancock. But as he worked with her to determine the truth, loner Garrett found he was changing his mind about a lot of things—especially falling in love.

Rachel Lee's Conard County series continues in January 1995 with A QUESTION OF JUSTICE, IM #613.

And if you missed any of the other Conard County tales (see author series page for title listing), you can order them now by sending your name, address, zip or postal code, along with a check or money order (please do not send cash) for $3.50 for each book ordered ($3.99 in Canada for certain titles), plus 75¢ postage and handling ($1.00 in Canada), payable to Silhouette Books, to:

In the U.S.	In Canada
Silhouette Books	Silhouette Books
3010 Walden Ave.	P. O. Box 636
P. O. Box 9077	Fort Erie, Ontario
Buffalo, NY 14269-9077	L2A 5X3

Please specify book title(s), line and number with your order.
Canadian residents add applicable federal and provincial taxes.

CON8

JINGLE BELLS, WEDDING BELLS:
Silhouette's Christmas Collection for 1994

Christmas Wish List

*To beat the crowds at the malls and get the perfect present for *everyone,* even that snoopy Mrs. Smith next door!

*To get through the holiday parties without running my panty hose.

*To bake cookies, decorate the house and serve the perfect Christmas dinner—just like the women in all those magazines.

*To sit down, curl up and read my Silhouette Christmas stories!

Join *New York Times* bestselling author Nora Roberts, along with popular writers Barbara Boswell, Myrna Temte and Elizabeth August, as we celebrate the joys of Christmas—and the magic of marriage—with

JINGLE BELLS, WEDDING BELLS

Silhouette's Christmas Collection for 1994.

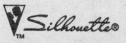

Silhouette®

JBWB

**Another wonderful year of romance
concludes with**

Christmas
Memories

Share in the magic and memories of romance
during the holiday season with this collection of two
full-length contemporary Christmas stories,
by two bestselling authors

**Diana Palmer
Marilyn Pappano**

Available in December at your favorite retail outlet.

Only from ▼ *Silhouette*®
™   **where passion lives.**

XMMEM

SILHOUETTE... Where Passion Lives

Don't miss these Silhouette favorites by some of our most
distinguished authors! And now you can receive a discount by
ordering two or more titles!

SD#05750	BLUE SKY GUY by Carole Buck	$2.89 ☐
SD#05820	KEEGAN'S HUNT by Dixie Browning	$2.99 ☐
SD#05833	PRIVATE REASONS by Justine Davis	$2.99 ☐
IM#07536	BEYOND ALL REASON by Judith Duncan	$3.50 ☐
IM#07544	MIDNIGHT MAN by Barbara Faith	$3.50 ☐
IM#07547	A WANTED MAN by Kathleen Creighton	$3.50 ☐
SSE#09761	THE OLDER MAN by Laurey Bright	$3.39 ☐
SSE#09809	MAN OF THE FAMILY by Andrea Edwards	$3.39 ☐
SSE#09867	WHEN STARS COLLIDE by Patricia Coughlin	$3.50 ☐
SR#08849	EVERY NIGHT AT EIGHT by Marion Smith Collins	$2.59 ☐
SR#08897	WAKE UP LITTLE SUSIE by Pepper Adams	$2.69 ☐
SR#08941	SOMETHING OLD by Toni Collins	$2.75 ☐

(limited quantities available on certain titles)

TOTAL AMOUNT	$_____
DEDUCT: 10% DISCOUNT FOR 2+ BOOKS	$_____
POSTAGE & HANDLING (\$1.00 for one book, 50¢ for each additional)	$_____
APPLICABLE TAXES*	$_____
TOTAL PAYABLE (check or money order—please do not send cash)	$_____

To order, complete this form and send it, along with a check or money order
for the total above, payable to Silhouette Books, to: **in the U.S.:** 3010 Walden
Avenue, P.O. Box 9077, Buffalo, NY 14269-9077; **In Canada:** P.O. Box 636,
Fort Erie, Ontario, L2A 5X3.

Name:_____

Address:_____ City:_____

State/Prov.:_____ Zip/Postal Code:_____

*New York residents remit applicable sales taxes.
Canadian residents remit applicable GST and provincial taxes.

SBACK-SN

Silhouette®

"HOORAY FOR HOLLYWOOD" SWEEPSTAKES

HERE'S HOW THE SWEEPSTAKES WORKS

OFFICIAL RULES — NO PURCHASE NECESSARY

To enter, complete an Official Entry Form or hand print on a 3" x 5" card the words "HOORAY FOR HOLLYWOOD", your name and address and mail your entry in the pre-addressed envelope (if provided) or to: "Hooray for Hollywood" Sweepstakes, P.O. Box 9076, Buffalo, NY 14269-9076 or "Hooray for Hollywood" Sweepstakes, P.O. Box 637, Fort Erie, Ontario L2A 5X3. Entries must be sent via First Class Mail and be received no later than 12/31/94. No liability is assumed for lost, late or misdirected mail.

Winners will be selected in random drawings to be conducted no later than January 31, 1995 from all eligible entries received.

Grand Prize: A 7-day/6-night trip for 2 to Los Angeles, CA including round trip air transportation from commercial airport nearest winner's residence, accommodations at the Regent Beverly Wilshire Hotel, free rental car, and $1,000 spending money. (Approximate prize value which will vary dependent upon winner's residence: $5,400.00 U.S.); 500 Second Prizes: A pair of "Hollywood Star" sunglasses (prize value: $9.95 U.S. each). Winner selection is under the supervision of D.L. Blair, Inc., an independent judging organization, whose decisions are final. Grand Prize travelers must sign and return a release of liability prior to traveling. Trip must be taken by 2/1/96 and is subject to airline schedules and accommodations availability.

Sweepstakes offer is open to residents of the U.S. (except Puerto Rico) and Canada who are 18 years of age or older, except employees and immediate family members of Harlequin Enterprises, Ltd., its affiliates, subsidiaries, and all agencies, entities or persons connected with the use, marketing or conduct of this sweepstakes. All federal, state, provincial, municipal and local laws apply. Offer void wherever prohibited by law. Taxes and/or duties are the sole responsibility of the winners. Any litigation within the province of Quebec respecting the conduct and awarding of prizes may be submitted to the Regie des loteries et courses du Quebec. All prizes will be awarded; winners will be notified by mail. No substitution of prizes are permitted. Odds of winning are dependent upon the number of eligible entries received.

Potential grand prize winner must sign and return an Affidavit of Eligibility within 30 days of notification. In the event of non-compliance within this time period, prize may be awarded to an alternate winner. Prize notification returned as undeliverable may result in the awarding of prize to an alternate winner. By acceptance of their prize, winners consent to use of their names, photographs, or likenesses for purpose of advertising, trade and promotion on behalf of Harlequin Enterprises, Ltd., without further compensation unless prohibited by law. A Canadian winner must correctly answer an arithmetical skill-testing question in order to be awarded the prize.

For a list of winners (available after 2/28/95), send a separate stamped, self-addressed envelope to: Hooray for Hollywood Sweepstakes 3252 Winners, P.O. Box 4200, Blair, NE 68009.

CBSRLS

OFFICIAL ENTRY COUPON

"Hooray for Hollywood"
SWEEPSTAKES!

Yes, I'd love to win the Grand Prize — a vacation in Hollywood — or one of 500 pairs of "sunglasses of the stars"! Please enter me in the sweepstakes!

This entry must be received by December 31, 1994.
Winners will be notified by January 31, 1995.

Name _____

Address _____ Apt. _____

City _____

State/Prov. _____ Zip/Postal Code _____

Daytime phone number _____
(area code)

Account # _____

Return entries with invoice in envelope provided. Each book in this shipment has two entry coupons — and the more coupons you enter, the better your chances of winning!

DIRCBS

OFFICIAL ENTRY COUPON

"Hooray for Hollywood"
SWEEPSTAKES!

Yes, I'd love to win the Grand Prize — a vacation in Hollywood — or one of 500 pairs of "sunglasses of the stars"! Please enter me in the sweepstakes!

This entry must be received by December 31, 1994.
Winners will be notified by January 31, 1995.

Name _____

Address _____ Apt. _____

City _____

State/Prov. _____ Zip/Postal Code _____

Daytime phone number _____
(area code)

Account # _____

Return entries with invoice in envelope provided. Each book in this shipment has two entry coupons — and the more coupons you enter, the better your chances of winning!

DIRCBS